Wondering wh ⁣red
through the see
what was up, but ⁣.

Then his voice: "Norrie, come here.

I turned and saw him through the doorway to my room. He stood a few feet inside with the lights out.

"What are you doing in there?"

"Come here. I need to speak to you."

I headed toward my room. His voice sounded strange. I hoped he wasn't thinking it was sexual appetizer time because that wasn't going to happen.

"Why are you in here with the lights out?"

I reached for the switch but he roughly grabbed my arm. "No lights."

I felt a flare of anger. I don't like being manhandled. I reached for the switch again and he grabbed me and yanked me deeper into the room, then he shoved me against a wall.

"I said, *No lights!*"

"Trav, what's gotten into you? I told you not now—later."

Although with the way he was acting, I was beginning to doubt there'd be a later. I didn't like this new Travis. I made for the door but he grabbed me roughly again and slammed me back against the wall. Harder. It hurt this time.

"Stay there! You're not going anywhere!"

I had no weapon and he was bigger and a lot stronger... My heart hammered, my mouth went dry. I was trapped.

A Gordian Knot Books Production — Gordian Knot is an imprint of Crossroad Press.

Copyright © 2022 by F. Paul Wilson
ISBN 978-1-63789-867-3

For information address Crossroad Press at 141 Brayden Dr., Hertford, NC 27944
www.crossroadpress.com

First Edition

Rx Mayhem

F. PAUL WILSON WRITING AS
NINA ABBOTT

WHERE WE ARE AND HOW WE GOT HERE

Welcome to Rx Mayhem, the immediate sequel to *Rx Murder*. What follows is a refresher on *Rx Murder* in case it's been a while since you read it. Wait... what? You *haven't* read *Rx Murder*? Well, you'd better remedy that right away, because that is where you get to know and love our heroine, Noreen Marconi (yes, like the radio inventor) and all the quirky nuances of her character. This recap simply won't suffice. Go ahead. Yes, you. Go ahead and read it. We'll wait here until you're done.

For those of you who *have* read *Rx Murder*, here's a recap of what happened so far to Noreen (Norrie) Marconi, MD. She's 32, half-Irish, half-Italian, and a family practitioner in a suburban town outside Baltimore, the third doctor in Lebanon Family Practice Associates. Norrie grew up in the neighboring town of Carmel. Her fellow doctors in the practice are Sam Glazer and Ken Lerner, and they're due soon to decide whether or not to take her on as a partner.

Margery Harris, a patient of Norrie's who once gave her piano lessons, suffers a severe allergic reaction to peanuts. Norrie keeps her in the hospital overnight and sends her home on medications. Two days later she suffers a fatal reaction. But during her 911 call she gasps, *"He's killing me!"* Norrie suspects Marge's husband, Stan. Beth, the neighborhood busybody, says she saw Stan leaving a motel with Allison, the Harrises' cleaning girl.

As this is going on, Norrie receives a summons informing her that she's been named in a malpractice suit. She's crushed because she's sure she did everything right. This might hurt her future with the practice.

Norrie has fought her weight all her life. Her nickname in high school was "Macaroni" Marconi. As she says, "I was roughly the size of Asia when I entered college." She took control and is now a size 10 but wants to be slimmer. She starts taking a new diet pill, Tezinex, to help her along. So far, it's working.

The tenant in the apartment above her leaves the tub running, flooding Norrie's condo and rendering it temporarily uninhabitable. She moves into her old room at her mom's house. Her dad, a Baltimore fireman, died in the line of duty six years ago while she was in medical school. She finds that her father's spirit is trapped in the house but she's the only one he can contact. Her father suspects that's because they "share blood." He can manifest himself for only brief periods.

She winds up investigating Marge's death with Deputy Travis Lawton, her old high school crush (a one-sided crush). They grow close as they eliminate Allison as the culprit. When Travis goes to accuse Marge's husband, Stan, of murder, they find him stabbed to death. They finally pin the murder on Beth the snoop. She and Stan dated in college; she knows he's been cheating on Marge and sees this as an opportunity to move back in. Marge's first allergic reaction inspired Beth to spread a little peanut oil on an envelope glue strip and cause a fatal reaction. But Stan laughs at her when she suggests they get back together; in a rage, she stabs him. Then she slits her wrists but survives to face charges.

Rx Murder ends with Norrie in a pretty good place. She's solved a murder and Trav, her first love, is romantically interested in her. All that's left to do is deal with this malpractice thing and find a way to free her father's ghost from the family home.

MONDAY

1

Mondays tend to be a bit frantic here at Lebanon Family Practice Associates, LLC. People who fall ill after we close midday on Saturdays and aren't sick enough for the hospital ER, flood the office with calls for appointments first thing Monday morning. The two doctors in the office that day—meaning Ken Lerner and yours truly, Noreen Marconi—try to accommodate as many as we can, which means we're usually jammed.

But this Monday had started off great for me. Really, how often in life do you get to solve a murder, right? Especially the murder of a cherished person in your life. The morning had been going swimmingly until I stepped into the little consultation room situated between exam rooms, and found a familiar figure sitting in the patient chair alongside the desk.

Sam Glazer, senior partner, founder of the practice, my mentor, great doctor and all-around good guy, gave me a wan smile. "Hi, Norrie."

"Sam?" I said. "What are you doing here?"

He'd been taking Mondays off since I joined the practice two years ago. He should have been anywhere but here today.

"I need to talk to you and Ken. I asked Harriet to send him in when he's between patients."

An innocent enough statement but I was getting an ominous vibe off him. He didn't look good—hadn't for some time now. Before I could ask anything, Ken popped in. He looked as surprised as I to see Sam here on a Monday.

"Sam? Something wrong?"

Ken, a somewhat dumpy, middle-age man with medium brown hair and a receding hairline, apparently caught the same vibe.

Sam stayed seated but leaned toward us and tugged down the lower lid of his left eye.

I didn't mean to, but I gasped: The sclera was yellow.

"Oh, hell," Ken said softly. He looked as distraught as I felt.

Yeah. Oh, hell.

Scleral icterus... when the whites of the eyes turn yellow... the first sign of jaundice. It happens when the liver either can't process the bilirubin in the system, or can't excrete it through the bile duct. A whole list of differential diagnoses flashed though my head. Some of them really, really bad.

"Any pain?" I said. "Nausea, vomiting?"

He shook his head. "Not a thing."

Oh, double hell.

Painless jaundice. Sam wasn't a drinker so cirrhosis was unlikely. Hepatitis can cause it. So can gallstones but they tend to hurt like hell when they block the bile duct. The best news would be hepatitis A which Sam would kick and come out fine. The worst was, of course, the Big C.

The thought of Sam with cancer took all the wind out of me.

He said, "On my way out I'll tell Giselle to cancel my appointments."

"For how long?" Ken said.

I knew he was seeing all those office visit receipts flying out the window. He tends to keep a close eye on the practice's bottom line. Too close, maybe.

"We'll start off with just this week. Bamdad is admitting me for a workup this afternoon."

Smart. Sam might have been tempted to do his own workup, but we have a saying in our profession: A doctor who treats himself has a fool for a patient.

"Three-C?" I said, using the local name for Carson County Community Hospital.

A nod. "Two south."

A surgical floor. Bamdad Mesgar was a skilled surgeon.

Three-C may seem lacking in cachet for some of our local elites, but they forget that most of the specialists here trained at Hopkins—like Bamdad.

"Well, you're in good hands."

"He's got me scheduled for an MRI as soon as I get settled. I'll have him call you with the results, which should give us a loose prognosis and some idea how long I'll be out."

I said, "You're awfully calm about this, Sam."

He shrugged. "It is what it is, and Sofia and I will deal with whatever it turns out to be." He rose and extended his hand to Ken. "But that doesn't mean I can't use a little luck."

Ken shook it, saying, "Best of luck to you, Sam. You know that goes without saying."

Sam turned to me but I ignored his hand and gave him a big hug. He hugged me back.

"We'll miss you, Sam," I said. "Come back soon."

Another wan smile. "As soon as possible. You two mind the store while I'm gone."

He stepped into the hall and headed toward the front and Giselle.

Ken closed the door and turned to me. "He's been looking a little frail lately. I don't see how it can be good."

Neither did I. I have my issues with Ken, but they have nothing to do with his skill as a diagnostician.

"We should all go and visit him after work," I said.

Ken held up a hand. "Don't even consider it. Sam won't want a stream of visitors."

"But—?"

"I've known him lots longer than you, Norrie, and he's extremely private. Pretty much every nurse and doc on staff knows him and they'll all want to wish him good luck and get well soon and so on and so on and that would be a nightmare for him."

"But we're his partners."

He shrugged. "Keep visits to a minimum. Go with that for now. It's the way he'll want it."

Okay. I'd respect that. But Samuel Glazer, MD, had become an important person in my professional life. My medical father figure. I not only respected and admired Sam, I wanted to *be* him one day. I wanted him to know I was thinking of him.

Ken hurried off, leaving me to contemplate the practice without Sam Glazer... the *world* without Sam Glazer—

Wait-wait-wait. I was getting ahead of myself. Not even the preliminary results were in yet and already I had him buried. It could be something non-life-threatening and completely curable.

He's gonna be okay, I told myself.

But a little voice in the back of my head kept whispering *cancer of the head of the pancreas... cancer of the head of the pancreas...*

I had just two more patients on my morning schedule and I must have seemed pretty distracted as I examined them. Well, I was. Sam with cancer...

When the last morning patient had gone, Harriet, our super-efficient nurse, locked the front door for lunch hour which—typical for a Monday—would last much less than an hour. I settled down and forced myself to eat a power bar while I finished up my chart notes.

I'd started myself on a diet pill—Tezinex—over the weekend and had taken my third daily dose this morning. It seemed to be working, but even if it had been a placebo, I wouldn't have been hungry. The news about Sam had killed my appetite. Still, you've got to eat something.

2

I was gearing up for the afternoon when my phone sounded with a text *ding*—Donna, the Cobdica rep. The pharmaceutical reps know not to visit us on a Monday because there's no way we can spare time for a chat about their latest miracle drug. But Donna wasn't pitching, she was reminding:

> *Looking forward to seeing*
> *you and Dr. Lerner tonight.*
> *6:00 at Morton's*
> *300 S Charles*

Oh, crap. We'd promised to attend her dinner in Baltimore tonight. Cobdica was giving Tezinex a big launch and these dinners were a part of it. They serve a nice meal while an expert of one sort or another lectures on the wonders of their new product. I'd turned her down at first, as I turn down all drug company dinners. A lifelong battle with my weight has evolved into a lifestyle that avoids big meals whenever possible. But when I'd decided to make myself a guinea pig for Tezinex, she'd given me samples and extracted a promise to attend. I'd read up on it before feeding it into my bloodstream, but it couldn't hurt to learn a little more about it, right?

But Sam's jaundice changed all that. I got up and went down the hall toward Ken's consultation room. Along the way I saw the usually bubbly Giselle looking glum. Short, thin, and a fidgety bundle of energy, she's our amazing front-office multitasker, handling appointments, phone calls, payments, and insurance billing. Nearby stood our RN, the thickset Harriet, who's been a nurse since shortly after God said "Let there be light." She could be cast as Nurse Ratchet, but she's got a big heart and a wicked sense of humor. She looked like she'd been crying. The news about Sam's illness had hit everybody hard.

I found Ken on the phone. He held up a hand to let me know he didn't want to be interrupted, then pointed to the chair next to the desk. I sat and half-listened to a half-grunted "Uh-huh" followed by a "Right," and so on, but my ears pricked up when he said, "Oh, shit." When he said, "Any sign of mets?" I knew the subject of the call.

Finally he hung up and leaned back in the chair, his expression grim.

"Shit-shit-shit!" he whispered.

"Bamdad?" I said, remembering Sam had told us the surgeon had promised to call.

He shook his head. "No. Mort." Mort Weis, head of radiology. "I couldn't wait so I called him."

"And?"

"Not good, Norrie. C-A of the pancreas."

"The head?" When he nodded I slumped in the chair and mumbled the same one-word question he'd asked Mort. "Mets?"

"Nothing obvious. They'll be doing a PET to stage him. If he's clean it looks like he'll need a Whipple."

I suddenly wanted to cry. The Whipple procedure—officially a pancreaticoduodenectomy—is a brutal piece of surgery that involves removing the head of the pancreas, the gallbladder, parts of the stomach and small intestine. It takes hours and your gut is never the same afterward. Poor Sam.

Ken was shaking his head in dismay. "Two malignancies... damn!"

That jerked me upright. "*Two?*"

Ken's expression turned chagrined. "I misspoke." Then he shrugged. "Sam has wanted to keep a lid on it but I'm sure you'll find out soon enough. He has CLL."

"Oh, hell."

You can have blood disorders a lot worse than chronic lymphocytic leukemia. I've got a hypertension patient who's had it for thirty years and is as stable as can be. Often something else will bring you down before the CLL has its way, but you tend to have a low blood count. The reasons for Sam's low energy, pallor, and desire to reduce his office hours suddenly became clear.

If his CLL was stable, it wouldn't have a major impact on his recovery from the surgery, but it certainly wouldn't help.

We both sat in silence for a while, then I remembered why I'd come in here.

"When you check your texts," I said, "you'll probably find one from Donna about the Cobdica dinner tonight. I'm going to cancel."

He said nothing at first, but as I lit up my phone to respond, he put out a hand. "Let's think about this first."

What? I couldn't believe it. Ken Lerner was the cheapest human being I'd ever met, but after this news, even he couldn't be worried about missing a free steak dinner. Or could he?

"I don't think I can hobnob over a steak while Sam's in a hospital bed."

"It's not the meal. It's something else she said at lunch last week. Something about introducing 'revenue incentives' to participating practices."

Oh, yeah. She'd been coy about what they might be but guaranteed they were legal. But so what?

"I don't see what—"

"Put your emotions aside for a moment and think," he said.

I bristled at his words and his tone, redolent as they were of that antediluvian idea that women are too emotional for rational thought. I'm pretty good at critical thinking—in fact, I'm damn good at it.

"Think about what?"

He looked me in the eye. "Revenue, Norrie... *our* revenues, to be precise. With Sam not seeing patients for who knows how long—maybe never again—we're going to take a big hit. But here's the real kicker: Our overhead won't be dropping one cent. The group's employment agreement states that if one of the partners is disabled, we guarantee his full salary for ninety days. We have disability policies that'll help some, but they have a thirty-day waiting period, so even though he's not here, we're on the hook for Sam's paycheck."

Leave it to Ken to go straight to the dollar signs. But to be fair, his concerns were valid. LFPA's cash flow depended on the number of patients we saw. Without Sam, that number would drop, and so would receipts.

"But what's that got to do with Donna's dinner?"

"If Cobdica is offering 'revenue incentives,' we should know about them."

I leaned back. "Sounds a little shaky to me."

"We're going to be behind the eight ball financially until Sam gets back—*if* he gets back. Don't you think we should at least go and hear her out?"

If Sam Gets back... I didn't even want to think about him not coming back. But as for hearing about our options... I couldn't come up with a good reason why not.

"Yeah, okay, I guess so."

He slapped his palms on his desk. "Then it's settled. We'll take my car and drive in together."

Nooooooo!

It's not a long drive, but trapped in a car with Ken... no escape...

"Oh, gee, I don't know..."

"We'll leave directly from here. We have a lot to discuss along the way. You and I will have to put in extra time here. I've already told Giselle to schedule me for tomorrow morning and tell any of Sam's patients who can't wait that they can see me."

Tuesday is usually Ken's day off, just like Thursday is mine. Well, not anymore, apparently, because I'd be expected to put in an extra session too. Only fair, though. Bye-bye day off—at least for the time being.

"We have to work out a new call schedule too."

I guessed it made sense to drive in together—make use of that time on the road. I wondered if he'd ask me to chip in for gas.

That's not an exaggeration. The group has somewhat regular dinners out together with the spouses where business talk is discouraged and we try to be social. I haven't had a significant other since joining the group so that makes it a fivesome. Usually we go to the Lebanon Golf and Country Club where Ken and his wife Allie—his attractive, blonde, second wife, known in my head as "Barbie"—are members. Ken is sort of the treasurer of the group, so he always handles the bill. If it's like most country clubs, the club members are required to spend a certain minimum amount per month in the dining room and I'm sure our dinners there go to cover Ken and Allie's obligation.

These dinners are a chore for me. Sam and Sofia Glazer are lovely people. But Allie… let me be frank here: Allie is a status-obsessed airhead who has embraced every doctor's wife cliché you can think of. Ken is the table's self-appointed sommelier and he orders a single bottle of Chardonnay for the five of us. Because the Glazers and the Lerners barely drink, they assume everyone else is the same.

Ken uses his phone to calculate the tip, and it's never more than fifteen percent. As a former waitress, this rankled me, so one time during my first year with the group I slipped the waitress an extra twenty on the way out. Ken and Allie got their car first. I'm sure he graced the valet with a 50-cent tip. Maybe a buck.

On that night, as they drove away, Sam leaned toward me and said, "I saw that."

"What?"

"The extra money you slipped the waitress."

I shrugged. "I waitressed in college. It's hard work. An extra twenty bucks—what does that mean between the five of us? Nothing. But to a single mother or a kid paying her way through school, it can mean a lot. It's the difference between a heel and a hero. Small price to pay for being a hero."

"So you made up the difference on your own. I've always thought his tips were skimpy. Why didn't I ever think of that?"

I didn't have an answer so I limited my reply to another shrug.

"I like you, Norrie. I like you a lot." He handed me a ten. "Here's my half."

And since then, that's been our ritual at group dinners. And that's one more reason why I love Sam Glazer.

Not to belabor the point, but there's a lot not to like about Ken.

3

By 5:30 we were on Interstate 70 headed east to Baltimore in Ken's Lexus. I had to hand it to him: He kept his car in cherry shape. No litter of any sort, clean as the proverbial whistle, with WeatherTech floor mats and all. Of course, they protect the resale value too.

Lebanon is twenty miles from the Inner Harbor as the crow flies, but an airborne crow wouldn't have to take Route 40 through lots of lights and some rough neighborhoods. It's actually faster to take the long way around on the 695 Belt. But even the fast route meant thirty or so minutes cooped up with Ken and no exit.

I must admit riding together turned out to be a good idea. Mostly we talked schedule: We had to take Sam off the weekend call rotation, which meant Ken and I alternating weekends. That wasn't so bad. We worked out a rotation for the weekday call as well. As for covering the office appointments, we'd each add a morning—Tuesdays for Ken and Thursdays for me—which was the same as our vacation schedule when Sam was away.

"I just hope it's enough," he said.

"How do you mean?"

"If the appointments are backing up too much, you and I might have to add more hours. We've spoiled our patients. They're not used to waiting."

I knew what he meant. LFPA held to a tradition of a short lead time for appointments. If you were sick or hurting, we found a way to squeeze you in. Sam's absence would put a strain on that tradition.

But extra hours... extra hours might save Ken's take-home, but what about mine? For my first three years here I was paid as an employee. I had performance incentives, of course, but in general my income was pretty much locked in by my employment contract. LFPA, LLC, had to pay me my salary come hell or high water, no matter what happened to the receipts. An open-ended loss of my day off was a breach of my contract. I'd be perfectly within my rights to refuse.

But that would be a dick move, and that's not me. Also, I couldn't do that to Sam. I'd joined this team and I'd take one for the team. I wanted to stay here. Ken was a cheapskate but I could live with that, because he was also a good doc and a hard worker. He wasn't asking anything of me that he wasn't ready to put out himself.

One thing that might get to him was Friday mornings. Usually he shared it with Sam, then they both left for the day and I came in to handle the afternoon on my own. I wasn't about to volunteer my Friday morning off as well.

"How long do you think this will last?"

He sighed. "It'll take him a while to recover from the Whipple, and that'll be followed by radiation and chemo, so... who knows? It all depends on the stage and the grade, and we don't know that yet."

"So... a while."

"Yeah. A while." He shook his head. "And am I ever glad we never went electronic. What with the decreased productivity and paying off the software and hardware, we'd *really* be behind the eight ball."

In case you haven't noticed, "behind the eight ball" is a favorite Kenism.

Initially I'd been put off by the group's lack of electronic medical records. Electronic records were all I'd used through med school and my residency. EMR was second nature to me. But Sam was old school and Ken was, well, cheap.

When Obamacare passed back in 2010, one of its provisions was to convert all medical recordkeeping to electronic. EMR makes records easily searchable and transferrable and, of course, legible. I brought this up in my early discussions with

Sam and Ken. Sam called it cookie-cutter medicine, saying cookie-cutter notes lead to cookie-cutter thinking. He'll use the hospital computer on our inpatients because he has no choice, but here in his office, he'd always written his notes by hand and intended to continue doing so.

Ken's objections were, predictably, related to the bottom line. First off, adopting EMR was expensive; it involved lots of new hardware and the software was especially pricey. Secondly, the average doctor's productivity initially dropped by fifty percent when switching from handwritten records to EMR and in many cases it never returned to previous levels. Obamacare had set penalties for non-compliant offices but Ken had done his research and crunched the numbers—of course—and determined that the practice's revenues would take something of a hit with the penalties, but nothing like they would suffer after going electronic.

So if I wanted to join LFPA, I had to adjust to paper charts and handwritten records.

And you know what? I've discovered I like paper better. When I switched to making notes by hand, I found myself in control of how much I put down. With EMR I'm forced to click so many boxes, fill in so many blanks, and if I happen to skip something it lets me know and hounds me all day until I do what it wants. When I look back on all the EMR patient encounters during my residency, I realize a big part of my focus was satisfying the software rather than satisfying the patient. I was looking at the screen far more than I was looking at the human being in front of me.

I'm also more productive now. With EMR, the record keeping for an uncomplicated case of bronchitis in a thirty-year-old takes almost as long as sorting through the possible causes of dizziness in an elderly diabetic. With paper, the bronchitis gets a few jots for findings, diagnosis, and treatment, giving me more time to devote to the more complex dizzy old gent. Win-win.

4

Morton's was down by the convention center. I'm sure it killed Ken to valet park—he'd have to tip the guy—but that was the best choice. Inside, the receptionist directed us to a rear section where Donna and another rep were waiting to greet us. After a few pleasantries, I accepted a glass of wine and Ken got a cranberry and club. His phone took him away—he was on call tonight—and Donna used the opportunity to pull me aside.

She lowered her voice and said, "Have you tried the Tezinex yet?"

"Took the third one today."

"And?"

"It seems to be working. I'm not the least bit hungry. I'll just be ordering a salad tonight. In fact, if I were home, I'd have another of those shakes. They're really good."

She'd left me a supply of Tezinex's own branded power bars and shake mix.

"You'll be hearing more about them tonight. And the videos?"

"Those too—except for this morning. Missed it. Too rushed. They strike me as a sort of advertisement for the shakes and bars."

"Partly, I guess. But they've proven to be a great motivational tool too."

The Tezinex program involved one pill every morning followed by watching a two-minute online video. Clinical trials had shown significantly greater weight loss with the videos so I was complying.

Ken and I sat together for dinner. Not my first—or second or third—choice for dinner companion, but no way could I sit somewhere else. I told the waitress just bring me the salad; Ken got a New York strip—my favorite cut. But truthfully, I simply wasn't hungry. Yay, Tezinex.

A Dr. Phong from Georgetown University lectured us on the lipogenic enzymes, such as TBK1, that Tezinex theoretically blocked to achieve its weight loss effects. All very interesting, but frankly I was surprised it had been so successful in the trials.

Look, I know about fat storage. It should come as no surprise that someone who carried the nickname "Macaroni" all through high school would keep an eye out for research on fat metabolism. Every time a new paper is published, I'm there. One of the things I've learned is that over the course of millions of years the human body has developed quite an array of evolutionary survival mechanisms to prevent starvation. You know how survivalists hide stores of freeze-dried food to prepare for the collapse of civilization and the ensuing apocalypse? Well, the human body has a whole arsenal of survivalist enzymes whose sole purpose is to store fat for the inevitable lean times evolution has taught it to expect.

That's why most weight-loss meds fail in the long term: Because sooner or later the body finds a way to do an end run around them to build up those depleted fat stores. Tezinex, however, seemed to have won the contest. So far.

After Dr. Phong finished, Donna introduced Cobdica's line of nutritionally balanced protein bars and shake mixes to help our patients lose the weight and keep it off. And best of all, she said, physicians could sell these products directly to their patients. In fact, they would be sold exclusively in doctors' offices until the end of the year. After that, they'd be available in grocery stores and pharmacies and online.

Ken hadn't been too interested in Dr. Phong, but now he was all ears. Here was the "revenue incentive" Donna had mentioned. The whole idea struck me as ethically shaky, but Ken had no such qualms, as I learned on the ride back to Lebanon.

"First thing I'm going to do tomorrow is call Donna and tell her we're in," he said as we headed up the ramp to the Beltway. He seemed psyched and I sensed I had to be careful here.

"I can't see Sam going for that," I said.

"Sam, with all due respect, is out of the picture at the moment. If fact, his absence is the reason we need a revenue boost."

Carefully: "Do you think it's right for doctors to be selling what they prescribe?"

"Oh, absolutely not—one hundred percent not. That's a direct conflict of interest. But we're not prescribing these power bars and shakes or any others. You heard her: patients can choose any brand they prefer. We're just making it convenient for them to stock up on a healthy choice."

I thought about the two videos I'd seen so far. They were pep talks that warned against fast-food joints and made menu suggestions about what foods to eat. They also said that if you didn't have time to prepare a meal, a protein shake or 200-hundred-calorie power bar could be substituted. All well and good, but the products they always showed were Tezinex brand. Not touting them, not even mentioning them by name, but definitely present as a form of product placement.

I couldn't mention this to Ken, however, because I didn't want him or anyone else to know I was taking Tezinex.

Ken said, "This Tezinex sounds like an effective product. We're both seeing a ton of obese patients, many of them diabetic. If it will help them lose weight, that will help them control their glucose levels, even allow us to reduce their meds."

"Yeah, but it's so new. Shouldn't we wait a while and see how it does?"

I do tend to hold off on a new med with my patients, just to see how it shakes out with the public. And no, I hadn't waited to start myself on it. But that's not hypocrisy. I'm a board-certified physician. I'm with me every minute of the day and night and I can recognize side effects. If I sniff any, I won't hesitate to discontinue a med. But I can't monitor my patients like that. I have a responsibility to them, so I'm more cautious where they're concerned.

"The FDA has approved it," Ken said, "so I'll go with that.

But another reason we should get on this now is that doctors' offices will only have an exclusive till the end of the year. That's seven months. If our patients get used to buying the products from us, they'll probably keeping doing that even after they're generally available. I'd rather see their money going into our till than CVS's or Amazon's."

Bottom-line Ken.

Ken's problem was that he tended to live above his means. We family practitioners occupy—along with pediatricians—the bottom income rung among doctors. Even though we're on the frontlines of medicine, the insurance companies reimburse us the least. But when COVID-19 was running rampant, who stayed on those frontlines for you? Better believe it.

I'm not complaining, because even bottom-rung doctors make a good living—not as much as a plumbing contractor, maybe, but we can certainly live comfortably. Doing well while doing good, as the saying goes. I'm content with that.

But if you're a family practitioner and you've got a trophy wife like Ken's Barbie—sorry, Allie—who likes to keep up with the orthopedists' wives, then you've got to have a big house and luxury cars and belong to the country club, and so on. All fine and good as long as your cash flow remains steady. But even a modest drop can put you, as Ken liked to say, behind the financial eight ball. And worrying about that was probably going to keep Ken awake tonight.

Not me. I have a little two-bedroom condo—flooded and uninhabitable at the moment—and drive a used Jeep Liberty. My biggest expenses are my education loans, and I had plenty of those. I'd earned a full-ride to NYU undergrad, but had to borrow up to my eyeballs for med school. I've got six figures to pay back.

The talk veered away from turning our office into a bodega— okay, that's an exaggeration and I'm prone to those, but I viewed adding retail sales to a medical office as a slippery slope. I had a bad feeling about this. Nothing specific, but I didn't sense anything good coming from this. Something somewhere along the line was going to go wrong.

I had no inking how right I was, nor how far wrong things would go.

5

Ken dropped me back at the office to get my car. He headed home and I headed for my mother's. When I got to the old three-bedroom ranch, she was in her room, either asleep or watching reruns of *Murder, She Wrote* or *Quincy, ME* or one of those TV dinosaurs she loved so much.

I stopped in the living room and stared at that damned landscape painting on the wall. It still looked canted. I adjusted it. Now it looked tilted the other way. Well, damn. I was too tired for this.

After a shower I got into bed and waited for the light and the voice.

It didn't take long. First that eerie glowing blob appeared beside my bed, then the words sounded in my head.

Your Babbo has been waiting for you.

Was this his way of saying I was late? No, Hello, Norrie, how was your day? All about him.

But maybe that's the way ghosts of your parents are. And maybe I was a little—or a lot—cranky at how a day that had started out so well had ended so crummy. (Yes, I know that should be an adverb. Don't start.) It had begun with me solving a murder of an old friend and pretty much deciding to have sex with Trav, and ended with a man I admired more than anyone in this world facing the ordeals of pancreatic cancer.

"How do I even know it's you?" I whispered. "You're just a blob of light and a voice in my head that doesn't sound at all like my father."

We've been through this. I don't have a voice, so how can I sound like I did when I was alive?

Maybe a few questions were in order.

"What meat was in your meatballs?"

What? Why do you want to know? Planning on making some?

"Just answer the question, please."

Beef, veal and pork. Why?

"Where did you always buy it?"

Calabro's on Fawn Street. Are you testing me?

Yeah, Calabro's down in Baltimore's Little Italy. Dad had sworn by their meats and sausage. And as a member of the Steadman Station Firehouse, he worked just a few blocks away.

"Well, why not? I can't see you, I can't hear your voice, I can't touch you. And I don't even believe in ghosts."

You've got to believe in this ghost. Please.

"It's okay. I believe it's you."

Despite my very science-oriented nature, I guess I did believe. Considering the circumstances here, what choice did I have?

Did you find out anything about Corrado's fate?

"Have you moved any closer to forgiving him since we last spoke?" A whole 24 hours.

How can I? I don't know what happened to him. Maybe if I knew...

My father had come up with the idea that he was trapped here on Earth, in this house, specifically, until he could forgive his old friend for abandoning his daughter and sick wife back when I was about 12. I think my father was angrier at Corrado for abandoning *him*. Dad had been a couple of years older and they'd bonded as two immigrant kids from Calabria. Dad had called him his *fratellino*, and he'd disappeared without a word.

And as the only human he could communicate with, I'd been tasked with learning his fate.

"Well, I was busy like you wouldn't believe, today, Dad. Maybe tomorrow."

What makes you so busy you can't help your father?

Whoa. Parental guilt. This had to be my father.

"Well, in addition to my doctor duties and obligations, I was busy solving a murder."

You like solving a murder? Find out what happened to your Uncle Corry.

That came out of left field.

"You think he was murdered?"

Maybe. No one ever heard from him again. It could mean he was killed. I need you to find out what happened to him that last night. He had dinner here with us, he drove away, and was never seen again.

"But who'd want to kill him?"

That's what you need to find out. I'm weakening now. The glow began to fade. *Please, work on this for me…*

I lay there in the dark staring at a ceiling I couldn't see.

Uncle Corry, my godfather…murdered?

TUESDAY

1

I'd missed my morning run yesterday—my Crimestoppers activity had taken precedence—so I made a point of getting up and out early today. I turned the jog into a trip down memory lane, going past Trav's old house where his father still lived. I wanted to go past the old Piperno house where Uncle Corry had lived, but I wasn't 100 percent sure of the address.

We hardly ever went there when I was a kid. Corrado's wife, Marie, was "sickly" and preferred to stay at home. She'd been a semi-invalid for as long as I could remember—ankles always swollen and she couldn't walk very far. As kids we were told she'd had an infection that had weakened her heart. Later, as a med student, I figured out that she'd survived a viral myocarditis that had left her in chronic heart failure. My main concern today was whether or not she was still alive to answer my questions.

And really, Uncle Corry murdered?

I couldn't see it. He'd been such a jolly, friendly guy. Who would want to hurt him? My father had put that thought in my head and I couldn't get it out.

When I'd had enough running I called it quits near the shopping centers. Besides, I needed a coffee.

This strip mall had no Starbuck's—I share your shock—but grocery stores usually sell coffee in the bakery section, so I headed into the Safeway.

The Carmel Safeway wasn't my Safeway, it was my mother's, but the layout was pretty much the same. As I headed for the bakery department I saw a middle-age couple round the corner, pushing a cart.

I recognized the man: good old Theodore E. Phelan. Patient of Lebanon Family Practice Associates. Client of Stark the Shark. Plaintiff against Noreen Marconi, MD.

I'd been so involved in crime stopping and Sam's cancer and Tezinex bars and Uncle Corry's disappearance that Ted Phelan's malpractice suit had slipped off my radar. The summons had arrived last Wednesday afternoon, not even a week ago. I still remembered the shock and dismay and hurt—yes, *hurt*, damn it!—I'd felt as I read through the charges of conduct that was *"grossly negligent, wanton, reckless, and intentional."*

A year ago I'd ordered a chest x-ray on Phelan and it came back abnormal: loaded with vascular malformations. A congenital condition. I knew this sort of thing was beyond a family practitioner's role so I immediately referred him to a pulmonologist. I did everything exactly as I should have, yet he was suing me.

Ken said the pulmonologist must have goofed somehow and was the real target; I was simply collateral damage. Didn't cost the attorney—Edward "the Shark" Stark, in this case—a penny to add my name to the suit. So now I too was listed as grossly negligent, wanton, and reckless. Me. Tight-ass, dot-all-the-I's-and-cross-all-the-T's Noreen Marconi, MD.

His wife was listed as a plaintiff as well, claiming she'd been *"deprived of any and all services which would have been performed by her husband and deprived of his care, comfort, companionship, society and consortium."*

Oh, really?

I'd informed my malpractice insurance company and sent them a copy of the Phelan chart and the summons. They'd probably assign me a lawyer sometime this week and we'd soon be off to the land of interrogatories and depositions and such. But as a result, the company would raise my premium. And Ken would have a mini-stroke.

Great, huh?

Phelan saw me and looked flustered. He made a sharp U-turn with his cart and headed the other way. The woman with him, presumably his wife, Mary C. Phelan, co-plaintiff against Noreen Marconi, MD, started to tug him back. Ted whispered something and she immediately followed him. She gave me a quick, shifty glance over her shoulder, and then they were out of sight.

Feeling a bit guilty, maybe? I sure as hell hoped so. They knew damn well I'd done nothing wrong.

I'd never seen the wife before, but I could understand her guilt. She didn't look too deprived of a damn thing at the moment.

Where's your loss of companionship now, honey?

Liar. Fake. Fraud.

I could feel my muscles tighten as my anger rose.

Were I a different sort I might follow them, make sure I was always in sight, yet never acknowledge their presence. Keep them ducking from aisle to aisle before they could find what they were looking for, force them to push an empty basket from one end of the store to the other in a vain attempt to avoid me.

But I'm above that. I've got better things to do with my time. Like getting to the hospital to make rounds.

Well, not completely above it.

Okay, just once, I thought. I simply had to subject them to one more Norrie sighting.

So I went on the hunt, stalking the rear of the store till I found them in the soft drink section. I ambled up the aisle, ostensibly studying the labels, but watching them out of the corner of my eye.

Mary Phelan spotted me first. She nudged her husband and cocked her head in my direction. He looked, turned, and they hurried on.

I sighed as I watched them round the far corner. Hollow victory. Why was I wasting my time?

As long as I was in the pop-fizz aisle I picked up a six of Diet Mountain Dew. No calories and lots of caffeine—what's not to like?

I checked out without running into the Phelans again.

2

The morning session at the office started out messy and then the poop really hit the prop.

I'd been late getting back from hospital rounds and so I started the day behind schedule. Giselle had spent yesterday afternoon calling Sam's patients to cancel their appointments or shift them to Ken who, as promised, had shown up on his day off to take up the slack. Most of Sam's patients were intensely loyal and wanted to wait for his return. But when Giselle told them she didn't know when that would be, but could guarantee it wouldn't be soon, some of them agreed to see Ken, and some said they preferred me. So my schedule was packed.

Mid-morning I checked in at the reception area to see how many patients remained on my schedule and found Donna setting up a display case of Tezinex protein bars and shake mix.

"Doctor Lerner called me early this morning," she said, smiling. "You're pioneers—the first office in the area to participate in the retail end."

Giselle's frown was as dark as Donna's smile was bright. "You mean to tell me on top of everything else I have sell these things and make change too?"

Trouble already.

Ken caught me between examining rooms. "Say, did you hear? We lost two more patients yesterday. That makes three in the past week."

"'Lost'? Who?"

"Beth Henderson murdered Stan Harris. And they say she's

responsible for Marge Harris's death as well, so that makes three. Haven't you heard?"

I bit back a smile. "I heard something about it. But I understand Beth is still among the living."

"Yes, but from all accounts she'll be getting her medical care in Jessup from now on. A double murder and attempted suicide right here in little Lebanon. Can you imagine?"

"Mind boggling," I said. I really hadn't looked at it in terms of losing patients, but that's Ken. I switched the subject. "You really think selling this Tezinex stuff is a good idea?"

"Absolutely," he said, then lowered his voice. "Donna says the company is providing us with the original supply free." *Free...*how he loved that word. His favorite adjective. "They want us to try it just to see how sales go. That means pure profit on this batch. There's no downside for us. I've already started two of Sam's diabetics on Tezinex just this morning."

I couldn't see Sam being too happy with that, but I kept it to myself and got to work.

My next to last patient of the morning turned out to be Anna Divisova, a plump, forty-three-year old type-2 diabetic in for a routine visit. Everything about Anna was neat—her short black hair, her starched blouse, her creased slacks.

She said, "My mother told me that Doctor Lerner started her on that new diet pill, Tezina or something."

Her mother was one of Sam's patients who I'd seen on occasion. Also a diabetic, definitely obese, and poorly controlled because of her dietary excesses. A good candidate for a weight-loss med.

"It's Tezinex," I told her, "and I'm not ready to prescribe it yet."

"Why not?"

"It's brand new and who knows what side effects might pop up once it gets into wide use?"

I felt more than a little guilty saying this, having taken a dose of it earlier this morning.

"But that didn't stop Doctor Lerner from giving it to my mother."

"Do you happen to know your mother's most recent A-one-C?"

The last one I'd seen had been around nine-something, but I couldn't tell Anna without permission from her mother. She and her mom were close, but I confess to being a little obsessive about patient privacy.

"Yeah," she said. "Nine-point-one."

"That's way out of range. Your mother badly needs to get her eating under control. Your A-one-Cs, on the other hand, have been running between six-and-a-half and seven—"

She lifted her chin. "My last was six-point-six. I haven't been over six-point-seven in a year."

I smiled. "There you go. You're making my point: You have your diabetes under great control, all on a single Farxiga tablet a day."

"But I'm *fat*. I was a hundred and seventy-one pounds in my birthday suit this morning. My BMI is twenty-eight. That's the upper end of the overweight range, right on the edge of *obese*."

Anna doesn't qualify for a full-blown obsessive-compulsive disorder—it doesn't rule her life—but she's definitely got an O-C personality. As someone with a similar personality trait, I know one when I see one.

For Anna, if the BMI chart says a woman her height should weigh somewhere between 130 and 140 pounds, then that's where she wants to be. No, that's where she *must* be.

"Those are just numbers, Anna. Rough guidelines. I'm not saying losing a few pounds wouldn't be good for you—"

"But I *can't*!" She looked on the verge of tears. "I try and I try but I can't get my BMI down!"

The one thing in her life she couldn't control. Those damn BMI tables. I wished they'd all blow away.

I tried to temporize. "Let's give it six months. If Tezinex still looks good then, we'll give it a try. But at this point I'm not comfortable prescribing it to a non-obese person whose diabetes is so well controlled."

"A twenty-eight BMI is *almost* obese!"

"Just give it time and—"

"Fine!" She hopped of the examining table and headed for the door. "If you won't help me, I'll find someone who will!"

She was on her way down the hall before I could get a word out.

Was I wrong about this? The practice of medicine isn't black and white. It's got its science side, but there's also an art to it, especially in the gray areas. If Tezinex was good enough for me, who's not a diabetic, why wasn't it good enough for Anna, who is? I had an answer: Because I simply wasn't sure yet. I'm the last line of defense between the pharmaceutical company's hype—I expected Tezinex ads on my TV screen any day now—and my patient's bloodstream. I'm responsible for everything I advise them to add to that bloodstream. I need to be sure before I sign that Rx form.

For myself, however, I'm less demanding. I had no qualms about acting as my patients' guinea pig, their test case.

I heard Anna's raised voice coming from the reception area and went to investigate. I heard her saying, "She didn't give me the treatment I need. I wanted Texiva and she wouldn't give it to me, so I don't see why I should pay."

She still hadn't got the name right. I arrived in the reception area and saw her angry face. She was already a dissatisfied patient. I didn't want her to feel dissatisfied *and* ripped off.

"It's all right, Giselle," I said. "No charge for today."

I turned and found Ken behind me.

"Why wouldn't you prescribe Tezinex?" he said in a low voice.

"Told you last night: Not in my comfort zone yet."

"Well, maybe it should be," he snapped.

He slipped past me toward the front and I returned to the examining room to finish my notes on Anna, thinking my instincts last night had been right. I'd sensed this stuff was going to be trouble and it already was.

3

After my last morning patient, I whipped up a quick Tezinex shake and drank it as I drove to Carmel. But I wasn't going to Mum's. I was going to drop in on Marie Piperno, Uncle Corry's widow. I figured what better place to start tracking a missing man than the wife he'd abandoned.

Tom, the property manager at my condo, called as I drove to tell me that the cleanup service had arrived and he'd let them into my apartment to survey the damage so they could give my insurance company an estimate. Great. Let's get this cleanup rolling. I wanted my place back.

Corrado had lived less than two miles from my folks' place in Carmel but we'd rarely visited—Marie being sickly and all—and I'd been young and not paying attention those few times my father drove us. So I made a couple of wrong turns before finding the Piperno place, a sprawling ranch with a couple of extensions added on. Bigger than the house I'd grown up in. Uncle Corry had made a good living as a mason. The place appeared to be in excellent shape.

I hadn't been able to find a phone number for her—she wasn't listed—so I had little choice but to stop by in person. I just hoped she was still alive.

A prim, trim fortyish woman answered the door. I told her I was looking for Marie Piperno.

"I'm afraid you have the wrong house," she said. "There's no one by that name here."

"Well, she used to live here. She and her daughter Angelina."

Recognition lit her eyes. "Oh, yes. Angelina. She was the

one we dealt with when we bought the place. Her mother was the owner but apparently she wasn't well so Angelina handled everything."

Damn.

"Do you know if the mother is still alive?"

She frowned. "She might be. We were renovating a few years ago and found some old family records from Italy. When Angelina came by to pick them up, she mentioned that her mother was in a nursing home."

Oh, not good. COVID-19 had run rampant through Maryland's nursing homes and extended-care facilities, just like everywhere else, accounting for better than fifty percent of the fatalities. Marie's heart had already been weakened by a viral myocarditis. If the corona virus got to her, she wouldn't have stood a chance.

"Did she mention which one?"

She shook her head. "No. That's all I know, I'm afraid."

I thanked her and headed back to Lebanon.

Angelina Piperno...I hadn't heard that name in like forever. She'd been about Sean's age, maybe a year older. Corry and Marie's only child. Word had it that the pregnancy almost did Marie in, and her doctors told her the first had to be her last. Angelina was too much older to have any meaningful contact with me. When I was in high school, I believe she had already graduated. I seem to remember something about nursing school. But I recall her being about as fat as I. We could have bonded over that, but Angelina had been fairly remote and withdrawn. I knew nothing of any substance about her.

But her mother...Carson County didn't have many nursing homes. A few phone calls would track her down—providing she was still alive. I didn't have much hope of that.

Trav called as I was pulling into the office lot.

"Hey, there. I tried you at the office but you weren't in."

"Just running errands. What's up? They promote you to detective yet?"

He laughed. *"Not yet, but I'm definitely the fair-haired boy around the Sheriff's Department at the moment. But I'm calling to check if we're still on tonight for that dinner I owe you."*

"Absolutely. Do you want to meet someplace or—?"
"*No-no. I'll pick you up at your mom's. What time?*"
"How's 6:30 sound?"
"*Great. See you then.*"
I was really looking forward to tonight. A nice dinner and then back to his place for… whatever. And I knew what I wanted *whatever* to be.

4

B ack in the office, Ken stepped into my consultation room as I was checking a stack of lab reports—yes, we follow the Paleolithic practice of having them mailed or faxed to us and then filing them in paper charts.

"I defused the Anna Divisova situation," he said.

"'Defused'? I didn't realize she was about to explode."

"You know what I mean. She was angry and frustrated, and in these days of social media, I didn't want her badmouthing us all over the Internet. You know how it goes: She mouths off on Facebook and Twitter and Instagram and whatever, and next thing you know her complaints are the first thing that pops up when a prospective patient Googles us."

This sounded like a speech he'd prepared but the point had merit. Disgruntled patients have an unfair advantage online when doctors are the target. They can troll us but we can't respond in any substantive way. They can post anything they want about the doctor's treatment of them but HIPAA privacy laws prevent the doctor from countering the lies with facts. Those facts are all privileged. The whole online dynamic is lopsided because satisfied patients almost never post praise. The unhappy ones, however, are often relentless. Taking a few potshots won't suffice—they've got to pillage and burn.

"So how did you 'defuse' this?"

"I had Harriet put her in an examining room, let her vent, then prescribed her Tezinex."

I stared at him a few seconds, unsure how to respond. Finally I said, "So when are we changing the sign out front?"

He frowned. "What?"

"When do we officially change the name to 'Lebanon Family Practice Associates and Deli'?"

"I don't get it."

"She comes in here and orders a medication and we fill the order. Like a sandwich at a deli."

"That's not at all—"

"And if we don't fill the order right away—I told her I'd wait a few months and revisit Tezinex—she throws a tantrum and we give in because we're afraid of social media. You let her blackmail you."

"I did no such thing! It was medically indicated in her case."

"I won't argue with you there." I could have but it would be a waste of time. "But as I told you yesterday, it's hasn't entered my comfort zone yet."

"Well, it's entered mine. It's going to be a popular medication and this is not a time when we should be driving patients away. If you're not comfortable with it, send them to me."

With that he walked out.

Didn't he understand how my recommending a patient to see someone else to prescribe a med I was hesitant about totally missed the point? Revenue worries were fogging Ken's brain.

Before starting the afternoon's patients, I looked up the local nursing homes. Expecting a—literal—dead end, I started calling around, beginning with the Parkview because it was in Carmel. Miracle of miracles, Marie Piperno was not only still alive, she was a resident of the first place I called. What luck. I decided to stop by after hours on the way to my mother's.

But right now: Time to get to work. Sam and I usually covered the whole day. But with Sam out and Ken covering only the morning, I was left alone to handle the afternoon on what is traditionally our second busiest day of the week.

But no complaints. You do what you have to do.

5

Sam, Ken, and I all have our loyal patients, people you click with. It's not always easy to explain, but some sort of vibe you radiate as a physician triggers a sense of trust and confidence in a patient. In objective terms, you're not necessarily the best doctor they could see, but to their minds, in their opinion, you are just that. Mrs. Stearns, for instance, won't bring her son Jerry to anyone else unless he's acutely ill and I'm not available. That kind of loyalty is precious, and I reciprocate whenever I can. This afternoon that loyalty would cause a problem.

Harriet stepped out of one of the examining rooms and said, "Jerry Stearns."

"Great," I said and entered.

I'm always happy to see Jerry. He's such a sweet kid. As usual, the sixteen-year-old had come with his mother and, as expected, he started off with his signature question:

"You're not going to stick me, are you?"

I make sure to dose Jerry with flu vaccine every fall, so on every visit he wonders if this is the one where he gets punctured.

Jerry has the typical Down Syndrome stigmata: almond-shaped eyes, small ears curled at the top, flat nose, slightly protruding tongue, short neck and fingers. He's chubby, barely five feet, and has left extropia—known on the street as a wall eye or bent lamp. But I've always found him brighter than the average Down kid, and the fact that he has three palmar creases—most Downs have only two—has led me to suspect he's a mosaic Down.

As usual he smelled of soap and was neat as a pin in a plaid shirt and khakis. His mother took excellent care of him.

I reassured him about the shot and learned from his mother that he'd had a fever this morning and complained of a sore throat. I checked and saw a scarlet soft palate and white exudate on his tonsils. The quick strep test came back positive, so I gave him a prescription for ten days of amoxicillin and stressed to his mom to make sure he got the full ten days. Hardly anyone takes any med for ten days. As soon as they feel better, they forget. But a Down syndrome kid needs a full course of therapy. I knew Jerry's mom would follow through.

I watched him trail his mother down the hallway toward the waiting room as my next patient followed his mother in. He was a broad-shouldered kid, a good eight inches taller than Jerry, and as he passed the little guy he jerked out his elbow and slammed Jerry against the wall. It was all so casual. He didn't even look back. Neither did Jerry, but I saw him rub his arm as he kept on walking.

And that damn near broke my heart. It told me that Jerry got pushed around so much it had become routine, expected.

The anguish quickly blazed into anger. I have a hot temper—what do you expect from someone half Irish and half Italian?—and I was ready to get in the kid's face right then and there.

I spent my college, med school, and residency years in big cities, sometimes in their worst sections. I came away with a sharp tongue and an attitude—survival mechanisms—that I sometimes find difficult to keep in check.

Like now.

But that wasn't the way to go here. So I stepped into the consultation room to cool off before I saw him.

I'd composed myself by the time I finally opened the exam room door and stepped inside. His name was Damon Castanon, a sixteen-year-old who usually saw Sam. But since Sam was out for who knew how long, and this couldn't wait, his mother had grabbed one of my open slots.

The Castanon name is as close to celebrity as you get in Lebanon. That's because Damon's dad, Bert, owns three car dealerships that he hawks relentlessly in the Baltimore papers, on the radio, and on local cable TV—"*Leave the city and drive to Lebanon for the deal of your life!*" Everyone knows his face and the Castanon name. And if you drive through the Hill section of Lebanon you can't miss the huge Castanon castle.

Damon sat on the examining table with his shirt off. His musculature had weight-lifter definition with the six-pack abs so many men aspire to. I'd expected a load of attitude but couldn't sense any. He seemed pretty secure in his skin, which was pierced here and there—two rings in his left ear and a stud through his right eyebrow. I was willing to give good odds that he had one through his tongue too.

Piercing was old hat for me. After all, I'd attended NYU for my undergrad and medical degrees. But when I'd arrived in Greenwich Village a dozen or more years ago, piercing was pretty much limited to the gays and the S&M crowd. Now piercing had followed tattoos into the mainstream. Seemed like every third teen or twenty-something in Lebanon sported either ink or chrome or both.

I'd always thought it was pretty lame, and even more so now that it had become trendy.

Damon was dressed in the skateboarder uniform: backward baseball cap, baggy pants worn low enough to show off his plaid boxers, scuffed Airwalks on his sockless feet. His oversized T-shirt was draped across his mother's lap. I guessed no one had told him the look was way passé.

Mrs. Castanon told me that Damon had been sent home by the school nurse because she feared the rash on his neck might be contagious.

One look at that inch-wide circle of vesicles below his right ear and I knew she was right.

"You've got herpes," I told him.

His mother gasped.

"No way!" said Damon.

I said, "Way."

If his well-developed pects and biceps told me he worked out a lot, the rash told me why.

"How long have you been wrestling?"

He stared at me. "How'd you like know I wrestle?"

"Because your rash is known as *herpes gladiatorium*. Lots of wrestlers get it."

"But how?"

"Well, if you spend a lot of time rubbing against the sweaty bodies of other guys on mats that are rarely if ever wiped down with antiseptic, it's almost inevitable."

A little harsh, maybe. Definitely cold. But this trend-humping twit who'd hurt Jerry was not one of my favorite people at the moment.

"See?" His mother jabbed an index finger toward him. "I told you it was an awful sport!"

"Aw, shut up, Ma."

And she did.

I couldn't help but shake my head. If I'd said that to my mother at age sixteen, Dad would have had to leave work early so he could come home and use a paint scraper to remove me from the nearest wall. Even now I wouldn't dare tell her to shut up unless I was wearing sneakers and jogging shorts and the back door was standing open.

After an uncomfortable moment Mrs. Castanon said, "Can you treat it?"

I nodded. "Just like a fever sore. Same family of virus."

I gave him a quick once-over exam: ears, glands, throat—yep, a barbell stud waggled in his tongue—heart, and lungs. All clear. I told him he was contagious and no wrestling or any other contact sport until I rechecked him on Friday. He didn't like that, but accepted it. He *did* like staying home tomorrow and not returning to school until Thursday.

As he shrugged back into his shirt, and I started writing his prescriptions, I knew I couldn't let him go without saying something about Jerry. I handed the script to his mother and turned to him.

"Damon, I want to ask you something. I saw you knock Jerry Stearns into the wall as you passed him. Why did you do that?"

"What?" his mother said. "What did you say?"

Damon said, "Shut up, Ma," then turned to me. "That his name? I like see him all the time in school." He shrugged.

"He's just like a special-ed geek we kinda, like, you know, mess around with."

...just a special-ed geek...

I envisioned my stethoscope tubing around his throat, twisting ever tighter. But I took a breath, counted to three, then let him have it.

"He's not a *geek*, Damon, he has Down syndrome. By some genetic accident, he wound up with an extra twenty-first chromosome when he was conceived. It's not his fault."

Damon was looking uncomfortable now. "Yeah, well—"

"Yeah, well, nothing! Do you think Jerry wants to have Down syndrome? Do you think if he'd been given a choice he would have picked being short and different looking with an IQ of around seventy?"

Damon looked down. "Seventy? Oh, man."

"Yeah. *Man.* Something you should try acting like."

"Now just a minute!" said Mrs. Castanon.

I wanted to say, *Shut up, Ma,* but didn't. Instead I held up my hand and kept my eyes on her son.

"Let me finish. Jerry's never going to look like a normal guy, Damon. Never going to be as smart as you, never going to be as tall as you or as strong as you, and he's never going to live as well or as long as you."

That last snapped Damon's head up. "Whatta you mean?"

"If he's lucky he'll survive into his fifties, but that's a strange kind of luck since Down syndrome people usually have Alzheimer's by then."

Damon's head dropped again. I waited for him to say something. When he didn't, I went on.

"I look at you and see a guy who's a slave to the trendoids. Ever think of breaking free? Setting yourself apart from the crowd? You're a big, strong guy. You should be looking out for someone like Jerry, not bumping him into walls. Don't you think that poor kid's got enough to deal with without getting bullied by jocks twice his size?"

"That's enough!" Mrs. Castanon said, rising and coming to Damon's side. "I won't have you talking to my son like that!"

"Somebody ought to."

As she took her subdued son by the arm and tugged him toward the door, I added, "So next time you see him, Damon, break from the herd and say hello. If you haven't got the guts for that, just walk by. But if you're really feeling gutsy, next time you see somebody pushing him around, step in."

I tried to end on a lighter note by giving the kid a reassuring pat on the back.

"Give it a shot, Damon. See you Friday."

"Oh, I doubt that," Mrs. Castanon said as they left the exam room. "I doubt that very much."

I sighed as I watched them go. Me and my big mouth.

Great way to build a practice, Norrie. You should write a book on it someday.

6

The afternoon ran me ragged. I felt like a gerbil on a wheel until I stepped out of the office door at 5:15. I figured I could make it to the nursing home and talk to Marie, then run to Mum's place for a quick shower before Trav arrived at 6:30. But I'd have to hustle.

Maybe a park had once existed by the Parkview nursing home, but no longer—no park, so no view. The place was laid out pretty much like every other nursing home I'd ever seen: single storied with multiple wings. It also smelled like every other nursing home I'd ever visited: urine... the olfactory Muzak of nursing homes. No matter how often they change the patients and their bedding, that unmistakable tang pervades the air. In all fairness, because of the frail nature of your clientele, you can't open all the windows and let the breeze waft through, so you're stuck with that inimitable redolence.

I checked at the front desk and learned she was on Appletree Lane, which was the Parkview's name for its east wing. The nurse's aide at the desk there went to check on Marie but returned saying she was already asleep.

No problem. I'd stop back tomorrow on my lunch break.

I hurried the few miles to Mum's place and jumped into the shower. By 6:20 I was revived and smelling a lot better. Ready for anything. And I do mean *anything*.

"He seems like a nice young fellow," Mum said of Trav as I hung out with her and Timmy in the kitchen. They were drinking, I was abstaining. "If only he wasn't divorced."

"Some marriages don't work out, Mum."

"*Some* marriages?" Timmy said. "Divorce seems more the rule rather than the exception these days. Norrie's not exactly a teenager, you know, Kate."

"Thank you for the reminder, Uncle Timmy."

I didn't take offense. Timmy didn't have the most efficient filter.

"Well, it's true isn't it?" He winked at me as he turned to my mother. "Listen, Kate, at Norrie's age, if she was to limit herself to guys who'd never been married, she'd have slim pickings. She'd have to settle for a reject or wind up an old maid."

"Heaven forbid!" Mum said. "I want grandkids! Oh, by the way, I'll be visiting your Aunt Irene this weekend. I trust you'll be all right here alone."

Mum's sister lived in Jersey City and every few months one would visit the other for a short stay. I guessed it was Mum's turn to make the trip.

I said, "I'm hoping to be back in my place by then. The insurance company's dragging this thing out."

"Well, I've decided when I come back I'm definitely going to call some realtors and see about putting this place on the market."

Oh, hell. That would leave my father trapped here with strangers. I couldn't tell her that. I wouldn't even tell Dad that. But now more than ever I needed to free him from this house.

Just then the doorbell rang. She followed me to the front door where Trav waited. I invited him to step inside for a moment. That same uncomfortable look passed over his face again and I saw him rub his arms as if he'd felt a chill—just like the other night. Was he sensing my father's presence again?

"Hi, again, Mrs. Marconi," he said, shaking hands with her. "Thanks again for Sunday dinner."

"You're very welcome," she said. "And thank you again for playing that song. 'That's Amore' was my husband's favorite and it did my heart good to see Sean and Norrie singing it again after all these years."

We said our good byes and I pulled him out the front door.

"You're still on her good side," I said. "Just for playing 'That's Amore.'"

"Yeah," he said absently. He wasn't all here.

"What's wrong?"

"I got that weird chill again, as soon as I stepped through the door."

Had to be my father's presence. Hadn't he told me he thought Trav was "sensitive"? That must have been it. Because Trav had told me Sunday night that he hadn't been familiar with "That's Amore," yet he'd played it… Dad's favorite song. He'd somehow connected with my father's ghost… or vice versa.

Kind of creepy.

"How do you feel now?"

He shrugged. "Fine. Normal. That painting's still tilted by the way."

"I know, I know, I know. Does it bother you?"

He shook his head. "Nah. Not tilted enough for that. But it seemed to bother you the other night. What do you feel like eating?"

He was on a deputy's salary and paying alimony and child support. I wanted to be sensible here. And frankly I wasn't very hungry, thanks to Tezinex.

"I've got a hankering for Mexican."

He laughed. "A 'hankering'? Did you just say 'hankering'?"

"I believe I did. Juanito's would assuage my hankering."

He leaned close. "And what will assuage my hankering for you?"

"I'm sure we can think of something. But food first."

"You got it. But Juanito's has no bar, as I recall."

"Just as well. I'm on call tonight."

He frowned. "Is that going to be a problem?"

"We rarely get called after hours, and it's almost always something that can be handled over the phone."

During the short drive he updated me on how he'd been working with the detectives on the homicide unit of the county prosecutor's office and how they were handling the Marge and Stan Harris murders. He told me he'd worked very hard—at my request—to keep my involvement in solving the crime out of the papers. We'd "solved" Marge's murder in a very roundabout way. We'd managed to figure out the *how*, but twice we'd had the wrong suspect for the *who*. But eventually we sorted that and the sheriff's department thought Travis had sussed out the whole thing. I was more than happy to let them go on thinking that.

We arrived at Juanito's. Over the years, the tiny adobe-style building with about a dozen tables inside has become a Carmel landmark. Back in the day, my folks would bring Sean and me here on a Friday or Saturday night maybe once a month. Juanito would always greet us like long-lost relatives.

The place was only half full, as expected for a Tuesday night. We took a table in a rear corner. I'd been back only once since joining LFPA. Juanito, plumper and grayer, still acted as maître d' but hadn't recognized me then and didn't recognize me now. Which was fine. I was half the size of when he last saw me at the end of high school.

Though hardly hungry, I had to order something. I settled on two appetizers: espinacas con queso—which Trav and I would share—and the ceviche for an entrée.

"That's it?" Trav said. "Come on. This is my treat."

Exactly.

"One of the sales reps dropped off some of those fresh soft pretzels and I can never resist them."

Not exactly a lie. A rep did indeed drop off said pretzels at the office, just not today. And I truly can't resist them.

Trav ordered jalapeño poppers plus chips and guacamole for the table—one of which I would sample out of politeness but leave the rest for him. For his meal he ordered the burrito loco with green sauce which I knew from experience in my *baleena* days was huge.

"And what did *you* have for lunch?" I said. "Barbecued hindquarter of steer?"

A tolerant heh-heh. "The Burger King in Lebanon was having a special on Whoppers so I had a few."

"A 'few'?"

A shy look. "Well, three."

"And fries too, of course."

"Whoever heard of burgers without fries?"

Who indeed?

The guy eats like that from morning to night and never gains an ounce. But then, no sane person ever said life was fair.

"Oh, before I forget," I said, "I was wondering if you could do me a favor. It'll be work-related for you."

"Anything," he said, loading a chip with salsa.

"It's about a guy who went missing almost twenty years ago."

The chip stopped halfway to his mouth. "Twenty years? And you expect to find him?"

"No-no. He was a friend of my father's and I'm sure his wife filed a missing-person report. I'd just like to know what they found. There must be a record of it somewhere."

"It'll be with the state cops. They run the MCMUP."

Never heard of it. "Which is...?"

"The Maryland Center for Missing and Unidentified Persons."

"Quite a mouthful."

"Better believe it. Give me his name and I'll check with them tomorrow."

I wrote *Corrado Piperno* on a paper napkin and slid it across the table, saying, "He just up and disappeared. Left his wife and daughter and job and everyone he knew without a word of good-bye."

Trav gave a little grunt. "Just like my mother."

I was shocked. I'd never met his mother. His folks' divorce was old news by the time I'd met Trav, although I'd always thought it kind of unusual for him to be living with his father rather than his mother.

"I had no idea."

"Yep. She walked out, called my father from Florida, and basically said marriage and motherhood weren't for her. They got divorced and never saw each other again. I never once heard from her—not a birthday card or Christmas card—nothing."

"Oh, that's awful." My heart went out to him. "You must have been devastated."

"I was like three at the time so I don't even remember her. But it ate at me over the years."

"And you never looked her up?"

"Oh, sure. When I hit twenty I found out where she was in Florida and went down there. I watched her from afar. She was waitressing in a restaurant in Jupiter and living with some guy who ran a charter boat. Whether they were married or not, I don't know, but she has a kid who looks about ten and who she seems to love. From everything I saw she seemed like a good wife and mother."

He fell silent and blinked a few times. Were those incipient tears?

I put my hand on his. "Trav?"

"I couldn't help thinking, Why did she leave? My dad's a gentle guy—never raised a hand to me and rarely raised his voice. It's not in him to be abusive in any way, shape, or form. I saw how she was with her new man and kid. Why couldn't she have stayed and been like that with us?" He sighed. "I came back without making contact. If she wasn't interested in me, why should I be interested in her?"

"How strange."

"My folks' wedding date and my birth date were six months apart, so I figure I'm the reason they got married." His mouth twisted. "Same reason Diana and I got married. History repeats itself."

I didn't know what to say to that. As I fumbled for a reply, he added, "Except Diana and I both want to be parents to Maddy. We just can't do it living in the same house."

I was sorry I'd brought this up.

"I didn't mean to trigger bad memories. If it's painful—"

He smiled and squeezed my hand. I squeezed back. I liked his touch.

"Not painful at all. My mother was never part of my life, so I don't miss her one bit. My father, on the other hand… he raised me. My Aunt Sally helped out a lot, but he was always there for me."

"How is the kidney hunt going?"

He shrugged and kept holding my hand. "He's moving up the list, but it's slow."

His father was on the waitlist at the Hopkins kidney transplant center, hoping for a match. Travis had offered one of his own but he wasn't compatible. And since he had no siblings, they had to depend on the death of a stranger.

I noticed him staring out the window.

"Nickel for your thoughts," I said.

He glanced my way. "Nickel?"

I shrugged. "Inflation. Thinking about your dad?"

"No. I'm looking at Phil's and thinking about you."

I leaned forward and, yes, Phil's ice cream shop sat across the street and a few doors down. I'd heard that while I was away getting educated, Phil had passed on to the Great Sundae in the Sky, but his legacy of homemade ice cream lived on. Phil's had been the hang for the local high school kids—the cool ones. The uncool crowd—Trav and I were charter members—weren't welcome. Not that they'd try to kick out the uncool, but they'd honed shunning to a fine art.

I was momentarily baffled. "Phil's? Me?"

"Yeah. Remember that time we went? And Marsh and Barton tried to hassle you?"

Ohhh, yes. The one and only time we went together, and that happened only because I said it was my treat. I'd sort of forgotten that episode—forgotten on purpose. Danielle Marsh and Cathy Barton... *Mean Girls* had come out a year or so before and these two obviously thought the "Plastics" were the clique to emulate. It all came back in a rush.

Trav and I were at one of the small tables. He'd ordered a banana split—of course—and I was enjoying a small cone of Phil's chocolate peanut butter swirl. He'd just got up to retrieve some extra napkins from the counter when Danielle called out, "Better hurry back or Macaroni will finish your sundae!" And Cathy added, "Yeah, she needs it for her third chin!"

Laughs all around. I blushed crimson of course—from embarrassment but also rage at the totally unprovoked attack. I wanted to die but forced myself to give them a hard stare. And in so doing I noticed a pimple on Cathy's forehead. The words spewed in a rush.

"Hey, Barton, is that a volcano on your forehead? No, wait. Hey, everybody, Cathy Barton is growing a third eye!" As Cathy's hand flew to her forehead, I turned on the very pretty and just about perfect Danielle. She had no visible defect so I had to create one.

"And Marsh, you're the one who practically lives here. I see you're working on a second chin yourself." I patted my double chin. "I've got too much of a head start for you to catch up, but keep it up. You're coming on strong!"

Someone in the shop said, "Oh, *snap!*" as Danielle's hand darted up to cover her throat. In less than a minute they'd left the shop, probably rushing home to their magnifying mirrors.

I remember looking over to the counter and seeing Trav standing with his jaw hanging open.

Back here at Juanito's, I said, "Yeah. Not my finest moment."

Trav grinned. "Are you kidding? You were awesome!"

"No, I was nasty. I got down on their level. I could have used a little help from you, you know."

"Me? Those girls terrified me. They terrified everyone. Everyone except you, I guess."

They terrified me as well. And after that episode I went from being the fat brainiac to the fat, *shunned* brainiac. No one wanted to risk a dose of what I'd laid on Marsh and Barton.

I said, "Well, they'd embarrassed me in front of you and I sprang to the attack."

He frowned. "In front of me?"

"Surely you knew I had a humongous crush on you."

"On me?" He shook his head with a bemused expression. "I never had a clue."

Clueless, clueless, clueless...

"But you know..." he said slowly. "Thinking back now, I can see things I never picked up on. Like when you asked me to the Sadie Hawkins dance."

Ah, yes. In November of our junior year someone came up with the bright idea of having a Sadie Hawkins Dance. For those of you unfamiliar with this antediluvian custom, it's a dance where the girls invite the boys. I knew there was no way Diana Robinson was going to ask Trav, so I gathered up my courage... and didn't ask him.

I couldn't. What if he said no? I'd die.

Then, just two days before the dance, I told myself that time was running out and that if I didn't ask him today I'd be kicking myself for the rest of my life.

So I regathered my courage and, sure that I was only setting myself up for a week-long crying jag, stammered out the question.

Miracle of miracles, he said yes.

I almost fainted. I was sure this was going to change everything. He'd hold me in his arms as we danced and he'd realize that I, not Diana Robinson, was the girl of his dreams.

When you're sixteen, do things ever turn out as you hoped? Maybe for some girls. Not for Macaroni Marconi.

Trav was a perfect gentleman, but spent the whole dance mooning over Diana. He asked me—*me!*—if I thought he should ask her to dance. I remember biting my lower lip to keep it from trembling before telling him it wasn't allowed at a Sadie Hawkins Dance. The girl had to ask *him*.

We danced. Mostly fast dances where we never touched, but I gathered my courage and asked him to dance to Celine Dion's "Because You Loved Me." We touched then, we moved together, but he was not transformed.

The good-night kiss I'd been dreaming about never happened.

I cried myself to sleep.

He said, "I never made a connection between you asking me to go and a crush. I wanted to go because maybe I'd get a chance to dance with Diana Robinson. I thought you and I were just friends."

"I realized that. And we were close friends. So close you kept asking my advice about how to approach other girls."

He threw his head back and groaned. "God, what a dumbass I was! I hope I didn't hurt your feelings."

I shrugged. "I was okay." Not. "It's all ancient history anyway."

"But what about now? Any chance for me to bring back that crush?"

"I'm a little old for a crush these days. I'm more into lust now."

He blinked but recovered with a quick grin. "Lust works even better." He shook his head. "Looks like I've got a lot to make up for."

"I expect you to start reparations tonight."

"You are *on!*"

The appetizers came then and we dug in. Well, Trav dug in. I love spinach; stir it into melted cheese and I am so there. Except I wasn't all that hungry—a new experience for me. Used to be I was always hungry. *Always.* Had I gotten religion and joined a convent, I would have taken the name Sister Perpetua Famisheda. But now, after dipping a few chips into the espinacas con queso, I was pretty well done.

Trav pushed the guacamole on me and offered his jalapeño poppers. I dipped one chip into the guac and that was it. He finished the rest as well as my spinach. Then came the entrées. I was glad I'd ordered just the ceviche—the portion was manageable. Trav's burrito loco, however, was about the same size as the average bedroll. I watched him sprinkle a generous amount of green hot sauce onto the already spicy salsa verde. The man knew what he liked.

We were both eating like Juanito was going to take our plates whether we were finished or not. Because we'd pretty much come to an unspoken agreement that we were going to have each other for dessert. Trav finished his burrito in what had to be record time, then he paid the bill and we were on our way out the door. Fastest restaurant dinner I'd ever had. We'd just reached his car when my phone rang. The caller ID said Three-C.

"It's the hospital. I've got to take this." I almost laughed at Trav's stricken expression. "Don't worry. Usually just a clarification of an order."

But it turned out to be nothing so simple. Eighty-three year old Amelia Henderson, on the mend from her pneumonia, was spiking a fever to 104. I'd originally scheduled her for discharge yesterday, but that plan was sabotaged when her daughter and only caretaker Beth attempted suicide and was herself hospitalized. So I'd held Amelia over and got the social services people on her case to find her a place to go. I'd been hoping for discharge tomorrow. But now this.

I ordered a urinalysis, blood cultures, CBC and SMAC, and another chest X-ray. Amelia had been one of my first patients when I joined the practice. She'd become a little confused during her hospital stay and her daughter's current situation prevented her visiting her mother. Amelia needed a familiar face. I couldn't leave this to a house doctor.

I turned to Trav. "An elderly patient's having some problems. I've got to go in."

His face fell. "Really? But I thought you said—"

"Yeah, I know. Hardly ever happens. But 'hardly ever' is happening tonight." I gave my head a chagrined shake. "Typical."

"I'll drive you over and wait," he said.

I waved a hand. "I appreciate that, but I have no idea how long this will take."

Crap. I was, to put it mildly, horny.

He took me back to Mum's place where I switched to my Jeep. Along the way we'd devised a plan: I'd do what I had to do at the hospital, then meet him at his place. He gave me his address—I had no idea where he lived—and we went our separate ways.

So all was not lost. The evening would not be a bust. Or so I thought.

7

Amelia's chest X-ray showed her pneumonia pretty much gone, so I couldn't blame the fever and shaking chills on that. Her urine, however, showed infection and the white count in her CBC was way up. Blood culture results would take a while, but it looked like septicemia from a urinary tract infection, despite the fact that her catheter had been out for forty-eight hours. I had her IV restarted and got antibiotics flowing into her again.

"Where's my Beth?" she said, looking up at me with watery eyes.

I leaned over the bed. "She'd be here if she could, but she's sick too."

Very sick—in the head. Plus she had a big gouge in each wrist. But Amelia didn't need to know any of that.

"I'm going to die, aren't I?"

The question startled me. Elderly patients can be like kids in their directness. And the most honest answer to that is, *Yes.* Because eventually we're all going to die. But I can't think of a single patient who'd appreciate that sort of wiseass crack from their doctor.

"Not tonight, Amelia," I said, patting her hand.

She grabbed it and said, "When it happens, will you tell Beth? I don't want her hearing it from some stranger."

"Sure. If that's what you want. But I'm not going to let that happen, okay?"

"Thank you."

After tapping my notes into the hospital's EMR, I'd done all

I could do here, so I headed for the main exit. It had been nearly two hours since parting from Trav but I was not yet ready to call it a night. I phoned him as I walked.

"I'm free," I said when he picked up.

"*Well, then, come on down!*"

"On my way."

The exit was in sight when the PA system blared: "*Fifty-five, two north! Fifty-Five, two-north!*"

Oh, hell. I'd just left Two North. *Fifty-five* was the cardiac arrest code, and that was Amelia's floor. I darted to the nearest house phone and called the floor. When the clerk answered, I identified myself and asked her who was coding.

"*Henderson.*"

Oh, no.

"Isn't she a DNR?"

"*I just looked it up and she didn't sign the form.*"

I hung up and headed for the stairs. A frail, eighty-three-year old diabetic should have a "Do not resuscitate" order on the chart. I knew she'd been given the form on admission—it's routine—but I bet Beth talked her out of it.

The code was in progress when I got there, with one of the ER docs running it. I stood back and watched, pacing. The resuscitation team is practiced at this and they all know exactly what each of them is supposed to do. I could add nothing and would only get in the way. So I watched in dismay as her monitor remained flatlined. She'd come through the pneumonia but the septicemia had proved too much for that old heart.

The one bright spot was that she was going to her grave without knowing that her daughter was a double murderer.

I waited until they pronounced her, then entered a final note into the chart.

I was feeling pretty low as I headed again for the exit, and then I heard her voice in my head: *When it happens, will you tell Beth? I don't want her hearing it from some stranger.*

Aw, no. The last person I wanted to see or talk to was Beth Henderson. Bad enough she'd stabbed Stan Harris in a fit of rage, but she'd killed dear Marge in cold blood... pure, premeditated, first-degree murder.

But I had promised.

My best hope was that she'd been sedated and fallen asleep. But no such luck. A local cop sat outside the door to her private room in the south wing. He cleared me through and I found her wide awake. Damn.

"Oh, it's you," she said when she saw me. She held up her bandaged wrists. "I suppose you think I should thank you for saving my life. Well, don't hold your breath. The last thing I wanted was someone to save me."

I wasn't going to get into any of that with her.

"I came to the hospital tonight to see your mother," I said.

Her harsh expression softened. "Is something wrong?"

"She's gone, I'm sorry to say."

"Wh-what happened?"

"Her heart gave out."

She closed her eyes. "Thank God!"

It took me a while to process that. "You sound glad."

"More like relieved." She held up the wrists again. "I won't have to tell her about this and the mess I'm in."

All about you, isn't it, I wanted to say but bit my tongue.

I turned and started toward the door. I couldn't bear another second with this woman.

I said, "Well, she asked me to be the one to tell you if it happened."

"Was it quick?"

I nodded but kept moving. "Very."

As I stepped out of the room I thought I might hear a sob or maybe a moan—some sign of grief—behind me, but heard nothing.

My phone rang: Trav.

"Are you all right?"

"Yes. Things suddenly got crazy here. That elderly patient arrested just after I called you. She didn't make it."

"Aw. Too bad. I was getting worried when you didn't show."

"Sorry. Then I had to go see Beth and tell her."

"Beth Henderson?"

"Yes. It was her mother."

"Oh, Christ. You of all people. What a night you've had."

"Tell me about it." I sagged. Those lusty sparks I'd been feeling earlier had been thoroughly doused. "Look, do you mind if we take a raincheck on the rest of tonight?"

After a pause, he said, "*You're sure?*"

"Yeah. I feel like someone pulled the plug on me. But I'll make it up to you—and I guarantee I won't be on call. Deal?"

"*Deal. But make it soon.*"

"Don't worry about that. I'll make it *very* soon."

8

With no prospect of seeing Trav tonight, I just happened to wander over to Two South where Sam just happened to be a patient. I ran into his attending, Bamdad Mesgar, sitting at the nursing station tapping on a keyboard.

He smiled as I dropped into a chair next to him. Bamdad likes to say he's Persian, but that means Iranian. Word is that his father, also a surgeon, fled Iran after the revolution brought Khomeini to power. Bamdad was born here and has an accent one can only describe as Long Island.

I leaned back and sighed. "Anything more you can tell me besides head of the pancreas?"

"I'm shipping him to Hopkins tomorrow."

"Oh, shit. What's wrong? Did you stage him?"

"I'm too close to Sam, Norrie. We've known each other forever. He referred me a steady stream of patients when I first moved here, just to help me get started. I owe him and I love him, and as a result I don't feel I can be objective with him."

I understood. This is why doctors shouldn't treat family. Tonsillitis, okay, but anything serious, anything with potentially dire consequences, and emotions start to come into play, clouding judgement. You can miss seeing something important, not out of incompetence or negligence, but because you didn't *want* to see it, didn't want to believe anything serious could be wrong with a loved one. That's the danger. If you really love them, make them see someone else.

"Besides," Bamdad said, "Hopkins has a dedicated pancreatic surgical team. He couldn't be in better hands there.

They'll want to do the staging and grading themselves, so I'll let them. Right now it looks good. He lucked out—as if anyone with pancreatic CA can be called lucky. The tumor sits at the leading edge of the head. He became symptomatic early." Yeah, Sam did sound lucky. Pancreatic cancer is a sneaky bastard. The organ is soft and sits in a sort of no-man's land between the spleen and the liver and behind the stomach, so a tumor can grow freely without causing distress in any other organ—unless it's in the head. The head of the pancreas is close to the liver and its bile duct. As the tumor swells it can press on the bile duct and shut it down. When that happens bilirubin backs up into the blood stream, turning the whites of the victim's eyes yellow, and doing the same to the skin. Jaundice. Exactly what happened to Sam.

He woke up this morning with yellow eyes, which led to discovery of the tumor in an early stage. If the tumor had been in the body or tail of the pancreas it could have kept growing and spreading in secret. That's why most cancer of the pancreas is found too late.

"You see a Whipple in his future?" I said.

Bamdad nodded. "Depends on the staging, but yeah. Looks like it. Followed by chemo and radio."

"Will the CLL affect his recovery?"

"I don't think so, but that's another reason to send him to Hopkins."

His expression mirrored what I was feeling: Poor Sam.

I'd always respected Bamdad Mesgar, both as a surgeon and a man, but now that doubled. Too many of the surgeons I'd met—including the orthopedist I'd had that affair with—are prima donnas. God complexes abound. I knew Bamdad had done some of his training with the Hopkins pancreatic team during his residency. He'd performed Whipples and could have done one on Sam and not only collected a fat fee from the insurance company, but also basked in the glow of having been the guy to cut cancer out of a beloved local physician.

But as Bamdad had said, he was too close to Sam. So he'd done what every good doctor does: Choose what's best for the patient.

I stood. "Is he awake?"

"Yes, but not crazy about visitors, you know."

"So I've heard. I'm just going to say a quick hello."

I peeked into Sam's private room and found him lying there with the lights on but his eyes closed. He looked vulnerable, like he was fading into the sheets. I didn't want to disturb him, so I pulled out my little Post-it pad and started scribbling him a note.

"Norrie?" he said, startling me.

"Oh, sorry," I said. "Didn't want to disturb you. Just leaving you a note."

"I wasn't sleeping. Just resting my eyes. You've heard the MRI results?"

"Yes, dammit. So sorry, Sam."

During my first year with LFPA, he'd quoted Voltaire to me: *The art of medicine is amusing patients while nature cures the disease.* But nature wasn't going to cure this. Major surgery was in order.

I went over my conversation with Bamdad and his coming transfer to Hopkins. He seemed resigned to the move.

"You're here late," he said, switching the subject.

"Yeah. Amelia Henderson had some problems tonight, then arrested. She didn't make it."

"Oh, that's a shame. I gather she was the fifty-five code I just heard?"

"That was it."

"Too bad. But she had a good run."

I hope you have one just as long, I thought.

He asked how the office had gone today.

"Ken worked the morning, saw a bunch of your patients. I saw a few. One of yours isn't happy with me."

"Oh?"

"Yeah, I think I ticked off Mrs. Castanon."

His Einstein eyebrows gyrated. "Not *the* Mrs. Castanon, of the car dealership Castanons?"

"The one and only."

"Hmmmm," he said, drawing out the sound. "What did you do to offend the estimable Mrs. C?"

I gave him a capsule version of what Damon had done to Jerry, and how I'd teed off on him. When I was through, Sam simply looked at me.

Finally I said, "I guess I should have kept my mouth shut and just done my job, right?"

"Not necessarily." He folded his hands over his chest and smiled. "I've always considered patient education an important part of a physician's job, and it sounds like you gave Damon a quick course in trisomy 21."

"But that's not why he came to me. And he won't be coming back. At least not to me."

He shrugged. "Win some, lose some. Do you think you did the right thing?"

I nodded. Yeah, I did.

"Well then, you go with that. Don't forget: Damon isn't the only patient involved here. You have a duty to Jerry as well. Better to say what you did than go home tonight regretting that you kept mum."

"His mom is for sure going to bad mouth me to all her friends."

"Stop beating yourself up, Norrie. That malpractice suit has made you paranoid."

"Still... not a way to build a practice."

"Don't worry about building your practice. You're doing fine."

I was glad to hear he thought so. But I wondered about Ken.

I could see he was tired so I said good night and headed out.

Do you see why everyone loves this man?

9

When I got to Mum's, she was already in her bed and I went straight to mine. The landscape called for straightening but I forced myself to brush past it. Losing Amelia had been bad enough, but then to have to be in the same room as Beth... and seeing Sam looking so frail and helpless in that bed... the whole night had left a bad taste in my mouth and I wanted it over and done with.

But my father had other ideas.

Amazing... my dead father had first spoken to me last Thursday night, just five days ago, and already it had become routine.

That boy Travis was here again, he said from his glow.

"You saw him then?"

I told you I don't see anything, really. Especially in daylight. People are just various blobs of color. I sensed him though.

"Well, he sensed you too. He gets a chill when he steps into the house. Don't you like him?"

I like him fine. I'm glad you had him back.

"Then why not give him a warm feeling?"

He's sensitive and he feels what he feels. I can't control that. But he likes you very much... I can sense that.

Well, I liked him too."

Are you going to see him again?

"I hope so."

Good! I'm very happy to have him come around.

Well, that was good to know. Trav seemed to have won over my father, but he still had a ways to go with my mother.

"I stopped by Corrado's old place today."

Why?

"Why else? To ask Marie about him."

She knows nothing. He sounded annoyed.

"How do you know that?"

Because I spoke to her after Corrado disappeared. She was no help then and she was no help now, am I right?

"I wouldn't know. The house had new owners and Marie is in Parkview."

Is that so? I had no idea.

"A ghost should know those things."

How? I barely know what happens in this house. I know nothing about what's going on in the world outside these walls. Nothing.

He didn't sound happy about that situation.

"Nothing? You don't even know who's president?"

No, and I don't care.

He had a point. What did politics matter to a dead person?

"Well, anyway, Marie's got to know more than I do. I'm going to stop by Parkview tomorrow and—"

Don't waste your time. She's a dead end. Find out what happened to Corrado. I'm sure he's dead and that somebody killed him.

"But why?"

That's what you need to find out. Isn't this Travis is a cop?

"Deputy."

Same thing. He should be able to help you.

"I've already got him on the case."

Good. Find out who killed Corrado. The blob of light started to fade. *I have to go now.*

Cranky, cranky, cranky... did death make people cranky? Or maybe he was just tired of being stuck in a kind of limbo and wanted to move on. I couldn't blame him for that.

Silently vowing to help him all I could, I rolled over and went to sleep.

WEDNESDAY

1

Another jog, another Tezinex and its attendant video, and then off to the office. Wednesday morning turned out to be fairly normal, patient-wise, probably because that's Sam's normal day off and none of his regulars were looking for him. I did have quite a surprise when I walked into the reception area mid-morning and found the rack of Tezinex products empty.

"What happened?" I said to Giselle.

"A patient of Doctor Lerner's—Martin Gale—came in a little while ago and bought us out."

"Everything?"

"Everything."

I could tell she was delighted—no more making change.

Word came from the hospital then that Sam was on his way to Johns Hopkins. He was scheduled for a PET scan later today, and if that looked good, they'd operate tomorrow. They weren't wasting any time. I silently wished him the best of luck.

I stopped by Ken's consultation room to update him on our hospital patients and to tell him about Amelia. I also told him about seeing Sam last night and his transfer to Hopkins.

"I think that'll be best for him," he said. "They've got a top-notch team."

When I mentioned selling out of Tezinex products, Ken looked surprised.

"Really? Martin Gale? I started him on Tezinex yesterday. I wonder what prompted him to do that." He shrugged and flashed an I-told-you-so smile. "Well, no matter. I'll have to call

Donna and tell her to drop off some more. I think we can say
that selling Tezinex adjuncts is already a big success."

Neither of us realized that just a few days from now he'd
have to eat those words.

2

I finished the morning on time, made myself a Tezinex shake—glad now that Donna had given me my own supply—and hurried out for a few errands. My primary destination was the Parkview nursing home, but first I needed to make a quick stop at Lebanon's one and only carpet store.

Yesterday I'd called the owner—his name's Tony—and he'd gone out and measured my now-uncarpeted hall. He said he'd write up an estimate and pick out some samples at the store that would match the pile and color I'd need. I just had to stop by and choose.

Great. I wanted the installers ready to go the second the cleanup crew finished their work.

I entered Carpet Town and approached the counter where two teenage boys were deep in conversation. I listened in, fascinated.

"Hey, I like saw this thing on the tube last night?" the blond one said. "You know, like extreme boarding from Australia? And know what? It's like almost winter down there!"

The other kid, his dark hair buzz cut, made a face. "No way! Australia doesn't even *have* winter. It's like right next to Africa and everybody knows Africa's all jungles and shit."

The blond shook his head. "Duh! Australia's like over by Japan, you know where we like nuked that city during Viet Nam."

"Yeah, I heard about that. What was the name of that place? It's like famous."

"I think it's Akira."

Buzzcut's eyes nearly bulged. "Dude! That's the anime guy!"

"I know, but where do you like think Akira got his name?"

I felt my IQ draining away just eavesdropping on this, so I waved my hands for attention.

"Helloooo! Tony said he left some samples for me?"

The boys low-fived and the blond kid walked off toward the rear while the buzzcut turned to me.

"Sure. Tony's out to lunch but give me your name and I'll check for you."

"Marconi. You know, like the radio guy."

He tilted head and gave me this vacant, dog-hears-strange-noise look, then returned to staring down at his keyboard. "I don't listen to talk radio. I'm like so not into that stuff."

I stared at him, not knowing whether to laugh or cry.

Finally he looked up again. "What?"

"You mean to tell me—?" I cut myself off. What was the use? "M-A-R-C-O-N-I."

I spoke through clenched teeth, but he managed to understand me.

You can*not* make this stuff up.

He found the samples for me and I went through them. I picked one I liked and gave it to the kid.

"Do you do the installation?" I asked.

He shook his head. "Nah. Willie and I load and unload and move inventory around. Tony has mechanics to do the installs."

Thank God for that, I thought.

I took the estimate for my insurance company and hurried out.

3

Next stop: the Parkview nursing home. Once there, I made my way to Appletree Lane and eventually to Marie Piperno's room which she shared with another elderly woman. Her roommate lay on her back, snoring; a transparent green oxygen cannula ran under her nostrils.

"I haven't seen you before," said the aide who brought me, a portly black woman in pink scrubs with a nameplate that read *Tierra*.

"I knew Marie when I was a kid."

"And you haven't seen her since?"

"No. I won't be long. I just have a few questions to ask her."

She rolled her eyes. "Well, good luck with that, hon."

As she walked out I turned to Marie. She sat in a wheelchair next to her bed, wearing gray wool slacks and a light blue blouse that carried some remnants of her lunch. The crumbs taunted me so I took a tissue and cleaned them off her. Her feet, ankles, and lower legs were markedly swollen despite the heavy-duty surgical stockings she wore to reduce the edema. She too sported an oxygen cannula under her nose.

"Hi, Marie," I said, "I'm sure you don't recognize me but—"

"Sit up straight, Angie," she said, pointing to the empty guest chair opposite her.

Uh-oh.

I tried again. "Marie, I just wanted to ask you a few questions about Corrado."

"Angie!" Again to the chair. "How many times have I told you not to bite your fingernails?"

"Corrado, Marie—do you remember anything about when Corrado disappeared?"

"Oh, Angie, you're such a willful child."

I could see she wasn't going to be any help. My father had been right, but for the wrong reason.

The room had two small dressers against the opposite wall. I recognized a small framed photo of Angelina but Corrado was missing. I rearranged the few bottles there, lining them up to either side of the picture. I tried a few questions again but ran up against the same wall. No use.

I patted her shoulder. "Well, have a nice day, Marie."

As I turned to go, she said, "He beats us, you know."

I spun back to her. She was looking straight at me.

"What did you say?"

"He beats us terribly, me and Angie. He's an awful man. Awful."

Shock stole my voice. I'd never expected this.

Finally I managed, "Did you tell anyone?"

But her attention was centered again on the empty chair. "Angie, your posture is disgraceful!"

I tried to squeeze more out of her but she simply wasn't there. I said good bye again and found Tierra at the desk.

"She's tough as nails, that one," she said. "Caught the 'rona when it came through, but kicked it."

"Amazing," I said. "She's had heart problems forever."

"Yeah. Her mind's gone but her heart keeps pumping away. God needs to pay more attention to these people."

Amen to that.

"Does her daughter Angelina come around much?"

"Now and again. When she does, Marie doesn't know who she is."

I could see how that would be discouraging.

"Do you have a contact number? We knew each other when we were teens."

She hesitated, then looked it up and wrote it down for me. I thanked her and left with Marie's words trailing after me.

He beats us terribly, me and Angie. He's an awful man. Awful.

Was that really my godfather?

4

When I got back to the office I heard a raised voice coming from the reception area. I went to see.

A red-faced Anna Divisova stood at the window, crying, "This isn't fair! It's just not fair! You had no right selling all the stuff to one patient. No right! What about the rest of us? Did you ever think that someone else might need them too? Did you?"

The stuff? Did she mean the Tezinex products?

Giselle said, "I told you, Anna. Doctor Lerner contacted the company rep this morning and she'll be bringing us a new supply on her next swing through town."

"When will that be?"

"I don't know. She didn't give me her schedule."

"Well, you should have asked! Why didn't you ask? The video says I have to eat their bars if I want to lose weight."

Poor Giselle seemed at a loss for words. She spotted me and gave a pleading look.

"Perhaps Doctor Norrie can explain."

Anna's face twisted. "Her? She wouldn't even prescribe it for me."

I didn't want to get into this, but I couldn't leave Giselle hanging. Dealing with an obstreperous patient came with the territory but I doubted I'd find it in her job description.

"Anna," I said, "Are you talking about the Tezinex bars and stuff?"

"What else would I be talking about?"

Still the bad attitude.

"Well, I know for a fact that the video doesn't say you have to use the Tezinex brand at all."

Her tone turned to a snarl. "How would you know *anything*?"

"Because I checked out a couple of the videos to make sure they're not just ads for their products, and they're not. They even make a point of saying any 200-calorie protein bar will do the job."

The sudden uncertainty in her expression told me I'd scored a point. "Yes, well, but I want to do this *right!*"

"A Quest bar will get it done. So will a Kind fruit-and-nut bar." I could speak with authority because, believe me, I know my low-carb protein bars. I've tried them all. I've practically lived on them at times. "They're very similar to the Tezinex bar and they taste pretty good."

"It's not fair!" she said as she turned and stomped toward the door. "It's just not *fair!*"

Giselle slumped back in her chair and blew out a big breath. "Thank you! I didn't know what to do with her. She just kept going on and on."

Anna's obsessive-compulsive proclivities seemed to have ratcheted into high gear. Seeing the Tezinex products on the video must have planted them in her consciousness as the only brand that would do the job. Her obsessive component wouldn't stop thinking about them and her compulsive side had to buy them and nothing else.

I said, "She can't help it."

She shook her head. "Is it worth it?"

"What?"

"Selling this stuff?"

No, it wasn't, but I didn't want to look like I was siding against Ken.

"We're just trying it out. We're not locked into anything."

"A royal pain in the butt, if you ask me." She raised her hands. "But you didn't, so I'll say no more."

And neither would I, except: "Hang in there, Giselle."

No sooner had I stepped into my consultation room, hoping to get through the latest lab reports, when Giselle buzzed me that Deputy Lawton was on the line.

"Hey, Trav," I said. "Sorry again about last night."

"Like the song goes, 'Don't think twice, it's all right.' Comes with your territory."

"So what's up?"

"I heard from MCMUP."

Who? Oh, right. The Maryland Center for Missing and Unidentified Persons.

"Do they have a file on Corrado?"

"They do. An unsolved case. They weren't digital yet back then so they had to dig out the paper file and fax it to me."

"And?"

"I'll swing by with a copy. When do your hours end?"

Always glad to see Deputy Lawton. "I should be free by five thirty."

"Okay. See you then." A brief pause, then, *"So what is this guy to you again?"*

"Told you: My father's best friend from the Old Country. Plus my godfather." Something in his tone. "Why?"

"Oh, nothing. See you later."

Oh, nothing... really? Why didn't I believe that?

5

We worked through the patients and managed to stay on schedule. The highlight of my afternoon was a double appointment with the Fletchers. They're a highly competitive middle-age couple who can't help one-upping each other at every opportunity. Both had come in with sore throats and body aches.

Peg sat on the examining table while her husband Greg leaned against the wall, waiting to switch places.

"My throat feels like someone's using a blowtorch or maybe a flame thrower in there," Peg said.

Greg rasped, "That's nothing. Mine feels like I'm swallowing a thousand razor blades."

"Yeah?" Peg said. "Well, my whole body feels like I was run over by a truck—ten trucks."

Greg shook his head. "You're lucky. I feel like a thousand guys have been beating me with baseball bats."

And that was the way the whole visit went. I love listening to these two with their sicker-than-thou tag-team. Their strep tests were negative so I skipped the antibiotics they wanted and advised Tylenol and fluids and rest. They weren't happy leaving without a prescription—many patients aren't—but the world is already awash in unnecessary antibiotics. I see no point in adding to that.

We all finished on schedule and Ken and the staff were gone by the time Travis knocked on the back door. We hugged and then I led him to the empty waiting room. The cleaning service would be in soon but for now we had the building to ourselves.

After some small talk about how good dinner was last night

and such, Travis handed me the manila folder he'd brought with him.

"The MCMUP file on Corrado Piperno."

I opened it and glanced at the typewritten sheets. "Have you read it?" I was sure he had.

"I gave it a quick run through. Did you know he has a record—or *had* a record?"

Uh-oh. "He was arrested? No, I never heard anything about that." I wondered if my father knew. "What for? Not the Mafia or anything, I hope."

"Nothing mob related. They looked into that. The mob's been in Baltimore forever, but the Gambino family moved in during the fifties. They had their hand in all the usual—drugs, gambling, loan sharking, prostitution, unions, including the construction unions. Piperno was a mason but no one could find any ties. As far as anyone could tell he made an honest living laying bricks."

"Then what was the charge?"

"D and D—drunk and disorderly a couple of times in Baltimore. On the Block, to be specific."

The notorious Baltimore Block. Actually a couple of blocks, all lined with strip clubs and sex shops.

"What was he doing there? Or do I want to know?"

"Word was he was known around the Block—something of a semi-regular there, like a couple of times per month."

I had to ask: "Are we talking strip clubs or are we talking prostitutes?"

Trav looked uncomfortable. "Both."

Poor Marie. Did my father know any of this about his *fratellino*? I wondered. And then I had an awful thought: Did my father ever go with him?

"Do they think that's where he might have gone the night he disappeared?"

Trav shrugged. "Who can say? No one they talked to at the time could remember seeing him around that night, but one night is pretty much like any other down there. The consensus after the investigation, though, was that there was a good chance of some foul play."

That went with my father's contention that he'd been murdered. His parting words last night had been, *Find out who killed Corrado.*

"They found evidence?"

"Only circumstantial," he said. "A guy who's going to run off and desert his family usually has financial problems or is involved with another woman or in some sort of criminal activity. Piperno's finances were in good shape and, like I said, no ties to the mob. Another thing a guy does if he's taking off is pack up some clothes and withdraw some cash. But none of his spare clothing or belongings were missing. Piperno disappeared with the clothes on his back and the cash in his wallet."

"So... no evidence his disappearance was planned."

"The strangest part of the mystery was that his car was found parked and locked near a vacant lot about a mile from his house, with no keys and no sign of foul play. It appears he met someone there and together they headed for some unknown destination."

I thought about that. "So it had to be someone he didn't want his wife and daughter to see. We might be talking about another woman. And very likely the last person to see him alive."

"And maybe the only person who knows—or knew—what happened to him. We don't know if this person was male or female. It may have been his killer."

"How do you know he wasn't visiting someone right there in Carmel—someone who lived on that block?"

"Well, the police canvassed the neighborhood and nobody remembered seeing the car before, and nobody recognized Piperno's photo."

"So getting picked up by someone makes the most sense."

"It fits the best. It may have been someone who also frequented the Block. The Block remained part of the accepted theory: This Corrado Piperno had gone down to there, maybe with a friend, looking for pay-to-play sex like he'd done before, and got involved with the wrong people."

"'The wrong people'? What does that mean? Are any of the lowlifes who run that racket the right people?"

"Well, with some of them, what you see is what you get:

They trade sex for money, just like they advertise. Others use it as a come-on for shakedowns and blackmail schemes or just plain muggings."

"And what? They think he ran afoul of these people and his body's at the bottom of Baltimore Harbor?"

Another shrug. "Seems as good an explanation as any as to how and why someone like him vanishes without a trace."

Without a trace... that pretty well summed it up. Never seen or heard from again. Not a call, not a note, not a peep to anyone, not even an Elvis sighting.

I waved the folder. "This is all very... disappointing."

"I'm sure. A close family friend, your godfather, of all people, living some sort of double life. That's why I wanted to give it to you in person. But like you said last night, it's been twenty years. Why the interest now?"

I couldn't very well tell him I was doing it to help out my father's ghost, so I extemporized.

"Well, I guess it's from being back in the old family home. And you playing "That's Amore" the other night—although in our house it was known as "'At's Amore"—brought back all sorts of memories. Corrado only knew a couple of chords—"

"I learned Sunday night you can pretty much fake it with just two," Trav said.

"He used to pound it out as he and my father would sing at the top of their voices, Corrado playing in one key, my father singing in another, while Corrado tried to harmonize in yet another."

Their singing defined cacophony, but they'd be having such a great time. A warm, pleasant memory. But this folder... this folder was adding to the pall Marie's remark this afternoon had cast over it all.

Damn, I wish Dad hadn't asked me to look into this. How much did he already know?

I said, "Anyway, thinking about my Uncle Corry got me wondering about what happened to him." I sighed. "You know what they say about poking into the past: You always run the risk of digging up something that should have stayed buried."

My dismay must have shown on my face, for Trav said, "Sorry to bring you down."

I shook it off. "It's okay." On pure impulse, I said, "Hey, you free for dinner? I'll treat this time."

"Aw, I'd love to, but I already have a date."

I had a feeling I knew who that was. "Maddie, right?"

He nodded, beaming. "Right." He adored his daughter—as every father should. "She absolutely loves Taco Bell."

"And so do you, I'll bet."

"What's not to like?"

He probably planned on having a light repast of a dozen or so chalupas.

"You're welcome to come along," he added.

I waved him off. "No-no. It's father-daughter night. She'll want you all to herself."

Besides, I wasn't ready to meet his little girl just yet.

"Speaking of which," he said, rising, "I'd better be off."

Just then I remembered that my mother was going away for the weekend.

"Hey, are you free Saturday night?"

"Absolutely. I have the day shift."

"Well, I've got the weekend off so how about I cook you dinner Saturday night?"

"Your place is back up and running?"

"Not yet. At my mum's." I saw a little frown, so I quick-added, "She'll be in Jersey City all weekend. We'll have the place to ourselves."

Well, not completely to ourselves. But I think I can be forgiven for not mentioning the ghost wandering about.

"Sounds great. What can I bring?"

"Well, it's going to be Italian. I'm making my famous meatball and spaghetti dinner."

His eyes lit. "I love meatballs and spaghetti."

Was there a meal he didn't like? Anyway, it was going to be an absolute pleasure cooking for an appetite like that.

"So bring a Chianti, maybe. Or a Valpolicella will go nicely. And yourself, of course. Like five o'clock if that works?"

"It works fine."

He kissed me good-bye, then hurried toward the door, but turned at the last moment.

"Almost forgot," he said. "My father saw the folder and said he knew Piperno."

"Really? How?"

"Both were in construction. My dad was a carpenter and Piperno was a mason. Sometimes they'd all play cards when the weather got in the way of work or sometimes hit a bar after work."

"Did he know him well?"

"Well enough not to like him."

Uh-oh. More Corrado negativity.

"Did he say why?"

Trav shrugged. "I'll tell you exactly what he told me: 'He was a bum.'" He waved. "Gotta go."

Well, opinions about my godfather seemed to be unanimous. If he were a movie his Rotten Tomatoes Score would be *0% Fresh*.

I had the evening to myself, so I carried the folder back to my consultation room, planning to read it. But when I got there I decided why bother? Trav had already summarized it for me. I'd keep it for future reference, in the unlikely event I'd need to peruse it for more detail, but I knew pretty much all I wanted to know. *More* than I wanted to know.

But that reminded me that I wanted to talk to Corrado's daughter, Angelina. Or did I?

He beats us terribly, me and Angie...

Would she want to talk about him? I pulled out the number Tierra gave me and punched it in. A woman answered on the third ring with an impatient *"Hello?"*

"Is this Angelina Piperno?"

"Speaking."

"Hi. I don't know if you remember me. My name is Noreen Marconi and—"

"Noreen. Yes, I remember you. Rocky's girl."

"That's me. Look, I was wondering if we could have a little talk."

"A 'little talk'? About what?"

"Your father."

A pause, and then the temperature of her voice dropped about thirty degrees.

"Why do you want to talk about him?"

"It's complicated."

"I'll bet." She paused again… thinking about it? *"Okay, here's the deal. I'm at work and can't talk about anything at the moment. Call me tomorrow morning."*

"Okay, sure. I—"

She'd hung up.

Okay, I'd bothered her at work. That would explain the terseness. But I'd definitely sensed her withdrawing when I mentioned her father. Well, if he'd beat her as Marie had said, that was understandable. I was definitely going to call her tomorrow.

I was glad Trav was going to be busy with Maddie tonight because I was feeling kind of wrung out. Out of the blue, Marie Piperno had dropped that bombshell about Corrado beating her and Angelina, and then Trav chimes in with a missing-person investigation showing he'd frequented prostitutes. I mean, WTF?

Yesterday hadn't been so great, either, starting off with that encounter with Ted Phelan and his wife in Safeway, but I'd managed to shake that off. I'd found that if I stayed busy, thoughts of the malpractice suit receded; but during down time, they floated to the surface like a bloated corpse in a pond.

Like now.

I have a locked drawer in the desk. I pulled out my keys and opened it. I kept the original copy of the summons here, and this would be where I'd file all my correspondence regarding the case. Nobody's business but mine.

I pulled out the summons and fanned through it, pausing at those wonderful words *"grossly negligent, wanton, reckless, and intentional."*

The damn thing didn't even say what error or misstep I'd committed. Not a hint of what exactly they thought I'd done wrong.

Damn, this was infuriating.

For quick reference, I'd stored a copy of the Phelan chart in the drawer as well. I yanked it out and opened it. His home number was listed on the folder's tab. I grabbed the phone receiver and began punching it in, but paused after three digits. Froze was more like it. My palms had slickened with sweat. What if he tore into me? How would I defend myself? I couldn't argue my case as in a trial.

This was foolish.

Last week, right after the summons arrived, I'd wanted to call Phelan but Ken had stopped me. *Never call the plaintiff. And never, never call his attorney. The only time you speak is in a deposition or in court—and never without your own attorney present.*

He'd quoted part of the Miranda warning: *Anything you say can and will be held against you in a court of law.*

I returned the receiver to its cradle.

A heartbeat later I had it back in my hand with my fingers tapping the buttons.

Phelan hadn't looked angry in the Safeway, he'd look guilty. Not only that, he was still seeing me for his hypertension. Do you continue going to a physician you thought was grossly negligent, wanton, and reckless?

And anyway, since when do I let someone else speak for me? Never. Not that I'd ever be so foolish as to represent myself in court, but why couldn't I speak to Ted Phelan, person to person, just to ask him *why?* That was all I wanted to know. Why did he think I'd been grossly negligent, wanton, and reckless?

Okay, it went against conventional wisdom, but conventional wisdom too often turns out to be less than wise.

I had to know, damn it.

I listened to the rings: one... two... three... Maybe he wasn't home. A part of me hoped so. And then a man picked up on the fifth ring and said hello.

"Mister..." My throat was dry. "Mister Phelan, this is Doctor Marconi."

"Doctor Norrie?" He didn't sound angry or unhappy to hear from me. "Is something wrong?"

Talk about an opening...

"Well, yes, Mister Phelan, there is: You're suing me."

"Oh dear. I... I'm not really suing *you.*"

"The summons I received last week says differently. You are

most definitely suing me, and I'd like to know why."

"Oh dear... oh dear..." He sounded like a stuck record. "I'm really suing Doctor Saxton."

Ken had been right—I guess everyone is right once in a while, and this was his time: Lenny Saxton was the target of the suit.

But that wasn't the answer I was looking for.

"But you're *really* suing me as well."

"No-no-no. Oh dear, I told Mister Stark that I didn't want you involved but he told me it would help ferret out evidence against the real culprit, Doctor Saxton—he's the one who botched the diagnosis. And Mister Stark says you're partly to blame for sending me to someone who didn't know what he was doing."

Mister Stark... nerdy weasel Eddie Stark from Carmel High had gone to law school and come out specializing in personal injuries—"ambulance chaser" in the vernacular. He'd sue anyone for anything. According to Ken he had truly earned the name among his fellow attorneys of "Stark the Shark."

"Doctor Saxton *does* know what he's doing," I said. "He's board certified in his field and I've seen him save more than a few lives."

Lenny is not exactly Mr. Personality, I'll admit—as a matter of fact he can be pretty cold and brusque at times.

"Well, he didn't know what he was doing with me. I have HHT and he never told me."

Hereditary hemorrhagic telangiectasia. Quite a mouthful. Simply stated, it's a genetic defect that allows some of the body's smaller arteries to flow directly into veins without first going through capillaries. This results in swollen vessels called telangiectases. Phelan's chest X-ray and CT would have been consistent with pulmonary HHT. Trouble was, beyond cauterization and embolization of the bigger malformations, there isn't a whole heck of a lot you can do for it.

"Who's taking care of you now?"

"Doctor Adams at Johns Hopkins."

Good man. "What's he doing for you that Doctor Saxton didn't?"

"Well... right now he's just watching me."

"And what was Doctor Saxton doing?"

"Nothing."

I didn't see a whole lot of difference between "just watching" and doing nothing, but I wasn't here to argue Lenny Saxton's case.

"So that's why you're suing me and accusing me of negligence? Because I sent you to Doctor Saxton?"

"Oh dear. I'd never accuse you of negligence."

"Well, you did—plus being wanton and reckless."

"Oh dear. Mister Stark told me not to think of it as suing you, just your insurance company. He said that you never know, we might get some extra money out of them, and Lord knows I could use some."

"It wasn't my insurance company you accused of negligence."

"But Mister Stark told me you'd be out of the suit long before it ever went to court. He said whatever happened, it wouldn't cost you a penny."

The lousy lying weasel...

I was getting steamed.

"That's not true, Ted." I decided to switch to his first name— that was what I used on his regular blood pressure visits, and I wanted to narrow whatever gap Stark the Shark had caused. "Not even close. My insurance company has to hire a lawyer to defend me and that's expensive."

"But *you* don't pay for him."

"Not now. But I do later. Even if I'm dropped from the case or I go on to win, being sued causes damage to my reputation with the insurance company—you are, after all, calling me a negligent doctor—and because of that they'll jack up my premium. I *will* be paying for this, Ted—for years and years to come."

"Oh dear! I feel terrible about this. What can I do?"

I had a feeling that my telling him to have Stark the Shark drop me from the suit might be crossing some sort of line. I didn't want to go there.

"That's up for you to decide."

"But what?"

"Do what you think is right, Ted."

"Oh, dear."

Oh dear, indeed. He seemed stuck on that phrase. The call ended with Phelan making apologies and me making noncommittal noises. The man was clueless.

I hung up and leaned back. So what had the call accomplished? Nothing I could see beyond raising a little consciousness.

No, wait. Ted Phelan had told me he didn't think I was negligent.

...*I'd never accuse you of negligence...*

He was suing me only because his lawyer had advised him to. That added a spark of brightness to an otherwise very dark day.

Edward "the Shark" Stark... I hoped I never ran into him. I might do something rash... something he could legitimately sue me for.

6

I called Mum and told her not to hold dinner for me. This being
Wild Wednesday, I wasn't sure whether she'd make her beef
stew or her baked ham. Thanks to Tezinex I had no appetite
for either. Her world famous minute steaks used to be on the
Wednesday menu, but somewhere along the way she'd either
lost her taste or lost her source for those epicurean delights,
because they'd been dropped from the Wild Wednesday menu.

"I've baked a lovely ham," she said.

As a rule she studded her Polish ham with so many cloves
it looked like a model of the coronavirus by the time she was
through.

"That's great, but I'll take a pass."

"Big lunch at the office again?"

"Those reps just love us."

Absolutely true.

"Of course they do."

"You and Timmy chow down. I'll just fix myself a snack
here and be home in a while."

I mixed up a Tezinex shake and got all caught up on my
labs and diagnostic tests and consultation reports. Then I forced
myself to read the MCMUP file on Corrado Piperno. My dad's
bestie, his *fratellino*, going with prostitutes... I simply couldn't
correlate Uncle Corry with the drunk-and-disorderly adulterer
described in this folder.

By the time I got home Timmy had gone and Mum was
watching TV. She doesn't have wi-fi or Netflix but she does
have cable and so we camped before the living room TV and

watched a couple of episodes of *Family Feud* on the Game Show Network. Maybe "we" isn't entirely accurate. I kept watching that damned tilted landscape on the wall. Kept getting up to straighten it. On my third attempt Mum grabbed me and pulled me back.

"For God's sake, Norrie, leave it be."

So I let it be. But I didn't like it.

I held off going to bed but finally called it a night. I didn't want to have to tell my father about the beatings, even less about the arrests and the prostitutes. I was going on the assumption that he didn't know anything about it, and if that was true, these new revelations would break his heart. Okay, that might be taking it too far, but I knew he'd be hurt.

I showered, got into bed, turned out the light, and waited. Didn't have to wait long. The glow appeared beside the bed, and then...

Did you learn anything?

"A 'hello' would be nice, Dad."

Sorry. I've been waiting all day. Okay: Hello, Norrie, how was your day?

"Awful."

What's wrong? What happened?

"I learned things about Corrado...things I wish I hadn't, but now I can't unknow them."

A pause, then, Like what?

"Like he used to beat Marie and Angelina."

What? That's crazy! Corry wouldn't hurt a fly. Who told you this?

"Marie."

You spoke to Marie? Didn't I tell you not to bother?

"You asked me to find out what happened to Corrado. I need to talk to the last person to most likely see him alive, don't you think?"

But I told you I already spoke to her just after he disappeared and she was no help. Was I right?

"Her memory's pretty much gone."

What?

"She's got dementia, probably Alzheimer's."

Then how could she tell you that Corry beat her?

I was getting a little annoyed at his defensive attitude.

"Because she did. She just came out and said it."

She's lost her mind and yet you believe her about Corry?

"Look, Dad, Alzheimer's eventually affects the whole brain. But early on it's mostly short-term memory that's affected. You can't form new memories, but the old ones are left intact. That's why it's typical for an Alzheimer's patient to remember, say, everyone she danced with at Homecoming in her junior year in high school but can't remember what she had for breakfast—or if she even *had* breakfast."

See?

"No. You're not listening. Eventually the old memories are destroyed too, but it happens piecemeal. If a connection persists to a surviving old memory, especially if it's a strong one, it can be accessed. My mentioning Corrado to her may have triggered a connection and all of a sudden it popped into her consciousness and she blurted it out."

Well, what did she say… exactly?

"'He beats us terribly, me and Angie. He's an awful man. Awful.' And that's an exact quote. It's burned on my brain."

Well, you can tell right there she's not right in the head. Corry's not beating anyone anywhere. I mean, how can you trust someone who thinks she's being beaten by a man no one has seen for twenty years?

"Because she's unmoored from the past, even the recent past. She lives only in the present now, with no sense of time, and though she may be able to recall an old beating, it has no context in time. To her it might have happened that morning or twenty years ago. It's all the same to her."

I thought about what a horrible way that is to live. We *are* our memories, after all. With no memory of who we know or where we've been or what we've experienced, we've got nothing to make us any different from the next person with no memories. Without our memories we're all ciphers, zeroes. All identical blank slates. That's no way to live. In fact I question if that's living at all. It's mere existence and little else.

That all comes down to a roundabout way of saying she doesn't know what she's talking about. I knew Corry and let me tell you, my fratellino would never raise a hand to Marie and Angelina.

He was in denial. I had to shake him out of that.

"*Did* you know him, Dad? Did you really?"

Of course I did. Did you get that cop boyfriend of yours to help you like I asked?

What a perfect segue.

"As a matter of fact, I did. But you're not going to like it."

Hesitant now... *I'm not?*

"No. The State Police have a missing person file on Corrado back from when he disappeared and they went looking for him. They learned that he had an arrest record for drunk and disorderly."

He did? When was this?

"A couple of years before he disappeared."

Well, Corry did like his vino.

"The arrests took place down on the Baltimore Block where they learned he was a regular."

Corry? On the Block? Why?

"Prostitutes, Dad. He frequented prostitutes down there."

No, that's not true!

"Dad, those cops had no reason to lie. They didn't know Corrado. He was just another missing person they were looking for. They simply wrote down what they learned."

A long silence followed, which I finally broke.

"How much did you know about this, Dad?"

Nothing... nothing.

"Are you sure?"

Of course I'm sure!

"Your best friend never said anything about this to you?"

No, never. He had to know I wouldn't approve. Probably too ashamed to tell me he was paying for sex. He paused. *But I guess...* His voice trailed off.

"You guess what?"

Corry did mention a couple of times that he and Marie... that they weren't really and truly husband and wife anymore. Something to do with Marie's heart.

I took that to mean no conjugal relations... referred to as "consortium" in my malpractice summons, of which Mrs. Phelan had supposedly been deprived because of my wanton negligence.

Well, what with Marie's chronic heart failure and all, that was certainly possible. But did it give him the right to visit prostitutes? Not in my book. What happened to "in sickness and in health"? Not to mention the diseases he might be bringing into the house. The Block had to be STD City.

"Do you think that's why he beat her?"

He didn't beat her!

"We'll see about that. I'm going to talk to Angelina tomorrow and—"

No! Don't do that! She was always a crazy one. Corrado would tell me that she was off her rocker. That was why he never brought her along when he came to our house. He never knew when she would just come out and say something crazy.

So that was why we never saw much of Angelina. I'd just assumed she was staying home to keep her "sickly" mother company.

Dad added, *I thought you were going to find out why he disappeared, not dig up all this dirt on him.*

He sounded upset. I guess I'd be upset too if someone had told me a dear friend had been leading a secret life. It occurred to me that maybe it's not such a bad thing that I don't have any dear friends.

"The cops couldn't find any evidence to show that he planned his disappearance. It looked like he left his house with every intention of coming back. But he never did. The police think he ran afoul of some shady types down on the Block and they might have killed him."

How am I supposed to forgive Corrado if I know all these bad things about him? I'll be stuck here forever!

"Well, now you know there's a good chance he didn't just up and walk out on everyone. It's likely he was killed."

The glow began to fade.

I have to go now, Norrie. Too much to think about. Much too much...

Yeah, I guess there was.

But I still planned to talk to Angelina tomorrow. The truth about Corrado Piperno—I couldn't bring myself to call him "Uncle Corry" anymore—had become an itch I had to scratch.

THURSDAY

1

Thursdays are supposed to be my day off, but I had to cover for Sam this morning, so I did a quick jog, took a Tezinex, dutifully watched the day's video, and ate a protein bar as I headed to the hospital.

Thursday morning was always Sam's for hospital rounds but since I was covering him, the task fell to me. After losing Amelia, I had no inpatients, but Sam and Ken did. I checked on them and everyone was doing fine.

I was heading out when I heard my name paged to an extension I didn't recognize. I called and identified myself.

"Oh, Doctor Marconi. This is Symons from the dialysis unit. One of our patients here would like to talk to you. He says he knows you from when you were a kid."

"Really? What's his name?"

"Albert Lawton. Does that ring a bell?"

Lawton? Travis's father. He'd told me his dad had renal failure and was on dialysis.

"Yes, it does. I'll stop by on my way out."

I entered the dialysis unit and looked around. Though he'd aged a lot in sixteen years—I'd been about half my present age when I last saw him—I knew him right away. He lay on a recliner with tubes running in and out of the fistula in his left arm. One took blood from him and ran it through the dialysis machine at his bedside where it was cleaned of the impurities his kidneys could no longer remove, and then the freshened blood was run back into his circulation.

I stopped next to his recliner and said, "Hi. I remember you."

He looked up at me with a confused expression, then broke into a grin.

"Norrie! Or should I call you 'Doctor Marconi' now?"

"'Norrie' will do just fine."

"I can't believe you're the same girl who used to study and practice piano with Travis. My God, you've changed."

Yeah. So much less of me.

"For the better, I hope."

"Oh, absotootly."

"Sorry to hear about your kidneys," I said, moving the topic away from me. "How's the dialysis going?"

His smile withered. "It makes me feel better in the long run but it's taken over my life. I feel like I'm chained to this machine."

It took on average of four hours to complete a dialysis session and the average renal failure patient needed three sessions a week. Dialysis kept you alive while you waited for a transplant, but yes, it did take over your life.

"I'll keep my fingers crossed for a transplant soon."

"I appreciate that. They say I got antibodies. I'm not quite sure what those are, but they say it makes for a tougher match. Travis took the tests but didn't match up good, so I've gotta wait."

I held up my crossed fingers. "You wanted to see me?"

"Yeah. Trav tells me you're looking into Corrado Piperno?"

"Yes. He was my godfather." A fact I was growing less and less willing to admit.

"He was good friends with your father, right?"

"They were both kids in the same town in Italy, so they stayed close. I'm trying to find out why he disappeared. Can you help?"

He shook his head. "Me and Piperno go way back—we're talking thirty-plus years ago—but we didn't have much to do with each other by the time he stopped showing up for work. If you asked me the year that happened, I couldn't tell you. Gave us a lot to talk about, though. The whole thing was a big mystery. Nobody knew where he'd disappeared to, but I can tell you nobody minded much."

"Not popular?"

"He was a bum. He was always a bum. He'd cheat at cards and he'd always be short when we was chipping in to pay a bar bill. That kinda shit." He waved a hand at me. "Sorry."

"That's okay."

Did nobody but my father care for this man?

"I could put up with that petty stuff, but when he started sniffing around my girlfriend—"

"Girlfriend?"

"Yeah. I told you we go way back. This is before I got married, obviously. That girlfriend, Barbara, soon became my wife and, not too long afterward, my ex-wife. We were both single then, but Piperno had a way with the ladies and was always on the hunt for something new. Then he set his sights on Barbara and—"

I loosed an involuntary groan.

Mr. Lawton looked at me and nodded. "Yeah, I know. A low-rent move. One thing to make a play for a girl, but not when she's attached to someone you know. So anyway, I had to take Piperno aside and bounce him off a wall a few times to straighten him out. We kept our distance after that."

And the hits keep coming. This was consistent with him visiting the Block for prostitutes.

I said, "I don't remember: Did you ever know my father?"

"Rocky, right? Sorta. We met a couple of times during those things where Marge Harris got her piano students together. What'd she call them?"

"Recitals?"

"That's it. Yeah, your father and me'd say hello and good-bye at the recitals, and that was about it. Mostly I knew your dad by reputation."

"By reputation?" I prayed he wasn't going to say anything bad.

"Piperno always talked about his friend Rocky—called him his *fratello* or something like that—and what a great guy he was and what great friends they were. Now, I never heard a bad word about your father from anyone, only good things, so I had to wonder how he was friends with a bum like Piperno. I guess the home-country connection explains it some, but still..."

Yeah. But still...

He didn't have much more to tell so we finished with a little small talk. I wished him well and hurried for the office.

The more I heard, the more I had to agree with Albert Lawton's succinct assessment: Corrado Piperno was a bum.

2

Since my regular patients were used to me not being in on Thursday, my schedule was relatively light, most of the slots taken up with Sam's regulars.

Early on I got a call on my cell from the cleanup service telling me their estimate had been approved and could they schedule me for Monday. Monday? I wanted them there immediately and told them the property manager would let them in. They said that was the earliest they could make it.

Damn. I wanted to get things back to normal.

Otherwise, the morning was uneventful and passed quickly. As I came down to the wire, I took a moment to call Angelina Piperno.

"Hi," I said, trying my best to sound chipper and casual when she picked up. "This is Norrie Marconi again. I called last night and—"

"You wanted to talk about my father, right?"

"Yes."

"Why ever?"

I'd decided to use a variation of the excuse I'd given Travis.

"Well, I'm having a renovation done on my condo—actually repair work after a water leak—and so I'm staying at my mother's, and we got to reminiscing about my dad and how he and Corrado were such close friends and we're both still mystified as to whatever happened to him."

I'd babbled that out and run out of air.

"And you think I might know? Or care?"

The "or care" remark gave me a bit of a jolt but I guessed

I should have expected it if her mother was to be believed. I fumbled for a response.

"Well, I guess we thought, that, you know, as his daughter—"

"*Tell me something, Norrie: Why do you care?*"

"I just thought maybe we could talk—"

Her tone hardened. "*You want to talk about my father? Okay, but we'd better do it face to face. I still live in Carmel. When do you want to come over?*"

"Well, I-I-I'm off this afternoon." Where did the stutter come from? "So if you've got time—"

"*Fine. I have to leave around two thirty. Get here before then.*"

She gave me her address and hung up.

Wow. She sounded angry, almost hostile. Angry at me, or was this just a residual from her father? Dad said Corrado had told him she was "off her rocker" and he never knew what crazy thing she might say. What was I letting myself in for here?

Well, I had the afternoon off and pretty open. I'd have to decide whether I wanted to hear Angelina's story, or take my father's advice and stay away.

But was he telling me to stay away because she was unreliable, or because he was afraid she'd only confirm what Marie had said? Dad was still in denial about the physical abuse. I needed clarity on that... needed to know if the godfather I'd always thought of as this great guy was really a whoring wife beater.

Then I heard a now-familiar voice raised in the reception area. I'd visited up front when I'd arrived earlier and noticed that the Tezinex products rack had not been refilled. So I not only knew whose voice I heard, but had a pretty good idea why she'd raised it. I knew better than to go see, but didn't feel right leaving Giselle to handle this on her own.

I walked up front and there she stood—Anna Divisova, looking stressed out and angry as all hell.

"Well, where are they? You told me yesterday you'd have more today. Where are you hiding them?"

"I'm not hiding anything, Anna," Giselle said gently. "And I didn't tell you we'd be restocked by today. I told you the rep would bring more on her next swing through the territory."

"Well, when will that be?"

A slim, dark-haired woman arrived in the waiting room and stood behind Anna, looking irritated and impatient. I'd seen her once or twice, but her name eluded me.

Time to put in my two cents. I stepped forward and spoke in my most soothing tone. "Anna, I know you're upset, but we have no control over the rep's schedule. You don't have to check here every day. Giselle has your number. She'll make a note to call you as soon as the new stock arrives, okay?"

"She shouldn't *have* to call me! The Tezinex products would be here right now if she hadn't sold the whole stock to one person! She shouldn't have done that!"

"Darn right, she shouldn't have!" said the woman behind her.

Oh, no. Another frustrated Tezinex patient?

Anna turned to her. "Am I right or am I right? She shouldn't have done that."

The second woman nodded. "Especially to a man who can't afford it."

Whoa. What was she talking about?

"I don't understand," Giselle said.

The woman pushed ahead of Anna. "I'm Heather Norton and yesterday my father spent a small fortune on that junk you sell."

Heather Norton... I remembered now. She'd been fatigued. Also worried because her father had recently been diagnosed with diabetes.

"Oh, yes," Giselle said. "Mister Gale."

"Yes. Martin Gale. He's on a fixed income and he spent his entire month's food budget on that junk. And let me tell you, it's not going to last him a month."

"Well, there was no way I could know that, and he was quite insistent on buying us out."

"Of course he was. He's Doctor Lerner's patient and not only does he have a weight problem and diabetes, he also has a hoarding disorder. When he learned this was the only place you could buy that stuff, he had to have it all."

What a mess.

I said, "Giselle, get Doctor Lerner, will you?" I turned to the woman. "I'm sorry about your father, Mrs. Norton. What can we do for him?"

"Well, for one thing, you can take back all that stuff he bought."

Anna was standing behind her. She grinned and pumped a fist. At least someone was happy.

"I don't see why not," I said. "I'll check with Doctor Lerner and see what we can work out."

Ken appeared then. He must have heard her on his way down the hall, because he said, "I'm afraid we can't take returns, Mrs. Norton."

The relief that had started growing in her features suddenly vanished.

"Why the heck not?"

Ken shrugged. "We can't resell something that's already been sold and moved from our premises to a private residence. We can't take it back and sell it again. It's simply not allowed."

The daughter said, "What is he supposed to do?"

"Hey, I can help!" Anna said. "I've been looking to buy but they don't have any here. He can sell some to me!"

The daughter looked at her. "Can you buy it all? Because he has a *lot*."

Anna said, "Well, I can buy *some*. I really need some."

The daughter looked at Ken. "Really? You can't take it back?"

He gave a helpless shrug. "Sorry. It's against the law."

As she and Anna wandered out the door, deep in conversation, I turned to Ken.

"'Against the law'?"

"Well, if there isn't a law against it, there should be. They might come back contaminated with something and then we'd be liable. Chain of custody and all that."

He had a point, but I think we could have found an accommodation.

"His daughter says he's a hoarder."

"We have no evidence of that and no one's ever mentioned it before. What I do know is that he's an obese diabetic who needs to lose weight, so I started him on Tezinex."

"When?"

"Tuesday. And apparently he's taken the diet to heart. Good for him."

There was no talking to this man. I left it at that. I wished we'd never got involved in this.

I'd pretty well finished my extra morning session by then so I tidied up my desk and headed out to the rear parking lot where I found Heather Norton and Anna Divisova waiting by my car.

Oh, boy. What now?

"I know you can't overrule Doctor Lerner," Heather said as I approached, "but do you think you could convince him to change his mind?"

"Oh, I don't know about that," I said. "I'm sure he feels terrible about this situation."

I knew damn well he didn't, but I could hardly tell her that.

Heather said, "Look, I'm going to take this nice woman—Anna, right?" Anna nodded. "I'm taking her to my father's place to let her buy some of his hoard. It's just around the corner. Would you mind terribly coming with me just so you can see what I'm dealing with?"

I hesitated. I'd decided to bite the bullet and stop by Angelina's, but I had a steadily narrowing window if I wanted to see her today.

"I have a meeting."

Heather got a pleading look. "Please? It'll just take a minute."

Normally I would have begged off, but Ken's hardline attitude had left me feeling guilty. Don't ask me why. No good reason. I didn't prescribe the Tezinex and I didn't block the return of the products. In fact, I hadn't even wanted them in the office. Yet who was on the spot here in the parking lot? Not Ken. Me.

"All right," I said, "but I don't have a lot of time, so let's get a move on."

I started my car and waited for them to get theirs from the other side of the building. Heather led the way, Anna followed her, and I followed Anna. Heather had exaggerated how close it was—not "just around the corner"—but it turned out to be a fairly quick trip. She pulled into the driveway of a ramshackle old Victorian with a turret and lots of gingerbread molding.

Anna pulled in behind her, I parked out at the curb—ready for a quick, clean getaway.

As I approached on the slate walk I noticed that the wraparound porch was stacked with weathered cardboard boxes, many of which looked like they were ready to fall apart. We all met on the wooden front steps that badly needed a paint job.

"I don't know how receptive he'll be," Heather said. "He knows he has a problem—the family's talked to him about cleaning the place out many, many times—so he may not want us inside. If we get in, don't react when you see all the junk. An 'Oh, my God' will shut him straight down. I talked to him this morning about the diet food. We'll just have to play this by ear but I wanted Doctor Norrie to see firsthand how he lives."

I simply nodded. The front porch had already signaled a problem.

Heather used the tarnished brass knocker. The curtain over the side window pulled aside, then the door opened to reveal an elderly gent, balding and obese, in a stained gray sweat suit.

"Heather?" he said with a puzzled expression.

"Hi, Dad. May we come in?"

"Why are you here?"

As she replied, Heather casually pushed the door open wider and eased her way in. "Remember this morning I told you I was going to the medical group to see if they'd buy back some of that stuff you bought?"

Hiding her hand behind her, she motioned us to follow.

"Um, yeah," he replied, not sounding too sure.

"Well, I brought Doctor Norrie along to help me carry it back. You know Doctor Norrie, don't you?"

Not a shred of recognition lit his eyes as he said, "I think so."

I saw Anna wrinkle her nose at the pungent smell. I'd worked in an animal research lab for a summer once and recognized it right away: rodents. The place was infested with rats or mice or both.

We all followed Heather out of the foyer and into a large space that probably had once been a living room, but was now reduced to a narrow path through six-foot high stacks of newspapers and magazines. No question where the rodents had taken up residence. You couldn't see them but you could smell them.

I'd seen that TV show about hoarders a few times—*Buried Alive*, I think it's called—and Martin Gale's place would easily qualify for an episode. My own obsessive-compulsive tendencies were itching to straighten all this clutter. I glanced at Anna and she looked ready to scream.

As we reached the next room, the path widened slightly and suddenly Martin was squeezing past us until he was in the lead. "Wait-wait-wait," he said, raising his hands as he stopped and turned to face us. "I'm not so sure about this anymore."

"Come on, Dad," Heather said. "We discussed this. You can't afford all those supplements."

Martin's attention focused on Anna. "Who are you and why are you here?"

Anna didn't realize at first he'd spoken to her. Her expression was dazed, her mouth hung open as she turned in a slow circle.

"You!" Martin snapped.

Taken by surprise, Anna blinked for a second or two, then said, "I came here to buy some of your Tezinex stuff."

"Why mine? Why not get your own?"

"Well, I would if I could but you bought it all and they haven't restocked yet. Look, I just want a few bars and shakes and I'll pay twice what you paid."

I saw his eyes narrow and knew she'd said something wrong. I didn't know just what, but some sort of warning bell had rung in his head and he was instantly on guard. Was it the offer of twice the price, which was awfully generous, or...?

"Why haven't they restocked?" he said.

She shrugged. "Oh, I don't know. I keep asking but they have some lame excuse."

He nodded slowly. "Oh, I *bet* it's lame." He looked at me. "You *can't* get any, can you."

I didn't want to get into this but felt I had to say something. "That's not true, Mister Gale. The sales rep has a big territory and she'll be by soon."

"So she says, but that's not it. I get it: The company's got a shortage on its hands and they don't want anyone to know. All right, I see it all now. That's it. I'm going to have to ask you all to leave."

"But Dad," Heather said, "we agreed—"

"That was before I knew there was a shortage." He made pushing gestures without touching anyone. "Now, please... all three of you... please leave."

Anna whined, "If I could just buy a couple of bars and shakes to tide me over—"

"*No!*" he shouted, suddenly red in the face. "Get out! All of you! Get out of my house!"

We got, but slowly, Heather and Anna protesting all the way. I said nothing. I could see the hoarder in him had taken full control and no one was going to talk him out of it. Hoarding disorders involve two fear components: the fear of throwing out something that might come in useful one day, and the fear of running out of something and not being able to replenish your supply.

That was a big part of hoarding all that toilet paper during the COVID-19 pandemic. No one wants to run out of toilet paper, and yes, you will use more when you stay home all day instead of going to work or school, but not to the extent that you need to grab every roll you can find. But that was exactly what people did.

Anna's remarks about our office not being able to restock had triggered that second component in Martin Gale, and he'd instantly convinced himself that we hadn't restocked because the company had run out and couldn't supply us.

Half a minute later the three of us were back on the front porch again with Martin behind his locked front door.

"This is crazy!" Anna screamed at no one in particular. "Absolutely *crazy!*"

She stomped off to her car and roared away.

"Do you see what I have to deal with?" Heather said, on the verge of tears. "I don't know what to do."

"After what I saw inside," I told her, "I'm sure I can convince Doctor Lerner to soften his stance on taking back the products."

"It's too late! My father's now convinced there's a shortage which means he'll hold onto them tighter than ever!"

"We have other concerns here," I said. "Your father has a major problem. Not just psychologically. His home is loaded with rodents, and that's a health hazard."

"I know, I know. I've threatened to call the health department but haven't had the heart to do it. He's always been a 'shit saver,' as my mother called it, but she kept him in check by not allowing junk to pile up. She'd simply heave it. But after she died, he just stopped throwing stuff out. Wet garbage, like leftover food, yes, he'll put that out, but he's gone so far as to start going through his neighbors' recyclables, collecting paper stuff like magazines and newspapers. It's a fire hazard as well."

"Try getting him to a therapist. Depression is often involved."

"I've already brought that up but he won't hear of it. He doesn't think anything's wrong."

"When does he next see Doctor Lerner?"

"He started that new medication yesterday and he's supposed to check back in a month."

"I'll talk to him and see what we can work out about your father's emotional state on his next visit. Maybe start treating him for depression."

"But what do I do till then?"

"Just keep an eye on him. No overnight cure for these disorders, I'm afraid. It's a long, slow road."

I didn't want to tell her that success was elusive with hoarders because they think it's everyone else who has the problem, not them. But I'd give Ken a heads up before Martin's next visit.

3

With the help of Waze I reached Angelina's garden apartment complex at 1:30, leaving us an hour for our chat. Plenty of time. I'd called from the road to confirm that I was on my way. I wasn't sure what to expect. I had only a vague memory of her. By the time I started high school, she'd already graduated. I couldn't picture her face, all I remembered was that she'd been overweight.

So the woman who answered my knock on the door to apartment 2F was pretty much a complete stranger. A *large* stranger. I'd managed to shed a lot of weight since my teens but this woman had held on to hers. She had mousey brown hair pulled back in a bun and wore dark blue scrubs with a nametag that read *A. Piperno, RN.*

"Norrie?" she said as she stood in the doorway. "Is that really you?"

"In the flesh." I stuck out my hand. "Nice to see you again."

"You've changed," she said as we shook.

Apparently she remembered me better than I remembered her.

She moved aside and I stepped into a sparsely furnished living room that smelled like an ashtray. A beige rug and lemon yellow walls made for a bright look. A couple of landscape prints graced the walls—both of them hung straight. I noticed a tabby basking in the afternoon sun on the windowsill. It lifted its head and looked at me.

Angelina must have followed my gaze because she said, "That's Missy."

Missy kept staring at me. I looked away.

"She looks suspicious of me."

"She's not fond of strangers, so don't waste your time trying to make friends with her. Have a seat." I stepped toward the couch but she pointed to an easy chair. "Try there. It's more comfortable. Can I get you coffee or tea?"

As usual, I was coffeed out by this time of day. I didn't want anything to drink but I like to have a little something to do with my hands while I'm talking to anyone I don't know.

"I'd rather something cold and calorie free, if possible."

"Seltzer?"

"Perfect. And I don't need a glass."

She left for the kitchen and, out of the corner of my eye, I saw Missy leave her sill and hop up onto the back of the couch to get a closer look at me. I didn't look back.

I like cats. A lot of people don't, I think, because they're put off by a cat's apparent aloofness. They prefer having a dog slobber all over them. I find dogs fun and puppies adorable, but they're all too needy. They're pack animals and don't like being left alone. Cats are just fine alone.

Sean and I each had a cat growing up. I'd learned that the least successful way to get to know a new cat is to appear interested in them. They're perverse that way. The more attention you pay them, the more they avoid you. The more you ignore them, the more interested they become. Sort of like: *I'm so wonderful, how can you possibly ignore me?*

I glanced around—everywhere but at Missy—looking for a personal touch, like a photo of Angelina with a child or a guy or even another woman. All I found was one of her mother and a selfie of her and Missy on the sofa. Also a full ashtray next to a box of Marlboro Lights and a butane lighter. I did notice a book on the end table next to my chair: *The Wounded Heart.* Never heard of it. Novel? I picked it up and saw that it was intended for adult survivors of childhood sexual abuse.

Oh. Shit.

I quickly put it back down. Was that the next shoe that was going to drop: Corrado had been sexually abusing his own daughter?

I didn't want to deal with this. It's not an easy subject to listen to, but I can handle it just fine with patients, and I have. A number of times. Being a female family practitioner makes it easier—it's *never* easy—for women to talk to me rather than Sam or Ken about what happened to them as children or adolescents in their own home. When they do open up, I have to step back and view their situation from an objective and clinical standpoint.

But Corrado Piperno was my godfather, my father's *fratellino*, a frequent visitor to our house, a man I'd called "uncle." I didn't know if I could distance myself from him.

Would she bring it up? Maybe she wouldn't want to talk about it.

No, wait. That book hadn't been left there just by accident. It's not the sort of thing you leave lying around when you expect company. And she'd practically pushed me into this chair.

Obviously she'd left it there on purpose. Like it or not, I knew I was going to hear about this.

Angelina returned with a can of store-brand lemon-lime seltzer, saying, "I understand you're in family medicine. Good for you. I didn't have that much ambition so I'm just an RN."

I took a tiny sip as she dropped onto the couch near Missy's perch. It groaned under her weight. I continued to ignore the cat's stare.

"There's no 'just' to being an RN." I meant that. Doctors couldn't get by without nurses. "We're both in the frontline trenches."

She gave a little laugh. "That we are. I'm on the second shift at Howard County General and—"

That was when Missy decided to hop down off the couch to the floor and up onto my lap.

"Well-well-well!" Angelina said. "This is so very out of character."

The cat stood on my lap and stared into my face as if to say, *How dare you ignore me.* I held up my hand, palm out, and let her nuzzle it. Then she curled into a ball and started to purr. I can't think of many things more peace-inducing than a cat purring on your lap.

Angelina shook her head. "What's your secret?"

"I like cats and cats like me." I didn't mention the ignoring trick.

"Come on, Missy. Don't bother the lady." She patted her thighs. "Come to Mama."

Missy opened one eye for about two seconds, then closed it again.

"I don't believe this." She sounded upset.

"I don't mind." I put the seltzer can down and stroked Missy's back. I now had something else to do with my hands. "Like I said, cats like me."

She loosed an exasperated sigh and lit one of her Marlboro Lights. I wished she had asked but it's her place. I knew I'd stink like cigarettes when I left.

After blowing a stream of smoke from the corner of her mouth, she said, "Well, anyway, my shift starts at three. What is it you wanted to talk to me about?"

I launched my partially true, partially fabricated spiel. "It's like I told you on the phone, I'm back home for a week and we got to reminiscing about when my father was alive and we came to the time when your father disappeared. I remember my dad being completely crushed."

"Was he now?" A noncommittal reply but uttered in an ominous tone.

I pushed on. "I stopped by your old house the other day and learned from the new owner that your mother was in a nursing home, so I visited her yesterday."

Another little laugh. "You should have come here first and I'd have saved you from wasting your time."

Speaking of time, I knew we didn't have a lot, so I came straight out and said it: "She spent most of the time scolding an empty chair, but then she told me your father beat you two."

Her eyes widened for a second, then she shook her head. "I'm surprised. When I go to visit her she doesn't even know who I am."

"Well, someone beating you is a pretty traumatic memory that'll stick more than others if it's true."

"Oh, it's true," she said with a level stare. "If only that was all he'd done."

Here it comes…

"What are you saying?"

"I'm saying my father raped me when I was twelve."

And there it was: the awful truth, twitching on the carpet between us. Even though I'd been expecting it, I found myself temporarily mute.

Finally, I managed a weak, "I'm so sorry."

And I was. My heart went out to that poor preteen.

"You don't seem terribly surprised."

I nodded toward *The Wounded Heart* on the end table. "I assumed that book wasn't left there by chance. And I really am sorry it happened to you."

"Not as sorry as I am. And it wasn't just once. He did it for two years."

The thought sickened me. My father's friend, my godfather…

"Oh, God. And you couldn't tell anyone?"

"At first I didn't know—or at least I couldn't be sure. He was drugging me. Sometimes he'd be a lunatic around the house, raging at some imagined insult. Sometimes he'd be nice and make me and my mother something to drink when we were watching TV at night, like hot chocolate or a milkshake. Even if you didn't want it you drank it because he'd go into another rage if you wasted something he went to 'all that trouble' to make.'"

"He terrorized you."

"Totally. Next morning I'd wake up hurting and feeling sick and sense that something had happened to me, but no memory of it."

"Do you know what he drugged you with?"

She shook her head. "I figure either GHB or Rohypnol, but I never went looking at the time. I searched the house after he disappeared but never found anything."

The description of memory loss was leaning the doctor part of me toward Rohypnol because anterograde amnesia is one of its side effects. The rest of me was sickened.

"How *did* you find out?"

"One night I was feeling queasy, so I waited till he wasn't looking and dumped the hot chocolate he'd made. That night I woke up to find him pulling off my pajama bottoms."

"And you were twelve?"

She nodded.

Oh, God.

"I screamed and he choked me and told me to keep quiet or he'd kill me. I'd seen his rages so I believed him. And then he raped me."

I couldn't believe she was revealing all this to me. We were virtual strangers. And relating it all in such a matter-of-fact tone, like she'd separated herself from that child and broken off any emotional attachment to the atrocity.

"And your mother?"

"Oh, he made sure she got dosed too. He told me if she ever found out it would stop her sick heart dead."

Blind rage surged through me. A girl's father, the font of stability and safety and security in her home, the man she looks up to, the man she'll look back on as a model for all males in her life, is instead a predator who victimizes her in the most foul manner imaginable. I hated this Corrado Piperno. To hold a mother's weakened heart over his daughter's head while raping her. I wanted to scream.

Missy must have sensed something. She stopped purring and stared up at me. Scratching under her chin relaxed her and relaxed me as well—but only a little.

My dad had told me the reason Corrado never brought Angelina along when he came to our house: *He never knew when she would just come out and say something crazy.*

I now knew the nature of that "something crazy." He feared Angelina might blurt out something about being raped.

I managed to keep my voice level. "Why did he finally stop?"

"I don't know. Maybe because I packed on so much weight. Maybe I outgrew the age group he lusted after."

"Dear God, Angelina, I thought I knew your father but he's become a stranger with a double life. I've learned so many terrible things about him this week. But I never expected this. This is beyond anything I could have imagined."

"'So many terrible things'? You mean there's more than the violence and the sexual abuse?"

"The police missing person report said he was a regular with the prostitutes down on the Block. Did you know about that?"

Angelina's shocked expression told me this was news to her. "Prostitutes," she said in a hardened tone. "Why am I not surprised? There's no depth that man would not sink to."

"I'll say it again: I'm so sorry. No one should have to live through what you did."

"Amen to that. I can tell you that the best thing that ever happened to me and my mom was when he didn't come home that night or ever again. But that's all in the past. I've moved on."

"Good for you," I said, but didn't really believe it. I didn't see how anyone could truly be over something like that.

She gave me a penetrating look. "You seemed to have moved on too."

I froze with my hand on Missy's back. "Moved on from what? What do you mean?"

"Your abuse. I know your father abused you too."

Was she insane? "Never in a million years!"

"Oh, come now. You can level with me. You've slimmed down since then, but when I saw you put on all that weight after you hit your teens, I knew you were in the same boat as me. That's a sure sign of abuse."

I was aghast at the accusation. I went to stand and Missy jumped down. She gave me a reproachful look, then hopped back onto the couch.

"Come to Mama," Angelina said as she grabbed Missy. She pulled her onto her lap and began petting her. "Back where you belong."

"Whoa-whoa-whoa, lady," I said, standing over her. "You put the brakes on right there. Don't you go talking about my father like that. Ever! He never laid a hand on me—not for any reason. You're operating from a totally false premise. A fat teenage girl does not equal an abused teenage girl."

She looked up at me. "You're in big-time denial, aren't you. Wake up. They were besties—all that *fratello* and *fratellino* crap. Your father had to know. They probably compared notes."

I contained my anger. I had to take into account this was a damaged person I was dealing with, whose loathing and hatred for her own father painted every other girl's father with the same tainted brush.

"Tell me something, Angelina: Did you ever happen to go through memory recovery therapy?"

She shook her head. "Never needed it. If I'd been able to repress the memory of what he did to me, I'd never have wanted it back. But it never went away. It was always there."

"Just as well. That therapy was proved to be totally bogus. Although I almost wish you had gone through it."

"Why do you say that?"

"Because if you'd done recovery therapy to reclaim a memory of abuse, it's probable the abuse never happened. They discovered that the therapists were *creating* memories. It's called false memory syndrome. A lot of innocent fathers were ruined and families were torn apart because of it."

"This is not a false memory, I assure you."

"Just as I assure you that I have no repressed memories about my father. Whatever the reasons for my weight gain they had nothing to do with him—except perhaps for the pastas he liked to cook. But that's it."

I wanted out of here. She was projecting her own tragic history on me and probably any other woman with a weight problem.

I stepped toward the door. "Thank you for seeing me. I had no idea I'd be digging up such an awful past."

She gave me a weak smile. "Like I said: I'm past it."

"Okay, one more thing before I go. Do you have any idea what happened to your father?"

"Not at all," she said with a curt shake of her head. "But if he's not burning in hell, I hope he's in a gutter somewhere rotting from an STD."

Past it? No, I don't think so.

4

I sat in my Jeep in her parking lot, taking deep breaths as I stared through the windshield. Harrowing enough to hear about Angelina's abuse, but then...

...I know your father abused you too...

I was still shaken from hearing that. Not because I gave it an ounce of credence, but because I hadn't seen it coming. Totally out of the blue. And I hadn't been prepared for it.

You're in big-time denial, aren't you. Wake up. They were besties— all that fratello *and* fratellino *crap. Your father had to know. They probably compared notes.*

A semi-valid assumption... unless you knew my father. If it ever came down to it, he would, without a second thought, quite literally sacrifice his life for me, Sean, or Mum. Family was everything to him. One time he got on the case of a divorced fellow firefighter for not paying child support. They came to blows and he got suspended.

Compare notes...? No way. No, wait, make that no *fucking* way could that perv Corrado even mention beating on his wife and daughter. And God knows what my father would have done had he learned that a man he called "little brother" and allowed into his home had raped his own daughter.

It all goes with why my dad had been so upset that Corrado had deserted his wife and child. He'd betrayed the standard Dad lived by: A man takes care of his family. But Dad had no way of knowing that, as Angelina said, Corrado's disappearance was the best thing he'd ever done for his family.

Corrado Piperno had lived a double life: hardworking family

man in public, wife-beating daughter rapist behind closed doors, while whoring down on the Block. And he'd managed to keep that second life secret from everybody, especially my father.

But there was a woman in this apartment building here who was convinced that I'd been abused as she'd been abused. I could not leave that unaddressed.

I hurried back up to the second floor and knocked on her door. Standing directly opposite the peephole, I watched it darken as she peeked, then lighten.

A choked sob leaked through from the other side of the door. She'd been in complete emotional lockdown while I'd been there, and now she was sobbing. That was either good or very, very bad.

"Angelina? Open up, please. I..."

What did I want to do? I'd come back to straighten her out about my father, but now... those sobs... so much pain...

"I want to help."

She pulled the door open and stood there, holding Missy, tears streaming down her face. "You can't help! No one can help!"

I stepped inside and pushed the door closed behind me.

"You may think you're beyond help, Angelina, but you're not. You have a form of PTSD and—"

"What? You think you're telling me something I don't know? I've seen therapists, I've read all the books, I know all the lingo, all the buzzwords, all the bullshit, but look at me. Just look at me. I've been on three different meds and not one of them helped. I smoke too much, I drink too much, I eat too much, and the only relationship I've been able to sustain is with this damn wonderful cat!"

She burst into tears again.

I had no solution to offer. Her young womanhood had been stolen—ripped from her by her father, of all people. I used to get teased and shunned and rejected at school because of my weight and because of my brains, but I always knew I had a safe haven to retreat to. I could always go home and feel wanted and respected and protected and, most importantly, valued and cherished. *Loved.* I didn't know how Angelina had been treated at school, but she'd grown up in a minefield—a home that had become a torture chamber of physical, emotional, and sexual abuse.

What do you say to someone who's had to endure that? I couldn't think of any solutions to offer, so I simply put my arms around her and we stood there in her living room—the damaged woman, the visitor from the past, and the cat.

Finally she said, "I'm sorry for what I said about your father being like mine. I really believed it. That's why I opened up to you about all this. I thought we were both victims." She wasn't looking at me. "And then again, maybe I didn't really believe it. I'm such a fucking mess. Maybe I just wanted to hurt you."

"Me?" What had I ever done to her?

"I used to hate you," she said. "You were younger but that didn't stop me from hating you."

"But we hardly ever saw each other."

"Oh, you didn't see me but I used to see you. I used to sit in the bushes in Deerfield Park for hours and hours, just to be out of the house. And I'd see you and your dad walk through and he'd be holding your hand and you'd be smiling up at him adoringly, like he was the greatest thing in the world."

Dear God, I'd forgotten those walks. Sometimes he'd work the night shift at the firehouse and be home during the day and he'd take me out for ice cream or a donut or another secret treat we couldn't let Mum know about. That was before I'd started to balloon, that was when I could eat and eat and not gain an ounce.

"You have no idea how I hated you then," she said. "Here was my father's best friend out with his daughter and they're so comfortable together, and you *wanted* to be with him, *wanted* to hold his hand and be close to him. Why couldn't I have that? Why couldn't my dad be like Rocky? I wanted that. *God*, how I wanted that!"

We stood like that a bit longer and then Missy decided she'd had enough of this and struggled her way to the floor. Angelina backed off, wiping her eyes.

"I'm sorry the visit turned out this way."

"I'm sorry too. I didn't know I'd be opening old wounds."

A weak smile. "You didn't. They've never really healed, just scabbed over. But I get along pretty well. Really, I do. I live day to day, like most people. Nursing keeps me sane—that and Missy. And speaking of work, I've got to get moving or I'll be late."

"You'll be all right?"

"I'll be fine. And again, I'm sorry for saying that."

I made my exit and headed back to my car, leaving behind a member of the walking wounded. I wondered how many were out there, male and female, living with a horrible secret in their past.

I wanted to be done with all this delving into the past. I hadn't suspected I'd be turning over rocks and exposing all these hidden vermin. And I still hadn't answered my father's question: What happened to Corrado Piperno? I couldn't believe Dad still cared. I sure as hell didn't.

I felt exhausted. I wanted to go home, pull the covers over my head and take a long nap. But that wasn't in the cards.

My phone gave off its text chime. A message from Ken:

> Word from Hopkins. Sam came through the Whipple fine. Is in recovery. So far so good.

Finally some good news. I needed this. I could have cried.

5

I was overdue to pick up my mail so I swung by my condo.
"Well, well, well," said a voice as I reached the second-floor landing.

I'd been searching in my bag for my keys. I looked up and saw my stripper neighbor, Janie "Poochie Sutton" Ryan, grinning at me from her doorway. She was dressed in a too-large green Loyola sweatshirt and long-legged pink pajama bottoms. Somehow she made that baggy outfit look sexy.

"How are things with the hot deputy, doc?" she said, winking from under her long, dark bangs. "Is he good in the sack?"

I felt a blush coming on—I hate that I blush at nothing.

"The relationship is proceeding accordingly, Ms. Ryan."

"No kidding? 'Proceeding accordingly.' There's a non-answer if I ever heard one. Has he locked you up in those handcuffs yet or threatened you with his gun if you don't do what he tells you?"

"He's a gentleman, Janie."

"But you're hoping he's not *too* much of a gentleman, right?"

"Janie—"

"C'mere." She stepped back into her apartment and motioned me to follow her. "I want to check something."

I had a little time and nothing better to do, so I followed. I'd been in here once before. I knew I'd find a mess. And still I recoiled as I crossed the threshold—clothes scattered everywhere. I mean *scattered*. And I mean *everywhere*. They looked clean, like they'd been taken from the dryer and just plopped on tables and chairs and the couch.

Of their own accord, my hands grabbed a towel and started folding it.

"What are you doing?" she said.

"How can you leave stuff like this?" I placed the folded towel on the arm of a chair and reached for another. "That's what drawers and linen closets are for."

"Why bother? Why waste time folding when I'm only going to take them out and use them again?"

"But—"

Before I could finish my explanation she snaked a finger inside the waistband of my slacks and yanked it down a couple of inches.

Alarmed, I pulled away. "Hey! What are you doing?"

"I knew it," she said, staring at me and shaking her head. "I just knew it."

"Knew what?"

"Big undies."

"*What?*"

"At least they're not big white cottons, although I do know guys who get off on them."

"Have you gone crazy?"

"*Me* crazy? You're the one not wearing a thong. I mean, how can you go out with a guy like Travis Lawton dressed in big undies?"

"They're not so big. And... and they're high cut."

Why was I defending my panties?

"You should be wearing a thong, doc."

"A thong? I don't even own one."

Now it was her turn to look shocked. "You—you're kidding me."

"Not at all. They look... uncomfortable."

I'd always figured they weren't called butt floss for nothing.

"Well, they aren't. But that's beside the point. I mean, do you want Deputy Dawg to see you in those big undies?"

"That's not an issue." At least not yet. A situation I hoped to change soon.

"So you say now, but just wait. If it ain't happened yet, it's a-comin'."

"Janie..."

She vamped. "Oh my, I wonder if Deputy Dawg likes to do it doggie style."

"Will you stop?"

But considering how close Trav and I had grown and what had been about to happen Tuesday night, I have to confess that the image she evoked wasn't altogether unpleasant. I might even say I found it a little breathtaking.

"Got an idea," she said, holding up a hand. "Don't move."

She hurried into her bedroom—I knew it was her bedroom because I could see from her condo's layout that the room she'd entered was adjacent to my own bedroom. I didn't have to look to know the exact location of her headboard: directly opposite mine.

I could hear it now... *bang-bang-bang...*

I peeked anyway and saw the noisy bed in question. Unmade, of course. I bit my tongue. I already knew her response: *I'm only going to get back in it later.*

She popped out just then with what looked like a magazine.

"Here's what you need," she said, handing it to me.

A slim, barely clad blonde reclined on the cover. *Scarlet Seductions* ran along the top in sinuous red script.

"I need porn?"

"No, silly, it's a lingerie catalogue."

I thumbed through it. So it was—but from a country where they must have been suffering a fabric shortage of crisis proportions. And the prices... when you broke them down to dollars per square inch... maybe they used solid gold thread.

"Look at these things. There's nothing to them. Why even bother getting dressed?"

She laughed. "This isn't dressed—it's *un*dressed." She leaned over the catalogue and pointed to a busty brunette. "*That's* what you need."

I glanced at those large, barely concealed breasts. "Implants?"

"No, a teddy. Men go *crazy* for them."

Me... in a teddy. Right.

"I don't think so."

"Why not?"

"We don't need more crazy men. We've too many of them running around as it is."

"Seriously."

"Look at me, Janie. A teddy?"

"You don't seem to want to see it, but you're a snappy looking dish. Maybe you should get a new mirror."

I opened my mouth to reply, then shut it. Janie was right. Somehow this younger woman, who'd dropped out of high school and made her living peeling off her clothes for leering men, had nailed me: I have a lousy body image. In medical language I have a mild case of body dysmorphia: I always see a fat girl in the mirror. She was telling me to get over it, to get real.

Good advice. Easier said than done, but good advice.

"Maybe I should," I said. "But no matter what kind of new mirror I get, I doubt I'll be seeing myself in a teddy and a thong."

"Sure, you will." She pulled the catalogue from my fingers. "Are you off this weekend?"

"As a matter of fact, I am." Ken had the office on Saturday and the weekend call.

"Okay, Saturday afternoon you and me are going into the city to get you ragged out in some new dainties."

"Dainties?"

"Yeah. In fact, that's the name of the place: Dainties. It's near where I work and it's really cool. Whatta ya say?"

I didn't know what to say. Her smile and bright eyes radiated enthusiasm. She really wanted to do this for me. I was touched, but I still wasn't interested.

To paraphrase Ogden Nash: A thong? No thongx.

But I didn't want to douse that light in her eyes. And a trip into Baltimore was in the cards anyway. I'd been planning on frying up a couple of servings of my father's meatballs when I cooked dinner for Travis Saturday night. I've tried before with varying levels of success—always good but never as good as his—but to have a prayer of success, I'd have to buy the proper mix of meats—the beef, veal, and pork—down at Calabro's in Little Italy.

"Okay. I've got another stop to make in the city so let's do it."

"Excellent! And after we do Dainties, I'll take you into the

Shark Tank so you can meet Mako."

I remembered from a previous conversation that the Shark Tank was one of the strip clubs where she did her thing. But Mako...?

"Didn't you mention this Mako before?"

"Yeah. Vladimir Makovei. Owns the Shark Tank. I told him how I'd tried to talk you into an audition—"

"Oh, right. Because I'm 'bigger' and 'older.'"

Janie thought I should try stripping on the side because her boss was looking to add "bigger, older women" to his lineup and I fit the bill. Apparently thirty-two is "older" in her trade. Maybe even 'elderly.'"

She laughed. "You always get huffy at that. You're hot, doc. A definite MILF. That booty of yours would rake in the tips."

"Yeah, well, we'll never know, will we? I assume you told him that you *failed* to talk me into an audition."

"I did, but he said I should bring you down and he'll make you an offer you can't refuse."

I was about to refuse right now when a thought hit me. Before I could voice it she added, "But we need to get you a stripper name. What street did you grow up on?"

Same place as where I was crashing these days. "Guilford Road."

"And what was your favorite pet's name?"

"I only ever had one: a cat named Duffy."

"Duffy Guilford." She grinned and slapped my back. "That's you, babe!" She lowered her voice to an announcer's tone. "Now stripping at the Shark Tank: Duffyyyyy Guilford!"

Never, ever, ever.

I went back to my brilliant idea: "This Shark Tank... it's down on the Block, right?"

"Yeah, where else would it be?"

Corrado's old hang...

"How long has this Mako been around—the Block, I mean?"

"Like forever, I think. Always talking about the Good Old Days when the Block was bigger and badder and how he started out as a go-fer, then worked his way up to a manager, and finally got his own place."

I would take one more stab at finding out what happened to Corrado. If that didn't pan out, I'd call it quits and let it remain a mystery for the rest of eternity. I pulled out the Post-It pad I always carry, printed *Corrado Piperno*, and handed the sheet to Janie.

"I will listen to Mako's offer if he can get me any info on this guy who used to be a regular on the Block and disappeared twenty years ago."

Her eyes widened. "No kidding? You'd consider getting on the pole?"

No, not now, not ever, never.

But I couldn't help fantasizing... what would it be like to get naked in front of a bunch of strangers... so I played along a bit...

"I'm not committing to anything, but if I did agree, I'd have to wear a mask. I mean, because I couldn't let any of my patients find out. Would that be okay?"

Not now, not ever, never.

"Yeah, why not? Might be sexy. Might even start a trend. Who knows?"

Not now, not ever, never.

"Hey," she said. "Can I tell him you're a doctor?"

"Not on your life!"

"What a come-on that would be! Duffy Guilford, the Dancing Doctor!" She started snapping her fingers. "What else can we call you? How about the Gyrating Gynecologist?"

"That sounds awful."

"I got it! The Fantasy Physician! No-no. We'll spell it with a P-H: Duffy Guildford! Your Phantasy Physician! Holy shit, doc, the guys will be lining up out the door to see you! You'll have to wear extra garters to hold all the cash!"

Never, ever, never.

I tapped the note in her hand. "Can we concentrate on *this* name?"

She glanced at it. "Twenty years is a long time, but it's a weird name, so Mako might remember, or know somebody who does. What's the interest?"

"Old friend of the family."

Well, he was once, but not anymore.

"All right," she said, folding the note. "I'll give it to Mako. I'll be working that night so we'll have to drive in separately. We can meet at, say, one, because Mako gets in early on Saturdays."

I'd go to the butcher first and get that out of the way. Then I'd make my way to the Block. I'd never been there before. Of course over the years I'd driven through it on Baltimore Street, but I'd never stopped. What for? This would be a new experience, one I wasn't particularly looking forward to.

I gave her a salute. "One o'clock, on the Block. Got it."

"And hey, Duffy. In the meantime, take these for Deputy Dawg."

She shoved some foil packets into my hand. I glanced at them and when I saw the word "Trojan."

"No thanks."

I tried to hand them back but Janie refused to take them.

"No-no-no. They're yours. Poochie's Rule: Never be without them. No matter how much you like a guy or no matter how much he says he's clean, use protection. You never know where that ol' one-eyed snake has been."

"Really, Janie—"

"And check 'em out: They're ribbed."

I looked again, and sure enough, the packets said *Ultra Ribbed.*

"No, Janie. I don't want—"

She had me by the shoulders and was turning me around and guiding me toward her door.

"Sure you do. Those little ribs are da bomb. And if you think you like ribbed, wait'll you try Rough Riders. I'd have given you some of those, but I'm all out."

She opened her door and gently propelled me into the hall.

"Okay, Duffy Guilford. See ya Saturday."

I stood alone on the landing, staring at the packets in my hand, thinking, Ultra Ribbed?

Not that I was offended. Not even close. I'm not a prude. In fact, I think I'm a pretty modern woman, a card-carrying member of the free-to-be-you-and-me generation.

But did they really have condoms called Rough Riders?

6

Before heading to Mum's I stopped at the local Ace Hardware and picked up a laser leveler. That landscape painting was not going to beat me.

This being Thursday, Mum was serving a dinner of Tater Tots and boiled Thumann's hot dogs. I had no fixings to make a shake before getting home, and didn't want to answer the inevitable slew of questions if I made it there, so I sat down with Mum and Timmy and ate a hot dog without the roll. And that was all I needed. Normally I would stuff my face with the Tater Tots, but tonight I allowed myself one—just one—to experience the delicate flavor and contrasting textures. One can fully appreciate the entire Tater Tot experience with just a single piece. Any more is simply gluttony.

I sound so totally Zen, don't I? But it was all courtesy of Tezinex's appetite suppression. I'm also totally full of it. The true Tater Tot experience is to shove as many as will fit into your mouth, chew quickly, swallow convulsively, repeat until the serving bowl is empty.

As usual, Timmy went home right after dinner, and I went through my mail. I pay my bills online and so I did that via my phone before watching some Old People TV with Mum while forcing my gaze away from the landscape.

Finally she went to bed. I pulled out my brand new laser level and attacked the landscape frame. According to the laser, I'd made it perfectly level now. But when I stepped back, it still looked canted. I kept at it for at least half an hour. Finally, fed up and disgusted, I headed for bed.

As usual, it didn't take long for the glow to appear. My little protest last night must have made an impression, because he started off with, *Hello, Norrie. How was your day?*

"If you must know, Dad: terrible."

Again?

"Yeah. I'd thought yesterday was pretty damn bad but today topped that by a mile."

You must have gone to see Angelina. Even after I told you she was crazy, you had to go and see her anyway, right?

"How do you know she's crazy, Dad?"

Everybody knows that.

"*How* do they know? And what do you mean by crazy? What did you ever see her do or hear her say that would make you think she's crazy?"

Corry told me.

"So you've got only his word to rely on."

I realized I sounded like a lawyer, but I had a reason for this third-degree approach. First off, to be honest, it delayed my having to come out and tell him the awful truth I'd learned. But second, I knew he'd go into complete denial. If he couldn't accept his friend beating his family, I could only imagine how raping his daughter would sit.

Corry was her father. He'd know better than anyone else. I told you last night: that was why he never brought her over to our house. He never knew when she'd start acting or talking crazy.

"That might be what he told *you*, Dad. But do you know what Angelina told *me*?"

Probably not, but let's hear it.

Okay. Here we go…

"She told me that when she was twelve her father started drugging her nighttime hot chocolate and then coming into her room and raping her."

There. I'd said it. I'd dropped the bomb. Now I waited for the explosion. It took its time coming, but it came.

That is the most insulting, outrageous, utterly insane thing I've ever heard in my life! Or my afterlife! Corry raping Angelina, his own daughter? I told you she was crazy and that you shouldn't—

"You were just repeating what Corrado told you. He's the

only one who ever said she was crazy. And think about it Dad: Couldn't that be the reason he was keeping her away from us? In case she let something slip about what he was doing to her?" *She would have told someone! She would have gone to her mother for sure! And there, right there, is proof it never happened, because Marie never would have stayed with Corry if she'd known.* "But she didn't know." *How could she not know? It was happening right in her own house!* "Corrado drugged her as well. And he told Angelina that if her mom ever found out, it would kill her—stop her weakened heart dead. So you see, Angelina was afraid to tell her mother." Another pause, then, *I don't believe this. I can't believe this. Why are you doing this to me?* "I'm not doing anything to you, Dad. You sent me on a mission and I'm just passing on what I've uncovered." *I just wanted you to find out who murdered Corry and where his body's buried.*

Monday night he thought Corrado "might" have been murdered. Now he was sure. Well, not taking any money or clothing with him when he left was a pretty good indicator that he hadn't planned to disappear. Which left foul play as the most likely cause.

"We may never know what happened to him, Dad. He could be in a landfill or at the bottom of the Harbor. If his remains haven't turned up after all this time, I don't think they'll ever be found." *That means I'm stuck here forever.* "We don't know that, Dad. We don't even know if forgiving Corrado is the key to your getting out of here. That was just an assumption we've been working on." *Who would know? How can we find out? Do we need an exorcism?*

An exorcism? What did I know about that sort of thing? Like pretty much everybody else in the world, I'd seen that movie, *The Exorcist*, but that was the extent of my knowledge.

"If I remember correctly, an exorcism is supposed to release someone from demonic possession. So, unless you're a demon, that's not the answer."

There's got to be an answer. Someone's got to know.

"I don't go in to the office till noon or so tomorrow, so I'll do a little research when I can and see if there's any information out there."

I had no idea where to even begin, but I'd try.

On another subject, your cop boyfriend... what's his name again?

"Travis."

Will he be stopping by to play the piano again?

"As a matter of fact, he's coming by for dinner Saturday night."

Really? What's your mother cooking?

"She's going to visit Irene this weekend. How come you don't know?"

I told you: You're the only one I can communicate with. Otherwise everything is just blobs of light and gurgles of sound. But if your mother is gone, does that mean you're cooking?

"It does. I wish you could take over the kitchen for me. I'm going to try and make your meatballs."

I wish I could help... I wish I could smell them when they're done. Just a little whiff would be wonderful. I smell nothing, I feel nothing, I can't touch anything... get me out of here, Norrie. Please.

And with that he faded from view.

I had to do something—and before Mum sold the house. But what? Not like I could call Ghostbusters, right?

FRIDAY

1

Ever since I joined LFPA, the Friday schedule has been Sam and Ken in the morning, I alone in the afternoon. Ken and I had decided to limit our extra office time to one extra morning apiece for now, and so Ken would be handling the office alone this morning.

I did my jog thing, then the Tezinex thing with a pill followed by another of their pep-talk videos. I have to admit I was impressed with how my appetite had decreased and I was no longer subject to those cravings I used to get. I was curious about my weight. I had to have lost a few pounds, but my mother didn't have a scale and I didn't want to make the trip all the way back to my place just to weigh myself. I wasn't *that* curious.

Then I got on my phone and started looking up mediums—or should that be *media*? This sort of mumbo-jumbo thing was so not me. I was raised a Catholic—with an Italian father and an Irish mother, what else could I be?—but I'd become a non-believer in my teens. Skipping mass with my brother Sean led to questioning this and that about the Church and faith; before I knew it, I was what they call "a fallen-away Catholic." Also known as "a recovering Catholic," because you're never *ex*-Catholic. They're too damn good at programing minds for anyone to get completely free.

My professional life is, of necessity, science based. I'm a hard-headed skeptic. I've helped run clinical trials so I know how to read a scientific paper. I can spot errors in the setup, execution, and conclusions of a trial. And woe to the pharmaceutical rep who tries to slip relative percentages past me.

And as for all the paranormal mumbo-jumbo that so many gullible people buy into? I offer the expression I heard so often during my eight years at NYU: *Fuhgeddaboudit.*

However—and admittedly it's a *big* however—unless I've had some sort of psychotic break with reality, the ghost of my father has been talking to me every night since I moved back into my old house. Not just talking to me, but I'm talking back. We're having *conversations.*

Anyway, I did an online search for psychics and DuckDuckGo listed a load of them in Baltimore, just a short drive away. But best of all it also listed one right next door in Lebanon. I tapped on that link and found a dark-skinned fellow staring out at me.

ROCHA

Pedro Rocha Souza *was born with the ability to communicate with those who have transitioned from earthly life to an alternate mode of existence. For the past twenty years he has professionally provided readings and reconnected the bereaved with their loved ones. Private groups and sessions can be arranged.*

Well, he was convenient, if nothing else. The big question was could he free my father from his house? I sincerely doubted it. This guy had *CHARLATAN* written all over him in capital letters. But I had to start somewhere. Early next week I was hoping to move back to my condo and that meant leaving my father here and all alone again with no one to talk to. I had to try *something.*

The hour was early—Mum wasn't up yet—but I called this Rocha's number and left a message from "Noreen" to please call me back.

Twenty minutes later he was on my phone.

"*Noreen?*" said a lightly accented voice. I guessed from his name and his look he was Brazilian. "*I am Rocha. How can I help you?*"

Rocha, ay? Just the one name? Who did he think he was? Prince? Drake?

"Just give me a second," I said as I hurried out the front door and stood on the steps. I didn't want Mum to hear. "I need your advice."

"*É claro.* I live to serve."

Of course he did.

"I need ten minutes of your time."

"The length of a reading starts at thirty minutes."

"I'll need only ten," I said, and quickly added, "but I'll pay for thirty if I can see you this morning."

"I can be available at nine thirty."

"Excellent. I'll see you then at the Central Avenue address that's online."

I went back inside, thinking I'd gone totally crazy. Consulting a psychic medium about a ghost… so, so, *so* not me.

2

I found Rocha's office or séance parlor or whatever he was calling it in a modern office building on the edge of Lebanon's commercial district, not far from the LFPA office. I'd been expecting some place like Martin Gale's old Victorian house instead of this marble lobby with its big glass windows. I found his name on the directory and took the stairs up to his second-floor office.

Beyond his door I found a waiting area totally divorced from the bright, sterile hallway outside. Indirect lighting, a Persian rug on the floor and another on one wall, abstract paintings on others. A man stepped through a door in the opposite wall. Rocha. I recognized him from his online photo—sort of. He had the same close-cropped dark hair, sharp brown eyes, and a Van Dyke goatee. His skin appeared much darker than the photo—almost black. And he'd aged since that photo. He was now gray at the temples with salt in his dark beard. Plus he must have put on forty pounds in the interim.

"Noreen?" he said in his smooth, accented voice.

"That's me. Nice to meet you, Mister Rocha."

"Just... Rocha. Please follow me."

He led me into the adjoining room, very similar to the first, with more Persian rugs and abstractions, but lower lighting.

"I'm surprised to find you in such a modern office building."

He smiled, showing white, even teeth. "You were expecting maybe the Addams Family house?"

"As a matter of fact, that was exactly what I was expecting."

"Would you have preferred that?"

"I'll tell you frankly, all the way over here I was at a total loss as to what I'd find."

He smiled. "A crystal ball, perhaps?"

I shrugged. "I don't know. Maybe?"

Where was he going with this?

"Yes, well, my crystal ball isn't available at the moment. It's out at the paranormal repair shop for a tune-up."

I stared at him, not knowing how to take that. He had to be kidding...

He smiled again. "You're thinking, 'He's got to be kidding,' right?"

"Right."

He tapped his temple. "See? Psychic."

Well, what else would I be thinking after a remark like that?

He clapped his hands once and held them together. "Okay, time for me to get all sincere: I've tried to discard all the clichés that come with my calling. I've decorated these rooms to be comfortable and restful and allow my clients to relax, because so often there is much anxiety associated with these encounters."

"I'm feeling a little anxiety myself," I said. I didn't mention that the anxiety was more about getting ripped off in the real world than any threat from the spirit realm.

"The spirits are real, Noreen. You don't need crystal balls and rocking tables and tapping sounds and ectoplasmic displays to demonstrate contact. Those are for charlatans. All you need is someone with a gift."

"And you have that gift, I take it?"

He looked at me. "Duh!"

What was it with this guy? He was definitely goofy but I kind of liked that.

He indicated a comfy looking armchair. "Please." As I sat, he dropped into a similar chair opposite me. "What brings Doctor Marconi to my humble premises?"

I'd been waiting for that, so I didn't react. I don't block my cell number ID because I need patients to pick up when I call them. He'd seen my number. No problem for him to do a reverse lookup and find that it belonged to a Noreen Marconi. Hardly a common name, and searching it would bring him straight to me.

"Would you like me to tell your future?" he added. "Is that what you're looking for?"

"That isn't why I'm here."

"I'll tell you anyway: You're gonna die."

He had me off-balance here. "What?"

"You can take that to the bank: Sometime in the future you're going to die."

I got it. "Yes, well, aren't we all?"

"Exactly."

I wasn't sure what to make of this guy.

I said, "Do you have any code of confidentiality?"

"Of course. I don't have a doctor's protection in that regard, so if it comes to questioning by the police about a crime, I'd feel obliged to cooperate. But otherwise my lips are sealed. I don't blab about my clients."

"Okay, then. I'm here about a ghost."

"A ghost? Well, damn, my P.K.E. meter is in the shop with my crystal ball."

"P.K..."

"Psychokinetic Energy Meter. You know, like they used in Ghostbusters?"

I was getting annoyed now. "I happen to be serious. Are you trying to drive me off?"

"No, but I want all our cards on the table. You're a doctor. You've been through medical school and residency. You know science and you think you've got me all figured out. Well, you don't. So... cards on the table? Your turn."

"Okay. Here are a few cards: Let me preface it all by saying this isn't easy for me. I'm a hardheaded realist and I don't buy into any of this spiritualist stuff. Or at least I didn't until the ghost of my father showed up last week."

He didn't look the least bit surprised. In fact, he slouched deeper into his chair and looked a little bored. "I compliment you on your ability to squarely face this new wrinkle in your quotidian reality."

Well, if nothing else, he had a good vocabulary.

"Flattery will get you everywhere," I said.

"Are you sure it's your father?"

Strange question. "Why do you ask?"

"Well, someone could be pranking you—or gaslighting you, to use an older expression."

He was adding a skeptical note here. I liked that.

"I wondered about that, but I asked him a couple of obscure questions from our past and he knew the answers right off. As a matter of fact, he got a little annoyed that I was testing him."

"Does he move things around?"

"Not that I've noticed. He told me he can't move anything without a body."

"Hmmm. Very true. How does he appear? What's he wearing?"

"He's just a blob of light."

"Red, yellow, green, pulsing?"

"Steady and whitish."

"How does he communicate—echoey voice or by writing?"

He sounded as if he was reading from a list of questions—a well-worn mental list that bored him.

"No voice," I said. "His words come into my head."

He straightened in his chair, his ennui suddenly gone, replaced by intense interest. "Really? No sound?"

"Well, he doesn't have a larynx—he called it a 'voicebox'—so how can he speak?"

"Good point. Excellent point. And not clothed in any way, you say?"

"No. Not looking even vaguely human. I'd have expected him in the firefighter's uniform we buried him in, but he's just a blob of light and he can maintain it just so long, then he has to fade away."

Rocha sat in silence for a moment, looking at the wall and nodding to himself.

Finally, he said, "This is very interesting. So many people who think they've encountered a ghost have not encountered anything but a prank by someone else or a quirk of their own overactive imagination. You, however, might be dealing with the real thing. A voice in your head, you say?"

"That's what I said."

"Yes, you're either dealing with the real thing or you've had some sort if psychotic break."

He wasn't mincing words.

"Don't think the latter hasn't occurred to me."

He looked me up and down. "All in all I must say you don't seem terribly upset with the situation."

"I was at first, believe me. But it's amazing how you can adapt."

Still with that intense look, he said, "Why are you here? What is it you expect of me?"

"It's his old house. I grew up there with him. He's stuck there. He wants to move on but can't. Can you help him get free?"

"How long has he been there?"

"He first showed himself to me a week ago but he says he's been there since he died."

"How long ago was that?"

"About six years."

"Does he know why he can't move on?"

"No. He hasn't a clue."

I didn't want to muddy the waters with the whole forgive-Corrado business. I wasn't buying that anymore and I wanted to see what Rocha could come up with on his own.

He pressed his palms together as if in prayer. "Hmmm. Most unusual. Usually a spirit will know why it's in a given locale. Mainly because it has chosen that locale."

"Chosen?"

"Yes, it's there because it *wants* to be there."

"But my father says he wants to get out. Could it be unfinished business?"

"Certainly. If so, that's usually why the spirit chooses to be there—and I emphasize the word *choose*. It's there to see the situation resolved."

I was getting impatient. "Usually" didn't necessarily pertain to my problem, and who knew what "usually" meant in these situations anyway? Talking here in his office seemed all too remote to have much relevance. The only solution I could see was an on-site evaluation.

"Could you come over to my house tonight?"

Mum would be gone and we'd have the place to

ourselves—along with my father, of course.

"I'm sorry. I don't do site visits unless it's for a group reading."

"Fine," I said. "I'll pay the group rate."

I'd dig into my savings. I needed to get this resolved.

He thought about that a moment. He probably had something better to do on a Friday night. Then again, maybe not. I know I didn't.

"I'm still not clear what you expect from me."

"Neither am I. An assessment? Maybe a plan? I'm the newbie here, you're the pro."

"Very well… for the group fee I will come on site and do an assessment of the situation. I make no promises, no guarantee that I will be able to come up with a solution. This sort of situation is uncommon. I might even go so far as to say it's rare."

"You mean a genuine haunting?"

"If that is what you wish to call it. Hauntings in literature go on for centuries. But in reality they are ephemeral. Spirits are easily driven away by the living. They will linger for a while in a familiar place, then move on."

"'Move on' where?"

He shrugged. "To be honest, I don't know. Heaven? Hell? I've seen and heard nothing to confirm their existence. When the spirits finally move on to wherever they go, they don't come back, so no one has ever returned to describe the final destination."

"You can help him move on?"

"I'm sure I can. Or I can help you help him move on. This is an unusual case. I can communicate with spirits of the departed for a limited time after their deaths, but usually I have to seek them out on behalf of their loved ones. Here you have the loved one—you did love him, didn't you?"

"Adored him." I felt my throat tighten. "He was the best."

"Good. Okay, here you have the loved one coming to you. This is very interesting. When do want me there?"

We set eight o'clock as the time. I paid in advance by credit card.

"There's one condition I must insist on," he said.

"What's that?"

"Cheese."

"Cheese?"

"A nice soft Brie."

"You're kidding again, right? Like with the crystal ball out for repairs and such?"

"It helps me contact the spirits."

"Really?"

He shrugged. "Well, no. I just love cheese."

This rotund fellow obviously liked it a bit too much. He did not need more, but I agreed to go along.

As I was leaving I turned at the door. "How do you see this playing out?"

He shrugged. "I have no idea." Then a smile. "Do you think I can tell the future?"

"Well, you already did, in a way: 'You're gonna die.' Remember? But I thought that's what psychics did."

"I'm a *medium*, Noreen. A go-between. The departed don't know any more about the future than you or I. If I could tell the future, I'd have invested everything in Amazon at eighteen bucks a share and be a multimillionaire by now. But I didn't, so I'm here talking to you. I wouldn't take advice from the departed anyway."

"Why not?"

"We have a saying: Just because they're dead doesn't mean they're smart."

I laughed as he closed the door.

One weird guy. If he was trying to disarm me, he was succeeding.

But cheese?

3

I was stopped at a light about a block from Rocha's office when I heard sirens. A sheriff's department car raced by and I recognized Travis behind the wheel. Curious, and with my psychic medium obligation completed, I decided to follow. He got way ahead of me but I meandered around till I saw flashing lights and headed that way.

I found him pulled up before Martin Gale's place. I hoped there wasn't a fire because with all those newspapers and other junk, that old Victorian would burn like a match. But no smoke pouring from the windows and no fire trucks in sight. I stopped out front and saw his daughter Heather on the porch by the open front door with her hands jammed into her mouth as she looked down at Trav who appeared to be kneeling in the vestibule.

Martin! An elderly, obese diabetic... odds were high for a heart attack or stroke.

I pulled into the curb and dashed across the weedy lawn. As I approached I noticed how the wood of the front door was splintered. I found Martin on the floor of the vestibule, lying in a pool of blood.

"What—what happened?"

Heather sobbed and clutched my arm with both hands. "Doctor Norrie! Thank God! He's been shot!"

"Shot? What the—?"

Trav looked up at me. "EMTs are on the way, but you wanna take a look?"

I was already doing that. He was dressed in a ratty-looking old blood-soaked robe, with more puddled around him. I couldn't tell the location of the wound or wounds except that they all seemed centered in the torso. But the wounds themselves weren't my main concern at the moment because I couldn't do much about them. What mattered was keeping him alive until the EMTs got here with some IVs. Right now his face was ghastly pale and I couldn't tell if he was breathing.

Trav rose and I took his place beside Martin, jamming my index and middle fingertips against one of his carotids. He had a pulse but rapid and thready. And yeah, he was breathing, but shallowly.

"Martin?" I said. "Martin!"

No response.

"You know him?" Trav said.

"Patient of Doctor Lerner's."

"Not anymore, he isn't," Heather said.

Apparently she wasn't going to forget Ken's hardline stance on returning the Tezinex products. But the sad truth was Martin wouldn't be anybody's patient if we didn't get some fluids into him soon.

"He's lost a lot of blood," I said, "and he's shocky. Trav, raise his feet as high as you can."

He shook his head and I noticed he had his pistol out. "I can't tie up my hands. The shooter might still be here."

Oh, God, I hadn't even considered of that.

I looked at the daughter and nodded toward his feet. "Heather, will you...?"

"Yes-yes! Of course!" She grabbed his slippered feet and raised them to the level of her breasts. "Why am I doing this?"

"Blood pools in the legs. Raising them lets gravity bring it back into the system. He needs all the volume he can get."

Trav was examining the door. "Four bullet holes. Shot him right through the door."

"Oh, dear God!" Heather moaned.

"No, that might be a good thing," Trav said. "Slows the bullets, so they do less damage. And it looks like one smashed the lock so that one probably didn't hit him at all."

I keep a spare stethoscope in my glove compartment but hadn't thought to bring it with me when I'd left the car. I was worried about a chest wound and a tension pneumothorax. I was also worried about the shooter still being around and kept glancing toward the dark front room.

"Where are those EMTs?" I said, debating whether to make a dash for my car and the stethoscope.

As if in response, a siren wail grew and seconds later a first-aid rig pulled up. Two EMTs, one male, one female, jumped out with their trauma bags, pulled out the stretcher, and wheeled it this way. I moved off to the side to give them access. Martin needed an IV running into him ASAP to get his blood pressure up or, at the very least, keep it from dropping lower.

"Multiple gunshots," I told them. "Not sure where, what with all the blood and the robe, but his blood pressure's in the cellar. Looks like one shot may have hit the spleen and—"

"And you are?" the guy said.

"Doctor Marconi, family practice."

He smiled. "Doctor Glazer's group, right? Thanks for helping out. I'm Jake, this is Lani. We got this."

I wasn't so sure. Lani had tied a tourniquet around Martin's right biceps but was having no luck finding a vein with her twenty-gauge needle. I sympathized. Because of the thicker layer of fat under the skin, veins in obese people tend to be hard to find anyway. In a shocky patient, no matter what the weight, the pressure behind the venous blood is reduced and so the veins won't be as plump, leaving them flatter and harder to find. Add shock to an obese patient like Martin and tapping a vein can be a real challenge. Jake, using a twenty-two gauge—I could tell because they're color-coded by gauge—was having an equal lack of success in the left arm.

Phlebotomy has always been my forte. Can't explain it, it's a gift I have. In my training I'd been able to find a patent vein on pretty much anyone, even junkies. The hospital IV teams used to call on me when they were desperate. I was so good they canonized me as St. Phlebotomia. Okay, not really, but if the Pope had granted them the power, I'm sure they would have.

"How about letting me try?" I said.

"Just give us another minute," Jake said.

Some EMTs can get territorial. I don't blame them. It's their responsibility once they arrive and unless a conscious patient says they want to be treated by a doctor on the scene, the head EMT has the final call. Me—I'd take any help I could get.

A second sheriff's unit pulled up and the new deputy— last week Trav had introduced me to him as "Hank"—joined Heather in the doorway. Travis stepped around the EMTs and took Hank aside to give him a whispered update on the situation. A Sit Rep, as they like to say.

After Jake got another dry tap I looked at Heather and cocked my head toward the EMTs. We had to get a damn vein open.

She got the message. "Look, I'm his daughter and have medical power of attorney. I want Doctor Norrie to give it a try."

Lani glanced at Jake who nodded, then she looked up at me. "You want a new setup?"

"Yours'll do."

"Gloves?"

"Just give me room."

Yeah, I know. A big no-no. In a hospital setting I'd have insisted on gloves, but Lani had already alcoholed the skin and I had no time to spare. Plus I'd need my most delicate tactile sense. That's my secret: I go by feel. I don't care how good a vein looks, if it doesn't feel right, I search for another. Martin wouldn't have been easy on a good day; with his blood pressure bottoming out, he was going to be a real challenge.

But there, in the medial aspect of his antecubital fossa, I felt a slight bulge. I went for it and was rewarded with a dark red flashback. In.

"Nice!" Lani said.

I pulled the needle, leaving the flexible outer catheter in the vein. Lani taped it down, attached the IV connector, then held the bag high as she opened the line for max flow.

I stepped back. I'd done what I could. They needed to get him to the hospital ASAP. Travis holstered his pistol long enough to help the EMTs and the Hank lift Martin onto the stretcher. Heather followed it to the rig.

"I need you outside, Norrie," Travis said. He had his pistol out again. "This is a crime scene—"

"Which I've been all over this morning, not to mention going through the first floor here on Thursday."

"Really? What for?"

"A medical issue." I couldn't get into details. "Not relevant."

"Do you know any reason why someone would shoot him?"

And that's when it hit me full force: Someone had shot Martin Gale... a patient I knew. I'd been so caught up in the emergency of trying to save his life that the harsh reality of the situation hadn't struck home until now. Someone had shot four bullets at this old man's front door.

"I haven't the foggiest," I said. "But I don't know much about him. I met him for the first time on Thursday. As far as I know he's just an old man who lives alone with his junk."

"Still, I need you to step outside with Hank while I do a quick walk through to make sure it's empty."

I couldn't help a little laugh. "Good luck with that."

He gave me a strange look, then motioned me back. Skirting the puddle of congealing blood, I joined Hank on the porch as Trav started for the front room. Any second now...

"What the hell?" came from inside.

Yep. Now he knew.

I waited on the lawn as Hank stretched yellow CRIME SCENE tape across the front porch. I noticed a grease-stained sack from The Bagelry next to the front door. Finally Trav emerged looking dazed.

"Notice anything missing?" I said.

He made a face. "Very funny. What's the story with this guy?"

"I think that's pretty obvious."

He stared for a few heartbeats, then smiled. "Oh, I get it. He's a patient so your lips are sealed."

"You're catching on. As I said, I was in there on Thursday. I have a picture in my head. I could tell you if things have been torn apart or pretty much in the same disarray as before."

"Sorry. Crime scene. They'll have my head if I let you in."

He looked around. "Do you think the daughter might have—?"

"Shot him? Heather? Not a chance. She's devoted and worries about him. Why do you ask?"

A shrug. "She called it in. Told me she brings him breakfast on Saturdays and found the door open and him lying there."

That explained the bag from The Bagelry. Not a recommended breakfast for a diabetic but no point in mentioning that now.

"Four shots," I said. "And nobody heard them?"

He looked around again. "These old houses are farther apart than most. A cool morning, the windows closed... I guess not. You free for dinner tonight?"

"Wait," I said, holding my neck. "I just got whiplash from the change of subject."

"Sorry. Wanted to catch you before you ran off. Well?"

"Sorry. I've an appointment."

"On a Friday night? Well, damn. Can you break it?"

"Family matter." I didn't want to get into my consultation with the cheese-eating medium. "We're still good for dinner tomorrow night, though, aren't we?"

It seemed weird to be talking about something so mundane as a dinner date at the scene of what looked like an attempted murder. But the victim was on his way to the hospital and the crime scene folks had yet to arrive, so...

He smiled. "Yep. The day shift cuts me loose at three. Plenty of time to get to your place—or rather, your mother's, by five. It's still five-ish, right?"

"You got it."

I was really looking forward to tomorrow night.

4

Back at the house, I saw Mum off on her Jersey City trip and made her promise to call when she got there. Strange how she always told me the same thing way back when, now I'm telling her. Took a shower and headed for the office.

Some morning off, right?

Ken was driving out of the office lot as I was driving in. I was surprised to find the reception area totally restocked with Tezinex products.

"You missed Donna by maybe twenty minutes," Giselle said. "She was asking for you."

Probably wanted to know how I was doing on her new product. I'd have told her I had absolutely no complaints.

"I'll catch her next time. Now that we're restocked—"

"Yeah, damn it," Giselle said with a sour face. She'd have to make change again.

"Now that we're restocked," I repeated, "did you call Anna?"

"Are you kidding? Immediately. She'd already been in first thing this morning—as usual—and threw her usual fit when we had nothing to sell her. Donna shows up a couple hours later and I'm on the phone to Anna before she even unpacks."

"I'm sure you made her day."

"I don't know. Weirdest thing: When I told her we'd just been restocked, she screamed 'Oh, no!' and burst out crying. What's up with that?"

"Your guess is as good as mine. Tears of joy?"

Poor Anna. Her emotions seemed all over the place lately.

"I don't know what kind of tears. I do know I expected her

to be here practically before I hung up, but she hasn't shown yet."

"Maybe she's out of town and can't get here. That would explain the 'Oh, no,' right?"

Giselle shrugged. "I guess."

I went to my office and checked through the lab and consultation reports, then called the hospital to check on Martin Gale. Bamdad Mesgar had been the surgeon on call when Martin had been brought in. We talked a little about Sam's good surgical results, and then he told me that Martin had suffered three .38 caliber bullet wounds. Due to their passing through his nice thick front door first, two of the three slugs had caused only superficial wounds. The third, however, had entered the upper left abdomen and pierced his spleen. That had been the major source of his blood loss and subsequent shock. Bamdad had taken him to surgery and performed a splenectomy. Martin was in the ICU and hanging on. He was still unconscious but it looked like he'd make it. Good news.

With that settled, I stepped into Room One to see my first patient of the day, a newbie named Walter Simon who looked to be in pain—severe pain. He stood beside the examining table, leaning against it with both hands. A telltale sign of a back problem.

"You've got to help me, doc," he said in a hoarse voice.

He appeared to be about my age—early thirties—and well kept, dressed in pressed khakis and a dark green golf shirt. Longish hair and built like he made regular visits to a gym.

I used to shake hands with patients, especially new patients. COVID-19 changed all that. Now I simply nod and smile.

"I'm Doctor Marconi, Mister Simon. What's the problem?"

He grimaced. "Hi, Doc. It's my back. I threw it out yesterday and it's just killing me. I've got three herniated disks and I've been getting along okay, you know, but when I picked up my suitcase at the airport yesterday, *blam!* Like someone shot me."

I looked at his chart. He listed his home address as Boca Raton, Florida.

A warning bell chimed. A new patient in severe pain: Nothing wrong with that. But add an out-of-state address...

was he looking for opioids? I'd been tricked before in my early days in practice—a bit too trusting back then. I've developed an index of suspicion since. It stinks to have to be so mistrusting, but that's our world today.

"When did you injure your back?"

"Six years ago. Would you believe, lifting my little boy?"

"Did you have surgery?"

If so, I could at least check to see if he had a laminectomy scar.

He shook his head. "Didn't need it. I've been getting along fine by being careful and taking a pain pill now and then."

Ah... pain pills. The bell chimed a little louder. Still, he could be the real deal.

"And the pills aren't working now?"

He gave me an embarrassed smile. "Would you believe I left them in Florida? This was supposed to be a relaxing vacation visiting my brother. Who'd have thought—?" He stiffened and grimaced. "There it goes again!"

Real or faked, I couldn't tell. But I knew one surefire way to smoke him out.

I pulled out my prescription pad and started scribbling.

"I'll write you something for pain right now."

Then I waited for the magic words.

Leaning forward for a look at the pad, he said, "What are you ordering?"

Bingo.

That pretty well busted him. The average patient with severe acute pain might say something like, "Better make it strong," but they're not up on the names of painkillers. Abusers are. They tend to be looking for a specific drug, and don't want you ordering anything else. They'll often tell you they're allergic to everything else.

But I didn't shut the door yet. No sense in being hasty.

"Why do you ask?" I waited for a list of non-addictive drugs he was allergic to or made him sick.

Walter Simon didn't disappoint. He ran the whole list— NSAIDS burned his gut and codeine nauseated him and on and on. Gosh, gee willikers, would you believe there was only one medication he could take without terrible side effects. Imagine that.

"Yeah," he said, summing up, "the only thing my orthopedist found that works is something called..." He closed his eyes as if trying to remember the name. "Oxy-Continuous, or something like that."

Right. Like he didn't have it tattooed on his brain.

OxyContin, the top primo prescription opioid on the abuse list, selling for a buck per milligram and up on the street.

"Gee," I said, all innocent, "OxyContin's not indicated for acute pain. That's for chronic pain."

"Well, that's what he gives me and it works just fine."

Was that a note of testiness I detected in his voice?

"Maybe I should call him and check this out."

He let out a forced-sounding laugh. "An orthopedist? In on a Saturday? Only dedicated family doctors like you work on weekends."

I guess I was supposed to be flattered. I wasn't. And Walter Simon—if that was his name—had just told me why he'd showed up today instead of yesterday.

"What's his name? You never know until you try."

He just stared at me. He couldn't give me a name.

I leaned back against the counter and returned his stare. This fellow was more likely from Frederick, MD, than from Florida.

I feel sorry for addicts and abusers. I do. A lot of them are genetically disposed toward addiction; a lot are clinically depressed and self-medicate with one substance or another. They need a dose of something to bring them up to the level of how the rest of us feel on an average day. If they choose alcohol, they're simply drunks. Marijuana's been either legalized or decriminalized in a lot of places, but get caught with meth or cocaine and the law says you're a criminal. Then a small problem becomes a big one, and in many states you're now a felon. I've never understood what we accomplish when we lock up people for simply wanting to feel good.

But I wasn't in the business of fixing society. My job was to deal with medical problems one person at a time. And no doubt about it, Walter Simon had a problem. But it wasn't his back. I decided that we'd danced around long enough.

"Okay, Mr. Simon. Let's put our cards on the table. You came here for one reason: to get an OxyContin prescription."

"Like I said, it's the only thing that works."

"I can't give you one."

"Hey, why not? I'm hurting. You're a doctor. You're supposed to help me."

"Right on both counts. But feeding your habit is not helping you."

"Hey, you prescribe it for other people, why not me?"

So there it was. A new doctor moves into an area and the local prescription hounds check them out to see how willing they are to prescribe the so-called Controlled Dangerous Substances. I'd been naïve when I started practicing and perhaps a little loose at first with my CDS scripts. As a result I started seeing a steadily increasing number of new patients with chronic pain.

I didn't think much of it until Sam drew me aside and mentioned that he'd spotted a couple of known abusers in the waiting room. He and Ken had cut them off years ago and now they were back. Was I prescribing opioids for them?

Yeah, I was. Seemed my name had got around—abusers tend to know each other through sales and buys and trades of pills. I'd been tagged by their network as an easy touch.

Some doctors use opioid prescriptions to build or expand a practice. It guarantees lots of repeat business. If I stayed easy with the CDS scripts, pill heads from Frederick to Annapolis and all points between would fill our waiting room. You can do quite well as long as the State Board or the DEA don't catch on. But it's rotten ethics—you're hurting instead of helping people—and illegal as well. In effect you're selling prescriptions.

I didn't go through four years of med school and three years of residency to feed people's addictions.

So I put the kibosh on the opioids unless they were absolutely necessary, and only for a few days. Eventually the abusers went somewhere else. But apparently my name was still out there.

"What I *will* do for you," I told him, "is help you get off this merry-go-round you've got yourself on by getting you into rehab, or into a pain management program, if that's what you need."

He straightened and jabbed a finger at me. "Hey, fuck you! Like I need some candy-ass bitch telling me what to do. Just 'cause you got the power of the prescription pad and it lets you decide who gets what and how much and when, you think you're better'n everybody else. Well, just fuck you!"

My heart was taching at one-fifty or better. The rage in his red face scared me. Here was a bulky, furious male in an office presently staffed entirely by women. For a moment I thought he was going to attack, but he only flipped me the bird and stormed out.

A few seconds later Harriet rushed in and found me still leaning against the counter, shaking inside.

"What happened? That guy left without paying!"

"Let him go." My heart finally was slowing. "He decided that he didn't want me as his personal physician."

She gave me a strange look as she began to change the paper on the examining table.

I stepped into the consultation room to compose myself before seeing my next patient. This was turning into Freaky Friday: first, I consult a psychic, then someone shoots Martin Gale, and now a belligerent drug seeker. And still early afternoon. What untold wonders did the rest of the day hold?

5

I pushed Walter Simon behind me and got on with the afternoon. By three I was running behind, and then Giselle intercommed back with a call I had to take: An attorney named Edward Stark was on the phone and demanded to speak to me immediately.

Uh-oh. Stark the Shark... fellow Carmel High graduate and Ted Phelan's malpractice lawyer...

An uneasy feeling rippled through me. What did he want?

I excused myself from a patient and ducked into the consultation room.

"Hello?"

"*Marconi?*" said a whiny voice.

"Ye—"

The word didn't clear my lips before he launched into a machine-gun tirade.

"*Who the hell do you think you are to interfere in my case? Where do you get the gall to approach one of my clients? How dare you meddle in my professional affairs!*"

I was momentarily taken aback by his vitriol, and remembered Ken's warning about not calling the suing patient and never *never* speaking to the plaintiff's attorney without your own lawyer present.

But I couldn't resist this. He'd finagled a patient who had nothing against me to add my name to his malpractice suit. I intended to be very careful, and if what I remembered from high school about this human weasel still held true, I was pretty sure I could handle him.

"Excuse me?" I said in my blandest tone. "Who is this?"

"You know damn well who this is!"

"No, I'm afraid I don't. And if you don't curb your offensive language, I'll report this call to the phone company."

He sputtered and stuttered. *"Off-off-offensive! You've gotta be kidding me!"*

"Who *is* this?"

I could sense the effort it took to ratchet down his tone. *"This is Edward Stark, attorney at law. I—"*

"Edward *who*? You're an attorney? You must have the wrong number. I didn't call an attorney."

"No, I'm calling you, Doctor Noreen Marconi, to give you a warning: Stay away from my clients."

"You have clients?"

A pause. *"Oh, so that's how you're going to play it?"*

Holding to the Miss Bland role, I said, "I'm not playing anything, Mister Spark, I—"

"Stark!"

"Whatever. I don't know who or what you're talking about."

"You damn well do *know who I'm talking about: Theodore and Mary Phelan."*

"Theodore Phelan... that name sounds familiar."

"It should. And it's gonna sound a lot more familiar over the next few months."

"And why is that, Mister Park?"

More sputtering. *"He's suing you for malpractice!"*

"He is? Why would he do that? He has no reason. I don't believe he'd do that."

"You know damn well he is! And I want you to stay away from him—no calls, no visits, no contact whatsoever!"

I detected a new tone creeping into his voice. Anxiety? Interesting. I pressed him further.

"Well, Mister Sock, just what is it you think I've done in regard to this Mister Phelan?"

"You know it's Stark and you know what you did. I don't know if you used threats or blackmail or cried on his shoulder, but I want you to stay away from him!"

"'Threats or blackmail' against your client? Are you

accusing me of a crime, Mister Dark?"

"I'm accusing you of tampering with my client by attempting to exert undue influence."

And then I knew—or thought I did. Could it be?

"Why, from the way you're talking, Mister Bark, I'd almost think that Mister Phelan might have consulted you about altering his claims against me."

The sudden silence on the end of the line was all the answer I needed.

I pumped a fist. *Yes!*

When he finally spoke, his voice was tight. *"That information is restricted by attorney-client privilege, but consider yourself warned: No more client tampering."*

"You sound worried, Mister Spock."

A forced laugh. *"Hardly. Be warned: You don't want to get into a pissing contest with me."*

"I wouldn't think of it. I'm sure you're the local champ, Mister Hark."

"You know it, Doctor Mar—no, wait. It's Doctor Macaroni, isn't it. Hey, you still substituting for the Goodyear blimp?"

It might have stung if I were still a blimp, but Norrie Macaroni was long gone and never coming back.

"You must have me confused with someone else." I heaved a sigh. "I'd love to trade barbs with you, Mister Garp, but as my mother says, Never wrestle with a chimney sweep."

"What's that sup—?"

I didn't give him a chance to go on.

"Hey! Hear that noise? Why... it sounds like a siren. I know that means you've got to run, Mister Snark, so I'll let you go."

And I hung up.

Yes! I had a very good feeling that unless Stark the Shark could turn the Phelans back around, I was about to be dropped from my first and only malpractice suit.

The first somewhat bright spot in a dark, dark day. I'd find another, much brighter spot this afternoon, and then darkness would return full force.

6

Toward the end of the afternoon I stepped into an examining room and found a T-shirted Damon Castanon sitting on the table. He wore a fiberglass cast from his right hand up to his elbow, and sat alone in the room. I figured he was back for a recheck on his rash and, considering how the last visit had ended, I was a little surprised his mother had brought him back to me.

"Hi, Damon. Where's your mother?"

"She like didn't want to come in. Didn't even want *me* to come in. Wanted me to see Doctor Lerner instead. But I told her no way."

I could imagine that conversation: *Shut up, Ma, I'm going.*

He held up his cast. "Especially since she kinda like blames you for this."

That took me aback.

"Me? What happened?"

"Busted my hand." He traced his left index finger along the blade edge of his right hand. "Broke the bone right in here."

"Really? Who'd you punch? Or was it a wall?"

His eyes went wide. "How'd you know it was a punch?"

"You broke your fifth metacarpal—that's known as a 'boxer fracture.' But why does your mother blame me?"

"Well, because of what you said last time I was here. You know, about like how Jerry couldn't help being a geek—"

"Down syndrome."

"Yeah, right. And how you said he'd already been totally dumped on by life and how I should be standin' up for him instead of dumpin' on him some more. I didn't think much of it, and I guess I was kinda pissed at you, I mean, you callin' me a trendoid and all."

"I was probably a little out of line there."

He waved his free hand. "No-no, that's okay. I guess I kind of am, in a way. But so's everybody else I know, so no big deal, know what I mean?"

I wondered if I'd learn about his fracture before midnight.

"Anyway, I'm walking down the hall Wednesday and I see Tommy Akers like pushin' Jerry around. Nothin' bad, not hurtin' him or nothin', just laughin' and pokin' him and knockin' his books out of his hands, and I go, 'Cool it, Akers.' I don't even know why I said it, it just came out. And he looks at me and he goes, 'What's with you, Casto?'"

"'Casto'?"

"That's like my name. You know, what they call me."

I guessed "Castanon" had too many syllables for his peers.

"Anyway, he starts getting his 'tude on and I'm like, 'Just cut him some slack, okay?'"

I was stunned. "You did that? Really?"

He beamed. "Yeah. And if these other kids hadn't been hangin' around, Akers probably woulda just dropped it, but when he's got an audience he can be a real jerkwad. So he goes, 'What're you, some geek lover now? This you're new boyfriend?' That pisses me, so I go, 'You're the one who's got like your hands all over him. You gropin' him or somethin'?' That gets a laugh which turns out to be a bad thing."

I cringed. Jerry had been the butt of the laughter before Damon came along, but now the audience was laughing at the bully. I saw where this was going.

"I can imagine."

"Yeah, because Akers goes bugfu—kinda crazy and takes a poke at me. I mean, what's up with that? But I see it coming and I duck and swing at his face. He ducks too, but not fast enough. I connect real hard with his head, like right above his eye. It's like hitting a rock. I hear something pop in my hand and it hurts like hell and I know I'm sunk because that hand's not gonna be good for nothin' now. But I connected so hard he falls back and trips on one of the books he knocked out of the geek—Jerry's hands, and crashes into a locker. He lands on the floor with the back of his head bleeding. I don't know if he woulda got up, but one of the teachers showed up then and that was it."

I shook my head in amazement. For good or for ill, people never fail to surprise me.

"You should be proud of yourself."

He shrugged, suddenly self-conscious. "Yeah, well. Funniest thing was Jerry's face when it was all over, I mean, you shoulda like seen it. Like he's thinkin' *W-T-F?* Y'know? I mean like I don't think that's ever happened to him before."

"You mean like somebody sticking up for him?"

I'd just said "like." I wasn't trying to sound like Damon, honest.

"Yeah, I guess so, y' know?"

My heart was ready to burst with pride for this kid.

"It's good to be the first," I said. "Maybe you'll start a new trend."

"Hey, yeah. That'd be sick."

I walked around him, checking his neck. After all, he was here for another look at his rash and we'd got sidetracked. It looked good. The acyclovir had worked.

"You're clear," I told him. "Just finish up what I gave you."

"Got it." As he slipped off the table he said, "Anyway, both me and Akers got suspended for three days."

He didn't seem to want to stop talking about this, so I listened. He'd broken a bone defending the defenseless. That rated as much time as I could spare.

"I'll bet your mother's *really* pleased about that."

"Yeah, tell me about it."

Time for me to give him some props.

"I can see now I misjudged you, Damon. I didn't think you had the guts to step up but I was wrong."

"Yeah, well, when I saw Akers messin' with Jerry I remembered you saying how he didn't choose to be, you know, a geek, and how he already had enough to deal with, and well, you know the rest. But you know what's really, really cool?"

"What?"

"Chicks, man. They've been calling like crazy, and they all want to talk about the fight. Like it was some big deal. It was like two punches and one of them missed."

Boys—like men—are so clueless.

"The fight's not the big deal, Damon" I told him. "*You* are. They're interested in the big guy who stood up for the little guy. That's you."

His face lit. "Yeah?"

I nodded. "Yeah. You proved yourself to be a white knight."

He frowned. "A what?"

I know the term has become derogatory in the online idiotverse, but it fit Damon's act in the purest sense.

"A white knight. Someone who can be counted on to do the right thing, who'll take your back when everyone else is against you. Not too many of those around. And all those girls think you're one."

"Huh. Cool."

Yeah. Very cool.

I'd be deluded to believe I'd changed Damon. But I think he's a basically good kid who never looked at his bad behavior in a larger context.

I do know this totally made my afternoon.

7

After finishing up at the office, I left Giselle to lock up. She informed me that Anna still hadn't shown up for her Tezinex supplies. That could only mean she was out of town. On my way home I stopped at The Hill Wine & Cheese Shoppe—don't you love when they add that extra "-pe"? I don't. The shoppe is located in an upscale strip mall in, appropriately enough, Lebanon's hill section.

The owner seemed disappointed that I wanted a plain old everyday wheel of Brie. Well, to him it was everyday. He'd have preferred to sell me a much more exotic and more expensive goat's milk Camembert instead, with all its "mushroomy goodness." He explained that Camembert was traditionally made with cow's milk, but this was made with goat's milk which has smaller fat globules, blah-blah-blah. Nope. Sorry. Rocha had asked for Brie so Brie was what he was going to get.

The owner was doubly disappointed when I wasn't interested in the Riesling he suggested I pair with the cheese. I'm sure Rocha would have loved it—as would I—but I wanted him perfectly clearheaded for whatever kind of "reading" he had in mind. But I did buy the suggested water crackers.

So, as instructed by the shoppe guy, I kept the Brie out of the refrigerator for a few hours to bring it to room temperature and placed the wheel on a plate with some of the crackers. It looked like an undersized white cake.

Mum had dutifully called me upon her arrival in Jersey City so I felt safe that she'd never find out about this. First off she'd be hurt if she thought Dad's spirit had been drifting through the house since his death and he hadn't contacted her. It wouldn't matter to her that he could contact only a blood relative, she'd take it personally and be devastated.

Secondly, she'd be scandalized that I'd brought a psychic medium under her roof. She'd be all over me, ranting that the Catholic Church believes that only God can tell the future, and if these people think they're in touch with the departed, they're wrong. If they're in touch with anyone, it's the devil, the Father of Lies.

I figured it best to keep those cans of worms far, far away from the opener.

By 7:30 that night I was pretty well set. But while waiting on Rocha to show, I used my laser level again on the landscape but still couldn't get it just right. I forced myself to leave it be by doing something I never could do while my mother was here: I stood in in the middle of the living room and tried to contact my dad.

"Dad? Are you here?" No answer, so I tried the name I called him as a child. "Babbo? Are you here? Can you hear me?"

Again, no response, so I wandered into my darkened bedroom and repeated the "Babbo" entreaty.

No voice in my head, no glow. Nothing.

Well, he did tell me his existence consisted of wandering around in a house of blurs and babbles. And maybe he was gathering his strength for tonight so he could manifest himself to me again. It would be nice, though, to have something to show Rocha.

I hoped this wasn't all a waste of time. And money. Rocha's "group reading" fee wasn't cheap.

He arrived at 8:06. If I were my mother, I'd have informed him he was late. Then again, maybe I wouldn't have. I mean, what do you say to a man wearing a burgundy-colored velvet jacket—a jacket he'd obviously bought before his waistline had expanded? It may have buttoned back then but no way now. Black slacks and an open-collar white shirt—without ruffles, thank God—completed the ensemble.

He stepped inside the door and stopped in his tracks with an unsettled frown. "Something going on here." He looked around and nodded. "Oh, yes. Something most definitely going on."

"What does that mean?" I said. *"What* is 'going on'?"

He took another step beyond the threshold and stopped again. "Is anyone else here in the house besides you and me?"

"No one. Just the two of us."

"There's definitely someone else. I'm sensitive to these things and we're not alone."

Sensitive... that was what my father had said about Travis who'd felt a chill both times he'd stepped into the house. He'd said, *Maybe he's one of those people who are sensitive to the spirits.*

Sean and Kevin had come to dinner that same night yet neither of them had mentioned a thing.

"How do you become 'sensitive'?"

"You're born that way."

"I have a friend who feels a chill here."

"Then he must have been born with the gift—although sometimes it can seem like a curse."

"How do you mean?"

"Sometimes you'd rather be like everyone else: blithely unaware of the spirit realm." He rubbed his hands together. "But it can also make life interesting. And from what I sense here right now, I have a feeling this is going to be a *very* interesting evening."

Neither of us knew then just *how* interesting it would become. *Too* interesting for one of us.

"I have your Brie over here. The cheese man—"

"He would most likely prefer to be referred to as a *fromager,* as the French say."

"Well, he wasn't French, but, yeah, that guy. He wanted to sell me Camembert but you'd said Brie so I insisted on Brie."

"Camembert is a bit more pungent but basically a very similar cheese. The names are different because of geography rather than the process. That's why they're both always capitalized."

Had I somehow stepped into a cheese documentary?

I led him through the living room toward the dining room but he slowed along the way, staring at the landscape on the wall.

"That looks tilted."

"I know, I know," I said, averting my gaze as I pulled him along. I'd already been down that road tonight.

"Ah!" he said with a single clap of his hands when we arrived at the dining room table. "A lovely wheel. And water crackers. Excellent choice."

"Of course," I said, nodding as if this was all routine for me. "What else would I serve?"

I saw no need to mention that these had been thrust on me by the owner—make that *fromager*—of the cheese shop—make that *shoppe*.

"They're a variation of the traditional hardtack, you know," he said as he cut himself a generous wedge from the wheel. "Hardtack was a staple of the British Navy in the old days. Water crackers are made the same way: without shortening. They're neutral in flavor so they don't get in the way of the delicate essences of unadorned Brie."

He did tend to go on. It appeared I'd allowed a compulsive lecturer under my roof.

As he placed the wedge on one of the crackers and raised it toward his mouth, he stopped and looked around.

"Something wrong?" I said.

He looked uncomfortable. "Not sure." Then he shrugged and shoved the whole wedge-cracker combo into his mouth.

"Oh, you must try this," he said, speaking around it. "An excellent Brie. Subtle Earth tones and nutty hints."

You like nutty hints? I thought. I'll give you a nutty hint.

But no. Stay cool. I needed the help of this foodie psychic. But I had such an urge to do *something* to take a mansplaining gourmand down a peg. Just one peg. And then I knew how.

"You enjoy that," I said. He was already cutting a second wedge. "And while you do, I'm going to take just a minute to whip up a nifty little cheese treat that will send your taste buds into orbit."

"How exciting," he said. "I can hardly wait."

I scurried through the arch to the kitchen where I searched the cabinets until I found Mum's box of Ritz crackers—she's never without a supply of Ritz. I arrayed half a dozen on a small plate, then found the other staple she's never without: Kraft

Easy Cheese. I shook the aerosol can and pressed the nozzle to swirl generous, conical orange piles atop each cracker. Yes, it says "Cheese" and "Sharp Cheddar" on the can but in the interests of full disclosure it would probably be more accurate to refer to the contents as a cheese*like* substance.

My mother makes only one hors d'oeuvre and this is it. As a kid I'd sometimes eat Ritz with peanut butter. And sometimes—when Mum wasn't around, of course—I'd shoot piles of Kraft Easy Cheese directly onto my tongue. But I never ate Easy Cheese and Ritz together on my own. That was reserved for those special occasions when company stopped by.

The only time she makes them nowadays is when my brother Sean and his partner Kevin occasionally stop by for Sunday dinner. Kevin goes into fits of ecstasy over them. Can't get enough.

I carried my platter to the dining room where I found Rocha staring at the wall to his left. He seemed almost in a trance.

"Rocha?"

He snapped out of it. "Sorry. I keep getting a feeling..." He shook his head and shoved more Brie into his mouth. "Never mind."

I set the epicurean delights on the table next to the Brie platter. Rocha stopped in mid-chew and stared. His shocked, confused—I might go so far as to say *horrified*—expression was priceless.

"What... what...?"

"The specialty of the house," I said with all the pride of a new mother showing off her baby. "My mother's signature hors d'oeuvre. Try one."

He actually recoiled. "No, I..."

I popped one into my mouth. I'd been a big fan of this stuff as a kid but not anymore. That didn't stop me from rolling my eyes to the accompaniment of near-orgasmic moan.

"Oh, God! Soooo good! Hints of guluronic acid laced with tones of calcium alginate."

Rocha froze, then broke into a laugh. "Okay. I see what you're doing. Point made and taken. I confess to a passion for cheeses and I do tend to get carried away. I much prefer stinky cheeses like raclette and Pont l'Évêque, but I would not subject the uninitiated to such, shall we say, challenging aromas. That was why I requested Brie tonight."

I swallowed my Easy Cheese-Ritz combo and had to admit it wasn't bad.

"You do need to taste one of these," I said. "Seriously. Give it a try."

He regarded the array like Miss Muffet would a spider. "I don't know..."

"It'll rock your world."

He didn't look good. His face was pale and sweaty and his hand shook.

"Are you all right?" I said.

"I'm okay. First let me ask you about your father."

He didn't look okay. The prospect of processed cheese couldn't have this much of an effect on him. Could it?

"Are you *sure* you're okay?"

"Oddly enough, I've lost my appetite—a new experience for me. But about your father..."

"Shoot," I said.

"What kind of man was he?"

Was he trying to get a feel for my dad? Made sense. I answered the way I always answered.

"He was the best."

"And how did he die?"

"Heart attack as he was carrying someone out of a burning building."

"So he was a good man who died a hero?"

"Yeah." My throat tightened as it always did on this subject. "He'd never call himself a hero, but everybody else did."

I turned away as I felt tears start. I get so emotional about him.

"Okay then, I must tell you something," Rocha said, and then made a choking noise.

I turned to find him hunched over, clutching his chest.

The pallor, the diaphoresis, and now chest pain—

"Lie down on the couch there!" I cried. "You're having a heart attack!"

His mouth worked as if he was trying to reply, then his eyes rolled up and he crashed backward to the floor. My first instinct was to rush to him but I knew I had to get help, so I jumped to my phone instead. I punched in 911, gave my name and my mother's address and said, "Cardiac arrest! Send a rig *now!*"

I didn't know for sure if he'd arrested but the way he'd passed out made it a likely possibility. I hoped my mentioning that would prompt the EMTs to bring their defibrillator with them when they entered.

I hit *END* and dropped beside Rocha who was flat on his back and not breathing. I pressed two fingers against his carotid—déjà vu with Martin Gale from this morning but Martin had had a pulse. Rocha didn't.

Shit, he'd arrested.

I started chest compression. The rate of compressions should be at least a hundred per minute, ideally a few more. I started playing the Bee Gees' "Stayin' Alive" in my head. I've always used that as my CPR metronome. The "Ah-ah-ah-ah" of the chorus is the perfect speed.

As I pumped away I was taken by a sense that my life had become a loop. This was the second unconscious obese man I'd had to deal with today. Luckily for Martin Gale he hadn't needed CPR. As with Martin I once again longed for a stethoscope, but mine was in the car and I didn't dare leave Rocha long enough to get it.

I started perspiring as I kept up the compressions. Anyone who's ever done one hundred-plus compressions per minute on an arrested human being instead of a dummy knows it's real work. I'd check his carotid every so often in the hope his heart had restarted itself, but I was getting nothing. He'd either flatlined or had gone into ventricular fib. I hoped for the latter because then the defibrillator would help. But either way, his heart wasn't pushing any blood into his system and so I had to do it for him.

Finally a siren. Optimist that I am, I ripped open Rocha's shirt in order to make way for the defibrillator. I hoped I wouldn't have to send them back to their rig for it.

Moments later two female EMTs rushed in, one with a trauma

bag and the other with—thank God—a defibrillator. I recognized the first one—a patient of the group named Barbara... something.

"Doctor Norrie? Is that you?"

"In the flesh," I said, still pumping. "Get those electrodes ready and turn on your AED." I hoped we were in time.

When all was ready I stopped the compressions and slapped the two electrodes onto his chest. This model defibrillator was automatic: You attach the electrodes, turn it on, tell it to go, and then get clear. It will sense the heartbeat or lack of one and decide on its own if a shock will help.

We backed off. Rocha spasmed as it gave him a jolt, then he coughed and started breathing. I felt his carotid and found a steady, rapid rhythm. His immediate response to the shock was a good sign, though he hadn't regained consciousness. We left the AED attached as we started IVs and got him onto the stretcher—just in case he arrested again. But he didn't.

"A relative of yours?" Barbara said.

"No, just an acquaintance."

"He's still out so we'll need his name."

"Rocha."

"Is that first or last?"

"It's the only name I have. I just met him today."

"Wait," said the other EMT. "Rocha? The psychic?"

"That's him." I saw Barbara give me a funny look. "This is my mother's house," I told her, as if that explained everything. "Better get him over to Three-C ASAP."

I preferred to avoid any questions as to what I was doing with a psychic medium.

When Rocha and the EMTs had finally roared off in their rig, I came back into the house and dropped into one of the easy chairs. Wow. Cardiac arrest and resuscitation had not been in the evening's plan.

After a few minutes I got up and headed for the kitchen, passing the remains of Rocha's wheel of Brie along the way. I found Mum's bottle of Bushmills and poured myself a couple of fingers. After the day I'd had, I figured I'd earned myself a little nip of Irish whiskey.

I wandered back into the dining room and noticed that

Rocha had cut himself another wedge of Brie but hadn't had a chance to eat it. Figuring why not, I took a bite of it sans cracker and waited for the subtle earth tones and nutty hints to wow my tongue. Nope. Too subtle for my palate, I guessed. Kind of bland, to tell the truth, especially compared to Kraft Sharp Cheddar Easy Cheese. I hoped in the future Rocha would avoid both kinds of cheese—and all others, for that matter. No doubt they were big contributors to tonight's blocked coronary artery.

I called out for my father again but still no reply. I wondered if maybe we could communicate only under certain conditions.

I'd figure it out later. Right now I was in bad need of a shower.

8

Hello, Norrie. I sensed a lot of commotion tonight but I couldn't tell what was going on. I felt outsiders in the house... more than one.

With nothing better to do, I'd called it a night and hit the hay early. While lying here waiting for him, I'd debated telling him about Rocha and decided to keep it vague.

"I brought in someone who knows about ghosts and spirits."

A Gypsy? He said in a scandalized tone. *You brought a Gypsy into my house?*

"No, not a Gypsy. He's Brazilian, I think. A psychic. I wanted to know if he had any ideas on how to help you move on."

You mean, move on without knowing about Corrado?

"We don't know if Corrado is really the problem, do we? If that's been the wrong direction, I was hoping he might be able to point us in the right one."

And what did he say?

"He never got a chance. He had a heart attack as he was standing there eating a piece of cheese."

Cheese? Was it bad cheese?

"No. That's not the point. The point is his heart stopped and I had to bring him back and I went through all this *sturm und drang* and still don't know anything more than when I started."

I sensed more than one outsider.

"That would be the first aiders who carted him off to the hospital."

I'd called Three-C after my shower and got the word that Rocha was stable. Checked on Martin Gale too while I was at it and learned he was doing better and starting to come to.

So he was no help, Dad said.

"Not a bit."

Well, there's only one outsider I can think of who I want in the house and that's that Travis fellow. Is he still coming tomorrow night?

"Absolutely. I saw him this morning and he'll be here."

Good. Maybe he'll play my song again.

"Dad... I've got to ask you something."

Ask away.

"Corrado Piperno was an awful person. Everybody who knew him says so. Except you. And you were closest to him of all. How could you not know?"

He didn't answer. I waited, and finally...

"Dad?"

Corrado was my fratellino. *I knew he had a wild side. I talked to him every so often about it, how he needed to hold himself in check. I thought he listened. He looked up to me. If he did bad things, he hid them from me. Which makes sense. He would not want his* fratello *to know. Because if I knew these things about him I would cast him out and never speak to him again. If, as you say, everyone who truly knew Corrado thought he was an awful person, everyone except me, then maybe he wanted very much to hold onto that. Maybe he needed one person who thought he was a good man, an honorable man. And so he kept his bad, dishonorable self hidden from me. Can you understand that?*

I could. Maybe Corrado needed one person to feel about him the way I felt about my dad.

"I understand that. But didn't you have any inkling?"

Maybe I did. But I'm weakening now, Norrie. I have to go.

"Really?"

Really.

His voice was fading.

"Okay. Good night."

Maybe he had an inkling? Toward the end, before Corrado disappeared, could he have begun to suspect?

He'd weakened before I could pursue it. But that proved convenient for me in this instance. He never got around to asking me what my plans were for tomorrow—besides having Travis over for dinner. He might not want me poking deeper into Corrado's hidden life, but I was determined to make this one last stab at answering the riddle of what had happened to that awful man.

9

I woke up just shy of midnight with only one thing on my mind. Not Rocha's cardiac arrest tonight, not the trip to Baltimore tomorrow. Nope. I was thinking about that damn landscape painting.

Tired though I was, I forced myself out of bed and made my way to the living room. I never could have done this with my mother here. But with the house all to myself—except for a certain ghost—I had to do it.

I dragged a chair over to the painting and stood on it so I could place my laser level along the top of the frame. I adjusted the frame until the laser said it was level, then stood back. It still didn't look right. I kept this up till I was ready to cry.

Exhausted and defeated, I stumbled back to my bed and dropped off to sleep.

SATURDAY

1

A h. The weekend free... mine all mine.
I treated myself by turning off my phone alarm when it buzzed, and sleeping in. I needed it after being up so late with that damn landscape. What had I been thinking? It seemed almost surreal now. But my bonus sleep didn't last very long. My body is too used to early awakening and seems incapable of taking advantage of extra snooze time. Bah!

But I didn't leave the bed. I lay there awake, luxuriating in the decadent warmth under the comforter. This afternoon I had to be in Baltimore to hit the butcher and meet Janie, but I had the morning entirely to myself. I could stay here for as long I—

My phone gave off its reminder *ding!* Now what?

The screen read: *Golf lesson*

Oh, crap! I'd forgotten all about it!

Yes, I was trying to learn some of the basics of golf. I know what you're thinking, but I have my reasons. Still, I couldn't think of too many things I felt less like doing right now than getting out of bed and hitting a stupid white ball around. But I'd booked it and I couldn't leave Luis the pro hanging. I'd have to hustle if I was going to make it on time.

I jumped up, dressed in a light sweater and my good jeans, and debated whether or not I should take a Tezinex. I wanted to chow down tonight when I cooked Trav dinner. I figured I'd earned a big meal without guilt and the trouble with Tezinex was that it worked so well. I simply wasn't hungry anymore, and I was serving dinner to a fellow with a supermassive black hole for a stomach. I didn't want to make him feel bad or inhibit his appetite by sitting there and picking at my food.

Okay, no Tezinex today. But I did eat one of their bars. It made for a pretty good breakfast as I raced to Quail Hollow, the county's public golf course.

How trite—another golf-addicted doctor, right?

Not so. Don't tell the AMA, but I don't like golf, not even a little. If I play twice a year it's a lot, and only because I'm invited. Golf bores me silly. Too slow. I much prefer tennis.

But every June the hospital staff has this outing at the Lebanon Golf and Country Club. Last year, at the evening awards dinner, I received the "Bogeyman Award," the booby prize for the highest score. Everyone, including me, had a good laugh. Ha-ha-ha. The leather golf bag I won was more lavish than anything I'd ever buy for myself, but that wasn't the way I wanted to win a prize.

Come hell or high water, or even plagues of golf ball-eating locusts, I was determined not to place last this year. One way or another I was going to beat last year's 137.

My instructor was Luis Sanchez, a gray-haired fellow in his sixties who'd been playing golf since he was old enough to hold a club. Today, in the best sartorial traditions of the game, he wore a pink shirt and dark green plaid slacks.

A patient man, Luis. *Very* patient. He'd taken me through a few holes on our first day and determined that my game had three weak points: First, I don't hit the ball far enough; second, I don't hit it straight enough; and third, I'm a lousy putter.

Otherwise Luis says I have lots of potential.

The worst part is I spend most of my course time in the rough looking for my ball. Not too successfully either. I use a neon yellow model and can't find even those. I went through a box of twelve at last year's outing.

So there I was on the driving range, whacking my way through a bucketful, with Luis behind me, watching. I was practicing my slice, even though I'm an expert: one ball after another, starting off straight, then curving gracefully to the right. Perfect.

"You're trying to muscle it," he said. "How many times I tell you, let the club do the work."

He adjusted my grip and I tried again. This time the ball hooked into the fencing on the other side. I'm not quite as good with the hook, but I'm getting there.

My shank needs some work too.

Luis made another grip adjustment which returned me to slice mode.

As I said, a very patient man. But I think we were both relieved when the hour was up.

I drove back home in a stew. I usually succeed at what I set my mind to, but this damn stupid game was getting the better of me. But only for the present. Eventually I'd beat it. If I lived long enough.

Even if I couldn't play, I could dress the part. For the next outing I intended to wear a neon yellow shirt over a neon green skirt. Always wanted to look like a key lime pie.

One thing I had to say for golf, though. While I was concentrating on hitting that stupid little ball straight ahead instead of off to the left or right, I hadn't thought about my father's cranky ghost. Nor about Corrado Piperno and all the misery he'd caused. And was still causing.

2

I was already in Lebanon, so, on a whim, I decided to make the short hop to the hospital to look in on Martin Gale and Rocha. Ken would already have done hospital rounds on our patients but Martin was on the surgical service for his bullet wounds and Rocha was in CCU under care of one of the cardiologists, so Ken would not have seen them. I doubt he even knew they'd been admitted.

I hit the CCU first since Rocha had the more recent problem but found his bed empty.

"He's down in the cath lab," his nurse told me.

From which he'd probably return with a stent or two.

She added, "He said he's very grateful to you for saving his life, and he wanted to call you first thing this morning. Said it was very important. But that's a no-no."

NO CELL PHONES signs were all over the CCU, an archaic rule I expected to be changed soon. The telemetry really wasn't all that sensitive to cell signals. But another rule here was no calls in the first twenty-four hours after a myocardial infarction. They didn't want the post-MI patients subjected to any extra stress.

"You can say you passed on his thanks and tell him I said I just did what anyone else would do."

"I have a feeling he wanted to talk about something else," she said. "Something about warning you. But I'll pass it on."

"Warning me? Did he say about what?"

She shook her head. "Not a thing."

Warning me about the cheese? But I'd eaten some without a problem.

Oh, well. Next stop: Martin Gale.

When I reached the surgical ICU they told me he was conscious now but still on heavy post-op pain meds.

"Has his daughter been in?" I said.

His nurse nodded. "She was here last night and said she'd come by mid-morning. He's been in and out of consciousness, not always lucid, but a little better each time."

I eased over to his bed for a peek and to say a quick hello if he was conscious. No way could he remember me from yesterday but he might recognize me from when Heather and I stopped by his house Thursday.

Nope. His eyes were closed. As I looked him over, I saw how his color was much better. They'd probably given him some packed red cells to raise his blood count. Suddenly his eyes snapped open. They widened in confusion as he looked at me, then narrowed with recognition.

"You!"

"Hello, Martin," I said as he glared at me with watery eyes. "How're you feeling?"

"You!" he repeated, jabbing his finger at me. "You brought that crazy woman to my house!"

That put me completely off balance. "What? Who?"

"The one who wanted my Tezinex bars, who else?"

"Anna?"

"I never got her name. But you brought her and then she shot me!"

"*What?* Anna shot you?"

"Yes! Shot me! She came back again yesterday yelling like a mad woman that I had to sell her some of my bars and how I had no right to hoard them. I told her to get lost. But after I closed the door on her she starts banging on it like she wants to break it down. I was watching through the peephole and told her to go away or I'd call the cops. So what does she do? She pulls out a gun and start shooting!"

I think my jaw must have been hanging open as I stood there staring at him.

Anna Divisova had been the shooter? No-no. Not possible. It had to be his painkillers. Martin was on an IV morphine bolus and it must have affected his mind.

And then I remembered what Giselle had said about Anna screaming "Oh, no!" when told that the Tezinex products had been restocked. Could that be why? She'd shot a man for them when she could have bought them if she'd waited just a few hours? If she'd looted them from Martin, it would also explain why she hadn't shown up at the office to buy from the new stock.

No. He had to be delirious, disoriented, and delusional.

I finally managed to say, "You're sure it was Anna?"

"Of course I'm sure. You think I'd forget who shot me?" He repeated the finger jab. "And it's your fault! You brought her to my house! You told her I had all the stuff!"

No, his daughter complained about it to Giselle while Anna was present. And she'd been the one to bring Anna along, not me. But I had no intention of getting into an argument with him about it in the ICU.

"Have you told the police?"

"Not yet. I'm not allowed to call anyone. I'll tell Heather, though. And I ought to call them on you!"

I could see he was disoriented and angry and my presence was only making things worse. I said, "Get well, Mister Gale," and walked away.

"And where is Heather?" he shouted after me.

"She'll be here soon," I told him.

"She's at my house, isn't she? She's cleaning out my stuff. She always hated my stuff. Got to stop her!"

He started pulling at the bed rails and looked like he was trying to climb over them.

I was going to alert his nurse but she was already on her way.

"Calm down, Martin! Please. It's all right."

"No, it's not all right! My stuff! My stuff!"

Another nurse joined her and together they rolled him back to the supine position. He lay there sobbing about his "stuff." A pitiable sound.

Poor man. He'd left his familiar surroundings—all his *stuff*—and been put under anesthesia as he went under the knife. Now he was in a strange, scary place, dosed with pain meds and on IVs that could be affecting his blood sugar, making it fluctuate all over the place. On top of that, his hoarding obsession was pushing him into paranoia. They'd give him something to calm him down, but I had to have a serious talk with Heather about getting him into therapy after he was discharged.

I left the ICU and went straight to the doctor's lounge where I put in a call to Travis's cell. He'd told me he had the day shift this weekend, so I knew he was on duty.

"I just saw Martin Gale," I told him when he answered.

"*Yeah? How's he doing?*"

"They had to operate." I didn't see a need to get into the details. "But it looks like he'll come through okay."

"*Great. Is he conscious yet? We need to talk to him.*"

"Do you have any suspects in the shooting?"

"*Well, a woman was seen around his house.*"

"Description?"

"*Middle-age, short dark hair, overweight. Could fit an awful lot of women. Why do you ask?*"

But it fit Anna to a T.

"Okay, I was just talking to Martin and, according to him, a woman named Anna Divisova did the shooting."

"*What? He's sure?*"

"I asked him the exact same thing and he said, 'You think I'd forget who shot me?' Plus there's the fact that she was with Heather and me when we visited Martin on Thursday."

"*Anna Who again?*"

I spelled it for him.

"*Got an address?*"

"Not off the top of my head."

"*No problem. We'll find her.*"

"Go easy on her, okay? She's been a little bit wound up lately."

"*Gotcha. If she's really the shooter, then she's armed. So we'll be extra careful.*"

"Please be. I don't want to be cooking dinner for just myself tonight."

He laughed. "*Okay, now, that was cold.*"

"Just saying. Take care of yourself. Oh, by the way, do you like Brie?"

"The cheese? Yeah, I guess."

"Good. We'll have some tonight."

No use in letting it go to waste, right?

"*Great. See you tonight.*"

I ended the call but stayed in the lounge, thinking. Anna Divisova shooting Martin Gale over diet protein bars... how bizarre was that? How surreal. And how unnecessary. Martin could have sold her a few and none of this would have happened. And Anna could have controlled her overwhelming fixation with the brand enough to wait a little longer.

Both of them had become obsessed with the Tezinex products. Why? Was it the drug itself? The videos? But I'd been taking Tezinex and watching the videos myself longer than either of them and I'd had no problem eating something else on that day I'd forgotten to bring along my Tezinex shake. So it couldn't be that.

Both of them had been obsessive types to begin with. I guessed maybe the med and the associated products just gave their obsessive-compulsive natures something to focus on. Just bad luck that Martin's hoarding compulsion got in the path of Anna's product-specific compulsion. A form of immoveable object meeting an irresistible force.

3

I stopped off at the Safeway to buy some greens and tomatoes for a salad tonight, plus some fresh parsley for the meatballs. The bakery had loaves of pre-made garlic bread wrapped in foil and ready for the oven. I decided on angel hair for the night's pasta. Mum always has extra virgin olive oil and balsamic vinegar on hand, so I'd use hers.

Okay. All set.

No sooner had I got home and unpacked the bag than my phone rang: Trav.

"Norrie, I'm afraid we've got a situation."

Oh, no. Was he cancelling out? At least I hadn't bought the meat for the meatballs yet.

"What kind of 'situation'?"

"I'm really sorry to call you. I know it's your day off, but it's that Anna Divisova woman. I stopped over just to ask her a few questions about this morning and—"

Uh-oh.

"Please don't tell me you shot her."

"What? No. No way. But she's threatening to shoot herself unless she talks to Doctor Lerner."

"Did you call him? He's in the office this morning."

"That's just it. I called him and told him the situation and he says he's with patients and can't desert them for an unstable woman. He says it's a police problem and we should handle it."

Why was I not surprised? But I couldn't say I blamed him. His first obligation was to the medical needs of the patients who'd made appointments to see him this morning. And I also couldn't blame him for not wanting to confront an obviously unstable woman armed with a gun.

I had a bad feeling about what was coming next.

"Do you think you could come over and talk to her?"

"Yeah, about that, Trav: Anna and I had a bit of a falling out this week." How did I explain this without breaking doctor-patient confidentiality? "She wanted me to prescribe a certain med for her that I didn't think was indicated in her case. So she switched to Doctor Lerner."

"You don't think she'll listen to you?"

"She was pretty ticked off."

I remembered that day she'd learned that Martin had bought out all the Tezinex products. And how when I'd tried to calm her down she'd snarled and said, "How would you know *anything*?"

"Could you give it a try? Please? We're not set up for this kind of thing and I could use any help I can get."

He was making it very hard to say no. And for all I knew, Anna would say she wasn't going to speak to me and I should get lost. And that would settle that. But at least I'd have tried.

I suppressed a sigh of resignation and said, "What's the address?"

4

As I made the trek from Carmel to Lebanon for the second time this morning, I reviewed what I remembered about Anna Divisova. I could rattle off her last blood sugar and A1C, no problem. But her personal life...

I knew she'd been divorced for about five or six years now—not an amicable parting, if I read her right—but she got the house and had been happy about that. I couldn't recall whether or not she lived with her mother.

Her house turned out to be a tiny ranch on a quarter-acre lot. Two sheriff department units were parked out front with their flashers going. About a dozen neighbors were standing around, well away from the house. Some had their phones out and up, taking either stills or recording the scene. My, my, what a fun home movie this would make.

I spotted Trav by his unit and pulled into the curb half a block away. As I got out and started walking his way, he hurried up and took hold of my upper arm.

"Thanks a million for coming," he said.

I noticed how he placed himself between me and the house as we walked. I couldn't see Anna taking potshots at me but I appreciated the gesture.

I said, "Any changes since last we spoke?"

"No. I'd like to resolve this without calling in the staties. They're likely to arrive with a SWAT team and an armored personnel carrier."

"Really?"

He shrugged. "That's probably an exaggeration but not by a

hell of a lot. They buy Army surplus and get all itchy to use it."
He guided me behind his unit. "Keep the car between you and
her. I think she's more of a danger to herself than anyone else,
but she waved a revolver to show us she was armed, and she's
already shot someone, so better safe than sorry."

"Where'd she get the gun?" I said. "Martin's surgeon said
the slugs he removed were .38 caliber."

"I would have preferred something smaller, like a .32. At
least we know it's not a .45. She said she's alone in the house.
She married?"

Alone in the house... so I guessed her mother didn't live with
her.

"Divorced."

"Still, her husband could have left it behind."

A lot of people hunt around here. I'm not a fan of killing
something you're not going to eat—unless it's a tick or the like—
and I don't know much about hunting, but a .38 caliber revolver
didn't sound like something you'd use to bring down a deer.

He added, "We've no record of her having a gun license,
which doesn't mean much. I have no idea how well she knows
her way around a pistol, so at this point an accidental discharge
is as likely as an intentional one. And either one can be deadly."

He pulled out a slip of paper and started punching the
number written on it into his cell phone.

"Who're you calling?"

"Anna—so you can talk to her."

I couldn't pass up such an opportunity to pull his leg. "You
mean I don't get a bullhorn?"

"What? No. Not when she'll answer her phone."

"But I've always wanted to use a bullhorn. That's the only
reason I came."

I wondered how long I could play this out.

"Seriously, Norrie, we have the phone. We're causing enough
of a disturbance around here as it is."

I waved him off. "You're no fun. I'm leaving."

And finally he got it. He shook his head. "You get off
winding me up, don't you."

I couldn't fight a grin. "You're just too easy. Call her."

I turned off my own phone—now was not the time to be interrupted with a robocall. When he finished punching in Anna's number, he held it between us so I could hear.

"*Deputy?*"

"Yes, it's me again, Anna. I've got Doctor Marconi here."

"*I don't want her. She didn't want to help me with my weight so forget her. I want Doctor Lerner.*"

"As I told you, Doctor Lerner can't leave his other patients. It's Doctor Marconi's day off but she came here just to see it she could help out."

I took the phone from Trav and said, "How can I help you, Anna?"

"*You can't.*"

"Try me. Deputy Lawton needs to ask you a few questions about yesterday. Why don't you help him do his job?"

"*He just wants to arrest me.*"

"How about talking to me, then? I couldn't arrest you even if I wanted to, and I don't."

"*I don't know. You wouldn't listen to me before...*"

I was going to tell her that wasn't true but thought better of it. In her mental state she might interpret a correction as my calling her a liar.

"I did listen, Anna. To every word. But when I've got my doctor hat on, I've got to make judgment calls. Even if a patient disagrees with me, that doesn't mean I didn't have her best interests at heart. Do you understand what I'm saying?"

Was that folksy enough? I was speaking the truth but trying to keep it humble.

"*I think so,*" she said slowly.

I sensed a softening in her hard line against me. She'd been coming to me as a patient for a while now. But doing this over the phone wasn't going to cut it. I knew Travis would have a fit but I needed to be talking voice to voice, even if it was through a door. That would still be a lot more personal than through a cell tower.

"Anna, would you mind if I came up to the door and we talked person to person instead of over the phone?" I purposely avoided saying doctor to patient. "You don't have to open the door. Keep it locked. I'm sure we'll be able to hear each other."

Travis was violently shaking his head.

I added, "Deputy Lawton is afraid you might shoot me. Should I worry about that?"

I heard her sob. *"No! I don't want to shoot anyone ever again! Except maybe myself."*

And there was my big worry. She hadn't killed anyone, and she was in a dark place. She could be guided into a better place, but only if she stayed alive.

I started around the sheriff's unit but Travis grabbed my arm.

"No, Norrie! Please! That's crazy!"

I handed him his phone and pulled away. I was fully aware that what I was doing looked crazy and stupid and unnecessarily dangerous. I'm not a hero and not terribly brave. But I knew this woman—had treated her for almost two years now. She definitely had some emotional problems, but she wasn't a killer.

Trying my best to look relaxed, I approached along the short front walk. A quick glance around showed many more of the onlookers with their phone cameras up. Hoping to see a shooting, maybe? I fully intended to disappoint them.

I stopped on her front step and said, "Okay, Anna. I'm here. Want to tell me your side of the story? Martin Gale told me his side this morning and—"

"H-he's okay then?"

"Just as cranky and ornery as ever."

Three quick sobs sounded though the door. "Oh, thank God! Thank *God!*"

"I hope you're not thanking God that Martin's ornery and cranky," I said in an admittedly lame attempt to lighten the mood. "That man doesn't need an attitude adjustment, he needs a total replacement."

This elicited a faint, strangled laugh. "Oh, does he ever!"

"So anyway, he told me his side, now you tell me yours."

Another sob. Her moods were swinging all over the place.

"I don't know what's wrong with me these past few days. I can't seem to control my thoughts. Or myself. I was fine until Wednesday morning when your girl said you were all out of the

Tezinex bars and stuff. That was bad enough, but when she told me she'd sold it all to one patient, I flipped. And I mean that: I could almost feel some kind of switch flipping inside me."

I went into appeasement mode. "Giselle shouldn't have done that, but in all fairness, she couldn't know there'd be such a delay in restocking."

"I overreacted. And I *knew* I was overreacting. I was angry on the outside, but inside I was completely *insane*. I *had* to have the Tezinex stuff. It became the center of my life. When I left your office I went to every drug store and grocery store and supermarket in the county and not only did they not have any, they didn't even know what I was talking about."

I started to tell her that was because the company was giving doctors' offices an exclusive until the end of the year, but cut myself off. I didn't know how that news would go down— probably not well—so I didn't mention it.

She said, "I even started going to other doctors' offices but none of them had any. That night I dreamed about Tezinex bars and shakes. Can you believe it? *Dreamed* about them. And the next morning you were still sold out. But then I heard that woman talking about her father buying them all, and you know the rest of that day."

Yeah, she'd gone over to Martin's house to buy some, only to be turned down.

"If only Martin had sold you just a few things from his hoard, you and I wouldn't be having this conversation."

"Exactly! *Exactly!* I couldn't get the stuff out of my head. I had to have it, and he had it all and I had none! So yesterday I took the gun when I went back to his house. I wasn't intending to shoot it, just threaten to if he didn't sell me some of his stuff. But then he slammed the door on me and told me to get lost. I didn't get lost, I *lost* it and started shooting at the lock. I don't know what got into me."

She started sobbing in earnest now.

"I didn't mean to shoot him, I wanted to shoot the lock off, but the bullets went all over."

I gave her a few seconds, then said, "Nobody thinks you wanted to kill Martin, Anna. You didn't point the gun at him, you pointed it at his door. You couldn't know he was standing right behind it. And Martin's going to be fine. So go with Deputy Lawton and answer some questions and—"

"He's gonna lock me up! And that's just fine with you, isn't it!" New anger in her voice. Where was this coming from?

"No, Anna, that wouldn't be fine with me at all. I—"

"You don't care about me! If you did you'd've given me what I needed when I asked for it."

That was so wrong on so many counts, I needed to set her straight. The words came in a rush: "I made a medical decision in your best interests, Anna. And if you'd listened to me, you wouldn't have been started on Tezinex which means you wouldn't have thought you needed their products, which means that Martin Gale wouldn't have a bullet hole in him, and you wouldn't be standing behind that door right now holding a gun."

I immediately regretted my words. She'd constructed this warped scenario that cast her in the role of a victim and absolved her of any blame. Was it wise to challenge that? Would that push her into some desperate move?

"None of that matters," she screamed. "What does matter is you were my doctor, and you let me down. And if I can't depend on my own doctor, what's the use, huh? *What's the use?*"

"Anna—"

"I can't take any more of this! You failed me, Doctor Marconi. Just remember that when this is all over: *You! Failed! Me!*"

"Anna, no!"

And then the sound of a shot—a very loud shot—just the other side of the door.

Instinctively I recoiled and ducked, but nothing came through. Then I heard myself shouting, "Oh, no! Oh, no, Anna! No, please!"

Travis was beside me in an instant, gun drawn. "You okay?"

His fellow deputy—Hank, from yesterday—joined him.

I could only nod at first, then I said, "I don't think she shot at me. The way she was talking, I think she might have..."

He groaned. "Oh, crap. Just what we were trying to prevent. Anna!" he called. "Anna are you okay?"

No answer.

"Anna?"

Nothing.

He looked at me. "Okay, you need to move over there, away from the door."

As I moved to the side, he and Hank flanked the door. They nodded to each other, then Travis tried the door knob. To my shock and, I'm sure, theirs, it turned and the door swung open. They each peeked around their respective side, then entered.

I eased up and peeked myself. I didn't want to see what I expected to see, but I simply had to look.

Anna sat in a chair about ten feet away, head down, chin on her chest. Her arms hung limp at her sides, her hands empty.

The two deputies were approaching cautiously, but when they got to with a few feet, she raised her tear-streaked face and looked me in the eye.

"Gotcha."

Travis had his pistol pointed at her. "The gun—where is it?"

She jerked her chin in my direction. "On the floor there, right by the door."

I felt my knees go soft with relief. "Anna! What—?"

"How does it feel, Doctor Marconi? How does it feel to fail? You failed me and felt nothing. Now you know what failure feels like."

5

I sat behind the wheel of my Jeep, staring ahead. I'd been shaken by what I'd thought was Anna's suicide while talking to me, and then shaken again by the sight of what appeared to be her corpse, and then came the added nasty shock of her "Gotcha." I still wasn't over it.

I watched Trav bring the handcuffed Anna out to the other sheriff's unit and let Hank take her in. With nothing left to see, the curious neighbors started to drift away as he came over to me.

"I've got to follow them in," he said, leaning in the window. "You all right?"

I nodded. "Yeah. Pretty much."

"Do you *believe* that?" he said, shaking his head. "All this violence and drama over some power bars? That's one sick chick."

I nodded. Anna certainly knew how to hold a grudge. "She definitely needs help. When I heard that shot I thought my heart would stop. I was sure she'd used the gun on herself."

Trav said, "There's a bullet hole in the floor near the door. She could have put it through the door instead, you know, just like she did with Gale. Why did you put yourself in that spot?"

"I didn't see it as putting myself in danger. Yeah, she had a gun, but I sensed the only person in danger there was Anna."

"Still, you damn near gave me a heart attack when you walked up there. And what was she talking about there at the end with all that 'How does it feel to fail?' stuff? What was that all about?"

"In her mind I let her down by not prescribing a drug she

wanted but I didn't think was indicated, so everything that followed is my fault." Seeing Trav's bewildered expression, I added, "Don't expect it to make sense. Her reality is not quite ours."

"But you didn't fail. She's still alive." He shook his head. "I still can't believe she put a bullet in the floor and then sat in that chair trying to look dead."

"Fooled me, I'll tell you that. She wanted to shake my world and she did just that. Her way of getting even, I guess."

"All for not prescribing a pill?"

"Yep. Like I said, her reality took a left turn away from ours."

"Well, her reality is gonna be jail or a mental hospital for a while." He straightened. "Okay. Gotta go. Are we still on tonight? I'll understand if—"

"Oh, no. We are definitely still on. You don't escape my cooking that easily."

He laughed. "I'm looking forward to tonight—*really* looking forward to it."

He trotted back to his unit and roared off.

I was about to start my Jeep when I realized my phone was off. When I brought it back to life again, I had a text from an unknown number. A robotext? I considered deleting it but decided to take a look. The nice thing about a text is it leaves the recipient in control.

> Norreen this is Rocha I need
> to talk to u. Cant call.
> Borrowing this Phone to text.
> Please answer. If your not
> there to answer I will try to
> get to phone and call tonight.
> Very important. Urgent. I owe
> you.

Rocha... he'd misspelled my name and the message had a rushed feel, like he'd been given very limited access to the phone. *Urgent?* I'd have assumed from what his nurse had told me that he wanted to thank me for the CPR last night, but he could have done that in the text. Nothing urgent about thanks, so obviously he had something else in mind.

I couldn't help but smile. Did he want me to save his cheese? Not gonna happen, Rocha. Your Brie-gobbling days are *so* done. But no. Had to be something else. Then I remembered what she'd said about a "warning." What could that mean? Well, I'd find out when he called tonight—*if* he called.

Time to get home and shower and change for my afternoon in Baltimore—the butcher, Janie, and Mako. I was hoping the last one had some new info about Corrado.

6

When I got back to Mum's house I noticed the landscape print was way off kilter. Rocha's heavy frame had hit the floor pretty hard last night. I bet that contributed.

But you know... it didn't bother me so much today. Seeing the print like that had been on my nerves—bothered the hell out of me, to be honest—pretty much my whole stay here. But now...

I spotted my laser leveler on the couch end table. Had I really spent money on that? It hadn't cost much, but I'd actually gone to a hardware store and bought it. I remember thinking how I could have ordered it online but didn't want to wait. Two days was too long. I had to have it right then, because I couldn't live another day with that tilt.

And had I really been up past midnight last night trying to straighten this picture with it?

Then it struck me... parallels between Martin, Anna, and me. We all had some form of obsessive-compulsive trait to varying degrees.

Obsession is in your head: a string of persistent, recurring thoughts. Compulsion is something you have to do: an impulse, often irresistible, to act. In its milder forms it can be useful. You like things neat and orderly: a place for everything and everything in its place. Great for a secretary or a housekeeper, or even a surgeon.

My mild form—I prefer to think of it as a personality trait rather than a disorder—compels me to make the bed every day, fold all my towels straight out of the dryer, keep all my clean clothes hung up in the closet, all my dirty clothes in the laundry hamper, all my cabinet doors closed, and so on. Oh, and of course, my pictures must hang straight.

On the professional side it makes me keep all my charts up to date, all my medical journals properly filed, and keeps me thinking about certain patients after hours. The important thing is, it doesn't rule my life. That's the way I like my world, that's the way I keep it when I can, but I don't get wacky when I can't, and I don't insist others around me be that way. In my eight years of undergrad and med school, I had my share of slobs for roomies, but they didn't make me crazy. I insisted on cleanliness, but I didn't dwell on their disorganization. They had their way, I had mine. Live and let live.

But in its more severe manifestations it becomes what's known as OCD—obsessive-compulsive disorder—which can run the gamut from majorly annoying to debilitating and crippling. A common example is becoming obsessed with the idea that you've left a door or a window unlocked and so you get out of bed—or turn the car around and go back home—to make a check of all the doors and windows. And once you've reassured yourself that everything is as it should be, you can go back to bed or return to the car. Until, that is, the unlocked obsession starts reverberating through your mind again. And then once again you must go check.

All along I'd noticed obsessive-compulsive traits in Anna. I suspect her condition led to her divorce. It's not easy living with someone who has strong o-c tendencies. The food in the refrigerator has to be separated by type into certain areas and arranged just so; same with the pantries and the laundry closet, and the cutlery drawer, and so on and so on. Her last job had been as a tech in one of the local retail pharmacies. Among her duties was the task of filling prescriptions, which involves counting out pills and putting them in a bottle. Simple, right? But not if you become obsessed with the idea that you'd miscounted. Poor Anna would be compelled to go back, empty the jar, and start counting again. She couldn't get her work done on time and so the pharmacy had to let her go.

Martin had it the worst. Hoarding falls in the OCD spectrum, often involving compulsive shopping and an obsession with your belongings. Martin's purchasing all the Tezinex products is a perfect example. He'd had to buy them all and then he wouldn't part with a single item, even when offered twice the price. The truth is, he can't part with anything. His crammed house is evidence of that.

But as I stood here in the living room now, staring at that laser level, I realized that all our o-c tendencies seemed to have ramped up since we started Tezinex. For some reason mine seemed muted today—I was less bothered by the canted landscape. And then I remembered: I'd skipped my Tezinex this morning.

There had to be a connection. Throughout my training my teachers hammered into me that correlation does not equal causation, but this seemed more than a mere correlation. Was it possible? Had Tezinex amplified our obsessive-compulsive behaviors? If so, what other behaviors might it affect?

I hurried to my bedroom where I'd stashed my Tezinex pills and products. Somewhere among them... here: the Cobdica Pharma rep's card. Donna Wegener had written her personal cell on the back. I tapped it into my phone immediately.

When I identified myself, she said, *"Oh, Doctor Marconi. Is something wrong?"*

"Sorry to bother you on the weekend, Donna, but yes, something might be wrong with Tezinex."

"I'm so sorry to hear that. You're having side effects?"

I gave her a quick rundown of what had been going on with Martin and Anna. Somehow I neglected to mention my own adventures in picture straightening—imagine that.

I finished with, "Did the clinical trials record any incidents like this?"

"I never saw the raw data—I mean, it goes on forever—but nothing like that is mentioned in the side-effects list, and I can't imagine it would have received FDA approval if there was even a chance it caused anything like what you described."

"Okay, so there's nothing on the record about it. How about rumors, whispers? Don't take this personally, Donna, but it wouldn't be the first time a pharmaceutical company has buried inconvenient findings."

"*Truthfully, I've heard nothing. But between you and me, even if I had, I couldn't mention it. The FDA very strictly limits us as to what we can say and can't say about a product. No product info can come out of our mouths unless they tell us it can.*"

I knew she was right. She'd be putting her job in jeopardy if she stepped over the FDA line. But still...

"Here's my big worry," I said. "What if what I've seen isn't just a coincidence but true cause and effect? What if Tezinex did amplify the obsessive-compulsive tendencies in those patients? Might it also amplify other disorders? Like violence? Or suicidal tendencies? Or paranoia?"

"*But don't you think we'd have seen that in the clinical trials?*"

"That's what we all assume. But a clinical trial has a miniscule sample size compared to the numbers once a drug gets out on the market. My little town had a near tragedy involving just two patients on Tezinex. That could be total coincidence, but it's got me worried enough to call you."

"*And I appreciate that. Believe me, I really do. Here's what I can do: The company has a hotline for reps and managers to report adverse events. I'm going to call this in right now.*"

"Will that get you in trouble?"

"*Just the opposite. The FDA has its own adverse-events hotline for patients and, trust me on this, the company would much rather have an early heads up from within rather than hear about a slew of patient complaints from the government. Learning of a real problem on their own allows them to get out ahead of it.*"

We both knew the subtext here: If Tezinex needs to be pulled, they can look like good guys who have only the public interest at heart if they do it on their own.

"*I hope it's just coincidence,*" she said. "*Cobdica's got a ton invested in Tezinex.*"

"Plus the bars and shakes. Which, by the way, can stand on their own. Very tasty."

"I agree. I've had a few. But thanks for the call, Doctor. I appreciate your trusting me."

I hoped my trust wasn't misplaced, otherwise I'd soon be on the FDA hotline myself. I'd decided from the get-go to hold off on prescribing Tezinex—a temporary hold that now looked to become permanent. But what about Ken? First thing Monday morning I was going to clue him in on my suspicions. I was pretty sure he'd decide on a moratorium as well. If I was right, Tezinex could trigger a lot of suits, and he wouldn't want to be on the receiving end of any.

And then I thought of Uncle Timmy. A couple of weeks ago he'd remarked that if I had any extra money I should invest it in Cobdica because of a new product they were going to launch. He must have been talking about Tezinex. I decided to give him a call.

When he answered, his first words—pessimist that he is— were: *"Norrie! Is something wrong?"*

"Not a thing. I just wanted to check with you about that Cobdica stock you mentioned. Did you ever buy it?"

"Bought and sold already. For a nice profit, I might add."

"Already? Did you hear anything bad?"

"Not a thing. Buy on rumor, sell on news. Why?"

"Oh, nothing concrete. I've just got this feeling they might have a problem with their new product and I wanted to give you a heads up."

"Well, isn't that sweet of you. But are you sure?"

"Absolutely *not* sure of anything, Tim. Could be nothing. Probably is."

"Hmmm. Could be a sign to get back in—but short. Hey, if it works out, I'll give you a commission."

"No, wait—" But he was already gone.

Okay. I'd done my medical, ethical, civic, and familial duty. Now for a shower and a trip to Baltimore.

7

Sam was in the Johns Hopkins Medical Center and School of Medicine complex in East Baltimore, not to be confused with Johns Hopkins University—up on Charles Street in one of the nicer sections of North Baltimore—nor the Bayview Medical Center in *way* East Baltimore, a whole other country.

I was having second and third thoughts about this visit. He didn't know I was coming and I didn't know what I'd find. Sure, all the reports said he was doing fine, but I think you know by now how important this man has been to me. I didn't know if I wanted to see him in pain or compromised in any way.

But when I reached Sam's room in the Zayed Tower, I found him sitting up and alert. He still had a nasogastric tube in place, IVs running every which way, a urinary catheter, and nasal oxygen as well, but I expected all that.

"Well, well, well," he said, his voice hoarse. "I didn't expect to see you today."

I kept my tone light. "Well, you know, I was in the neighborhood—if Little Italy qualifies as the neighborhood—and figured why not?"

The lightness faded. I swallowed a lump and blinked back some tears. He looked so frail and pale and small in that bed.

My voice sounded choked as I added, "How're you doing?"

He noticed and said, "I'm okay, Norrie. And I'm going to *be* okay."

"Are you sure? What's the true scoop?"

"The true scoop is that the surgery came off without a hitch—they've done thousands of Whipples here—and they've declared me stage one and grade one."

"That's the truth? You're not just saying that to make me feel better?"

He held up three fingers. "Scout's honor."

Now I wanted to cry again, but this time for joy.

"Oh, that's great, that's really great. How are you feeling? Much pain?"

"I'm feeling exactly how a person is supposed to feel after having parts of his pancreas, stomach, and small intestine removed along with his gallbladder. The pain isn't so bad and when it acts up I have Sister Morphine waiting to help."

"Sister...?"

"A Rolling Stones reference. Way before your time. How's the office doing?"

I could see he wanted to move the conversation off him and his surgery. Big question: Should I tell him about our adventure in Tezinex retailing? I decided against it since the issue seemed like it was quickly going to become moot.

"Your patients miss you and want to know when you'll be back."

"ASAP, I guarantee that. I'm sorry you two have to put in those extra hours. I imagine Ken's worried about the revenues?"

"Not a bit," I deadpanned. "As a matter of fact, he's running a two-for-one promotion on office visits and gave Giselle and Harriet each a thousand-dollar bonus."

He laughed and then grimaced and clutched his abdomen.

"Are you okay?" I said.

"Yes!" he gasped. "Just don't make me laugh! *Please*, don't make me laugh!"

I pretended to write it down. "Duly noted: no humor allowed."

"Stop. You're going to make me laugh again."

We made small talk until one of the nurses appeared and said he had to go down to imaging. I left the Zayed Tower feeling a lot better about Sam's future than I had when I'd entered.

8

Next stop was the butcher shop—Calabro's on Fawn Street in Little Italy. This was where my father bought all his sausages and the only butcher shop he'd use for his meatballs. He never said why, exactly, but I've got to figure that for a guy born in Calabria, a butcher named Calabro seemed like a good fit.

The mix of meats in my dad's meatball recipe was two parts beef, one part veal, and one part pork—all double-ground. I bought a pound of the beef and half a pound each of the pork and veal. As long as I was cooking I might as well make sure I had a few leftovers—although, considering Trav's appetite, the possibility of leftovers was iffy at best. I also picked up a small chunk of Romano cheese because dad always grated his fresh. Plus some Italian breadcrumbs and minced garlic. I'd bought fresh parsley yesterday and already had that at home. I also bought a quart of Calabro's homemade gravy because it's excellent and I'd add a few extra spices when I heated it tonight, just to put my own stamp on it.

And as the final touch I bought a small tub of my father's coup de cuisine, the real secret to the taste and texture of his meatballs: lard.

With all the fixings for tonight safely stored in my trunk, I headed for the Block. Parking proved no problem. It would have been a totally different story had the Orioles been in town for a game. The rain that the weatherman had promised all morning arrived as a drizzle as soon as I stepped out of the garage. No problem: I'd worn a raincoat and brought an umbrella.

As I've said, I've driven through the Block but never actually visited. If you're walking east on Baltimore Street, you get your first indication from the big black marquee emblazoned with "Larry Flynt's *HUSTLER* Club" which used to be an old burlesque house called the Gayety. The *Gayety* name is still carved into the front up near the roof. "Club Pussycat" came next, followed by "Chez Joey," "The Jewel Box," and then "Dainties," the lingerie shop that was one of our destinations.

Across the street you'll find a place with the subtle name of "Lust," followed by "The 2 O'Clock Club" and "The Shark Tank," our other destination. I suppose all the flashing neon at night masked a lot of the shabbiness and added a certain glitz for those who liked this sort of stuff, but here in the drizzly daytime it all looked tawdry and, well, lame.

Only a three-block walk up from the determinedly family-friendly Inner Harbor, this was a whole other world. Janie had told me the Block's lifeblood was the attendees at the convention center's big events, plus the frequent gatherings at the numerous harbor hotels.

I was approaching Dainties and, speak of the devil, here she came, walking from the opposite direction: Poochie Sutton herself. She too wore a raincoat but hers was transparent, revealing the skimpy shorts and halter top she wore beneath.

"You showed up!" she cried, spreading her arms and breaking into a run.

She locked me in a big embrace like we were long-lost sisters.

"You had doubts?" I said as we broke apart.

"I was ninety-percent sure you'd chicken out."

I probably would have done just that if I hadn't had Sam and Calabro's as reasons to come to town.

I said, "Even if I had chickened out, I'd have called to let you know. I wouldn't stand up a friend."

Friend was perhaps too strong but I went with it. *Acquaintance* and *neighbor* were more accurate and fitting. I genuinely liked Janie. Or maybe I should say she fascinated me. I certainly envied her *joie de vivre*, but our values and mores were too divergent to allow us to be friends in the truest sense.

"Yeah, I should have known you were too classy for that."

As we stood before Dainties I got my first close-up look at

what the mannequins were wearing. Whoa. In a way I hoped I was too classy for a place like Dainties as well, but I bit the old tongue again.

Janie caught my stare. "Let's go in and get out of this rain. We'll buy you some goodies and then go see Mako. He's anxious to meet you."

I wished I could have said the same. I was sure he was anxious to meet me because Janie had told him I was a potential "bigger, older" woman for his lineup. Or how else had Janie put it? Mako was looking to bring a few "strong, mature women" to grace his stage. Or "MILFs," as she'd also described me.

"Has he learned anything about my godfather?"

"I gave him the name. He told me it rang a bell but he said he'd ask around to see what some of the other old timers around here remembered."

Well, I couldn't ask any more than that. I figured no one could tell me anything worse than what I'd already heard about the man. I didn't hold out any hope of learning his ultimate fate, but maybe I could gather enough of a hint to provide some closure for my dad. Though why he cared about what had happened to this monster was beyond me.

We entered Dainties. Janie led me around until we reached the bra section where she held up a lacy black model. Big deal. I had a number of black bras. And then I noticed...

"The cups—where's the rest of them?"

The front of the cups had been removed.

Janie smiled. "I was wondering when you'd notice."

"But—"

"The underwire provides lift and—"

"So does the one I'm wearing now."

"Do your boobies sag?"

Kind of personal, but it was just us girls. "A little. Maybe."

"Mine are fake so they don't, but I have one of these anyway. It lifts them and leaves the nipples, shall we say, accessible?"

"So does a nursing bra."

She barked a laugh. "You're too much!"

She dropped the bra and moved to the panty section.

"Here we go," she said, holding up a pair, also black and

lacy. I was seeing a trend here.

"Wait. It's got no crotch!"

She broke down laughing. "Oh, God, I wish we had a camera on you! Your expression is just… just priceless!" Still laughing, she motioned me to follow her. "One more thing I just gotta show you."

She led me to a shapely mannequin in a fishnet bodysuit. I turned to her. "Why, Janie? *Why?*"

"Why what?"

"Why wear this?"

"Why not?"

"Because it hides absolutely nothing so why put it on in the first place?"

She laughed again. "It's not *supposed* to be practical, Norrie!"

Bras with no fronts and panties without crotches, I get it, and then again, I don't. But a fishnet body suit? Beyond me. This stuff was for jaded people who needed to spice up their sex life. I got that. Well, sort of. But I *had* no sex life to begin with. I was hoping to start having one tonight with Travis, but any sex at this point would already be plenty spicy just by the very fact that it was present at all.

We went through the whole place and I'm glad to say I didn't see anything that was *me*. Fine. Call me a prude. I'll own it. I kept telling Janie "That's not me" and she kept saying, "Right, it's for a new and better you." Well, that was up for debate. She did shame me into buying a black thong. After all, she'd gone to the trouble of giving me a guided tour of the place so I felt obligated to buy *something*, just so she didn't think this was a total waste of her time.

"You're a piece of work," she said with a grin as we stepped back onto the sidewalk. "How're you ever gonna strip down on stage?"

I didn't have to worry about that because it was never going to happen. Not in this universe, and nowhere in the whole entire multiverse will you find a reality where Noreen Marconi strips before a room full of men. Or even women, for that matter.

But to Janie, I said, "I'm going to have to shed a few inhibitions before I do that."

Another laugh. "Ya think?"

"Can we go see Mako now?"

"Let's do it."

We crossed the street to The Shark Tank. The sign on the door said it was open from noon to 2 a.m. seven days a week. Janie pulled open the front door and a wave of cold air and loud dance music enveloped us. The bruiser at the door smiled at Janie.

"The one and only Poochie Sutton!" he said.

When he raised his eyebrows at me, Janie said, "Mako's expecting us."

The guy nodded and we moved on. I wondered how he could hear after prolonged exposure to that monotonous thump-thump-thump beat at this volume. As we entered the main room I was surprised to see it had two levels. A wide stairway curved up and away on the right; a sign with an arrow pointing up read, *V.I.P. ROOMS*.

The lights were low and red, reflecting off the black lacquered surfaces and chrome trim. The walls were red and all the cushy chairs and banquets were covered in tufted red velvet.

I leaned close to Janie's ear to be heard. "Just a wild guess but I've got a feeling this Mako guy likes the color red."

She grinned and nodded. "He says"—her voice deepened and took on a bad Russian accent—"'is blood in water... think of color as blood in water.'"

The Shark Tank... blood in the water... I got it. I guess it made sense on some level.

Maybe a dozen customers, all—surprise!—male, sat as singles or in pairs at the tiny black tables arranged around an oval central dance floor equipped with not one but two brass poles. A skinny topless blonde twirled and gyrated and hung from one of the poles. The girl looked bored and the watchers looked bored. I mean really, guys, can't you find something else to do on a Saturday afternoon?

The second level had a glass-floored pole-dance stage suspended over the first—I guessed so those below could watch the dancers up there as well. That stage was not in use at the moment.

Janie led me on a winding path through the red chairs and black tables to an office in the rear. The door was decorated with a brass plaque that said Бос. Janie answered my question before I could ask it.

"It means 'Boss' in Ukrainian."

Her knock was answered with "Come" from within and we entered a very plain office. After all the excesses of the rest of the décor, I'd anticipated something much more elaborate. Mako—or Vladimir Makovei—was supposedly the owner so I'd expected a mahogany partner's desk at least. But no, he sat behind a spare pedestal desk that might have come from Ikea. The rest of the office décor consisted of a couple of extra chairs, file cabinets, wall shelves piled with binders, and the inevitable desktop computer.

"Ah, Poochie!" he said, rising from his rolling office chair. He had a deep voice and a thick Russian accent. "I see you have brought your friend."

I'd expected a cliché—a bear of a man with a shaved head and a collection of gold chains gleaming at his hairy throat. Instead I found a slim, dapper fellow in a dark suit and tie with slicked back, thinning hair—more of a barracuda than a mako shark. Give him a monocle and he'd be Baron Barracuda.

He gripped Janie by both upper arms and gave her the traditional Euro kiss on each cheek. Then he surprised me by doing the same to me.

"And who is lovely lady?"

"This is Norrie. I told you about her."

He made a little bow. "Norrie, I am Mako. You wish to dance for me?"

Not ever, never.

But I'd told Janie I'd listen to his offer to hire on as a pole dancer if he got me some info on Corrado, so I played coy but spoke the truth.

"Well, I have no experience. I've never done anything like that before."

And never will.

"It is easy. You just move to the music. Poochie teach you. Right, Poochie?"

Janie's grin said she was really enjoying this. "Oh, absolutely!" I said, "Did you find out anything about that name I gave you?"

"Yes-yes. Corrado Piperno. But first I want to see you without that raincoat."

"Without—?"

"I'll hold it," Janie said, her grin wider as she held out her hand.

The things I do for my father.

"All right," I said, unbuttoning it. "But that's all I'm taking off."

I shrugged out of the coat and stood there in my hospital-visit-to-a-colleague-on-a-Saturday outfit of black slacks and a light sweater.

Mako was all smiles. "Yes, Poochie, she tell truth about you. You are a strong woman."

He made a horizontal circular motion with his hand, so I did a slow turn. I felt like a side of beef at a meatpacking plant.

"You mean I'm overweight," I said.

"No-no-no! Do not think this. You have curves. Men like women with curves. You are just what I am looking for. Many customers will go nuts for you. You will be cleaning up tips."

I wasn't feeling so bad now. What woman doesn't like to be appreciated for what she has—especially when she always thought she had too much.

"You can start tonight," he added.

I put on a disappointed expression. "Oh, damn. I have another commitment I can't break. Let me get back to you next week."

He beamed. "Excellent. I shall await your call." He indicated the two chairs. "Now, we talk. Sit, sit." When he was ensconced behind his desk again and we were seated out front, he leaned forward and said, "Who is this Corrado Piperno to you?"

"My godfather."

"Godfather, eh? I have seen movie. He was powerful man? He had influence like Don Corleone?"

"No, not at all. Just a mason—a bricklayer."

"But is important person to Italians, yes?"

I shrugged. Knowing the sort of man we were discussing,

the questions were making me a little uncomfortable. "Sort of. I mean, traditionally, yes, the godparents are important to the family. Not so much in mine. It's all part of the Baptism ceremony and comes down to the godfather and godmother promising to take spiritual care of the child should something happen to the parents."

A sudden epiphany sent a wave of horror and revulsion through me. What if something awful had happened to my folks back when I was a kid? With no other relatives to turn to, would I have wound up in the Piperno house? Would I have been beaten too? And would Corrado have been making visits to my bedroom as well?

I couldn't repress a shudder.

"Something is wrong?" Mako said.

I shook my head. "I'm okay."

"So, this man was close to your family?"

"He and my father knew each other from the Old Country and always stuck together."

"And now after so many years you want to know where is he?"

I used my cover story. "My father always wondered what happened to him when he disappeared. My father passed years ago but I thought I could tie up the loose ends."

Why all these questions?

Mako drummed his fingers on the desktop. "I have small memory of name but not of face. So I ask about him to others who were here back then." He drummed again. "You may not like to hear. Was not such nice man."

Ah, now I got it. He'd uncovered bad things about Corrado. What a shock.

"Oh, I appreciate your concern, Mako, I really do. But believe me, I've already heard some terrible things about him. From what I've learned, he was an awful man. So whatever you have to say, I've probably already heard. I know he used to frequent prostitutes down here, so that won't be news."

"Good, then. Well, not so good, eh? But I was not liking to make favorite uncle or godfather look bad. I ask around about him, hear of prostitutes. I speak to people who know of such things." He raised his hands. "I am not involved. Mako is strictly legit player, but I know people."

I merely nodded. Of course he knew people. He ran a strip club. He was in the sex business. Ostensibly a look-don't-touch sex business, but he was still playing to and preying on the male libido. What with cover charges and overpriced drinks and VIP rooms, I was sure he could make a lot of money running his club in a perfectly legal fashion, and maybe he did. But anyone would be naïve to think some of his girls weren't doing extracurricular work after hours with the conventioneers. No way could I tell if he had his hand in that or not. And not my business anyway.

"Some people I know tell me he like young stuff. Early to mid-teens. That sort of girl."

Nausea replaced the revulsion. It fit. I thought of Angelina. She'd told me she'd been only twelve when her father drugged and raped her.

I managed to say, "I suspected."

"Was very strong about that. Must be young or he will not be interested. I hear story that one pimp send him girl who is not young but looks and dresses young to fool Johns. This Piperno guesses truth and beats her."

Well, that fit too.

What a sterling character was my godfather. Not only goes whoring but beats up prostitutes who aren't young enough.

"He disappeared," I said. "He didn't run away because he didn't withdraw any money from his bank account and left behind all his clothes except what he was wearing. The police believe that's a pretty good indication that something happened to him. And they think it might have happened to him down here on the Block."

A massive shrug. "Is possible. You beat up girl, bruise face, she can't work. That costs pimp and he take revenge. And some girls you shouldn't mess with. You punch her, she stab you. She and pimp get rid of body. Each is possible, but I hear nothing either way."

I remembered how his car was found a mile from his house, and how it seemed he'd parked it there and was picked up by someone else.

"Was he ever with anyone else? Did he make any friends down here?"

"Is barely remembered. Nobody care. He was nobody. Good riddance. Whatever happened is long forgot. You too should forget, pretty lady."

Yeah. Easier said than done. But I couldn't stay here any longer. I wanted out of The Shark Tank and off the Block and out of Baltimore. I rose and extended my hand.

"Mako, that's the best advice I've heard all week. But I'm afraid I must go. Thank you for your efforts."

He rose and clasped my hand in both of his. "It was my pleasure. You will call and we will set up audition, yes?"

"As soon as I am able," I said.

Of course, I would never be able.

Poochie—I mean Janie—walked me to the door.

When we reached the sidewalk, she said, "My shift starts in a few hours so I'll hang around here. I'm guessing Mako shouldn't hold his breath waiting for your call."

"Not unless he's a real mako."

She smiled and shrugged. "Well, I tried."

I gave her a quick hug. I'd always liked her and I liked her now more than ever. "You've got a good heart, Janie. I'll be back in my place next week and I'll take you up on that chess game."

"You're on."

The rain had stopped—or paused, I couldn't tell—so I hurried to my car and found my way back to 695.

On the drive home I decided I was through with the quest. For good. I'd uncovered everything anyone could find on Corrado Piperno. I kept returning to Trav's father's assessment of the man: *He was a bum.*

Indeed he was that, and so much more. Or maybe so much less. Whatever, I was done with him. My last word tonight to my father on Corrado's disappearance would be that he died by virtue of being a rapist and a pervert. He'd been known to beat up a prostitute if he wasn't satisfied that she was young enough, and it's not a stretch to assume that on the night of his disappearance he beat up the wrong one. Or perhaps he crossed the path of the pimp of one he'd previously beaten. Either way, a score had been settled and Corrado's remains had most likely settled to the bottom of the harbor, never to be seen again.

That was it. That would be enough to provide closure. And if not, well, it would have to do. Because I was done with Corrado Piperno.

9

When I got home I went right to work on making my chopped salad, which I stored in the fridge. Then came the messy task of making the meatballs. You mix the beef, veal, and pork in a large bowl with the chopped parsley, grated cheese, garlic, salt, fresh-ground pepper, and two raw eggs. The meat and eggs are the easy ingredients because they're pre-set amounts. The real challenge comes with the garlic, cheese, salt and pepper. How much of each? My father could never write it down because he didn't really know. A bit of this, a sprinkle of that, a handful of that—those were his measurements. I used to help him and thought I knew until I tried my first batch of meatballs during college. Everyone swooned over them, raving that they were the best meatballs they'd ever tasted—everyone except me. They weren't like Dad's. Not even close.

I figured I could ask for some input from the master here, even though he hadn't responded last night before Rocha's visit.

Which reminded me: Rocha hadn't called back like he said he would. I'd got the feeling he wanted to tell me something… something more than thank-you. Well, if he got access to a phone, he'd call. If not, I was sure it could wait.

"Dad?" I called to the walls of the kitchen. "Can you hear me? I could use a little advice here on your meatball recipe."

No answer. So, like last night, I tried my childhood name for him. "Babbo? I really could use your help."

Still nothing. I was on my own, I guessed.

So, I did my best with the cheese and garlic and all. Everything was in the bowl. Now came the messy part: You get in there with your hands—my father used his bare hands but I'm comfortable with latex gloves so I always don a pair—and mush everything together. Mush it really, really well. Then you add two cups of bread crumbs and some water, and get your hands in there again.

When the texture of the mix is consistent, you form your meatballs. You don't want them too small like Swedish meatballs or like ping-pong balls—they'll fry up dry. And you don't want baseballs because they won't cook enough in the center. You want somewhat smaller than a tennis ball. I made a bunch of those and placed them on a sheet of aluminum foil. I'd fry them up tonight.

I hunted through the kitchen cabinets and found the big iron pot my father used for frying his meatballs. All the standard recipes recommend a skillet but he felt he got less splatter with this pot, so that was what I intended to use. I set up two more pots. I emptied the quart of Calabro's gravy into the smaller one and added some cayenne pepper flakes to spice it up. I'd seen the amount of hot sauce Trav put on his burrito loco so I knew this wouldn't bother him. I'd put it over a flame later. In the bigger pot I salted some water and brought it to a boil, then turned off the heat. It would come to a boil more quickly later when I was ready to cook the angel hair. The garlic bread was ready for the oven.

When the time came, I'd be able to cook everything fresh and quick, just before I served it.

10

Travis arrived promptly at five-ish, as promised. By that time I'd had my second shower of the day—I needed to wash off the Block. I liked the way the short sleeves of his golf shirt stretched over his biceps.

But I didn't like the sudden uncertainty in his expression when he crossed the threshold.

"That chill again?" I said.

He rubbed his arms as he always did. "Yeah. What *is* that?"

"I can't say, Trav. I've never felt it."

Both true: I *had* never felt it and I truly couldn't say. How could I tell him he was sensing my father's ghost? How does a person who wants to be taken seriously as a science-based physician get those words past her lips? Answer: She doesn't. Not even to Travis Lawton.

The other thing I couldn't say was why he felt it and no one else did. I'd have to go with my father's explanation that he was "sensitive."

To change the subject I pointed to the bottle in his hand. "Oh, is that what I think it is?"

He held it up. "If you think it's wine, you're right. It's a kind of Valpolicella called 'Ripasso.' The guy at Corky's told me it's better than plain Valpolicella."

"Oh, it is. Same grape but thicker and richer."

"So you know it?"

"I'm half Italian, remember? My father introduced me to Ripasso della Valpolicella when I was a teen. This is good stuff. Be perfect with the meatballs. Let's open it and let it breathe a little."

"It needs to breathe?"

"Trust me. It'll make it better."

I didn't want to get into an explanation about oxidation and tannins. My dad tried to make his own wine when I was a teen—I kid you not, he called it Guinea Red. Being the curious sort, I did research on the subject and learned about fermentation and tannins and oxidation and all that. My dad's career as a vintner lasted one batch. It. Was. Awful.

On the way through the living room Travis said, "Hey, you know, that landscape—"

I held up a *stop* hand. "Yeah, I know. And it's going to stay that way. I'm going to let it do its thing and hang whatever way it wants."

He followed me into the kitchen. I didn't have an aerator, so I handed him a corkscrew and put him to work.

"Get it open, then pour two glasses and put them aside. After that, help yourself to some cheese."

To bring the remnant of Rocha's Brie wheel to room temperature, I'd placed it on the kitchen table about an hour ago. The leftover water crackers surrounded it like siege works.

"There's an open Gavi in the fridge to go with it."

"Gavi?"

Obviously not a *paisan*.

"White wine. We can drink some of that while I start cooking."

You're sounding bossy, I told myself. But Trav obviously didn't know his way around a kitchen, so I preferred to think of it as merely providing firm guidance.

"Or you could have one of Timmy's Guinnesses," I added. "He won't mind."

"I'll try this Gavi stuff."

I started a low flame under the gravy pot and turned the dial to max for the pasta water. Then I emptied the tub of lard into my father's iron pot.

"Hey, this cheese is great," Trav said as he handed me a glass of Gavi. "Wait—is that lard? I've never seen anyone cook with lard."

"Yep. My father's secret. Heat it till it's just beginning to smoke, then pop in the meatballs. Gets them crispy outside and soft and juicy inside, and gives them an extra layer of flavor you can't get from olive oil. A holiday for your mouth."

"Can't wait."

I had both hands busy so he settled a piece of Brie onto half a cracker and slipped it into my mouth.

"What's the menu for tonight?" he said as I chewed.

"At the moment I'm serving wine and cheese. And very, very soon we'll be sitting down to spaghetti and meatballs with garlic bread."

"Sounds like heaven. I could have brought dessert."

I kissed him on the cheek. "You did. We'll have the same dessert we planned for Tuesday night."

He looked confused for an instant, then he got it and slipped an arm around my waist. "You're for dessert?"

"Well, I'm your dessert, and you're mine. But not here. We'll have to move to your place for that."

He gave me a puzzled frown. "Oh?"

I could *not* make love to this man with my father's ghost hovering nearby. Just. No. Way. But I couldn't tell Trav that, so I fibbed. Just a little.

"My mother's not due back till tomorrow but she and my aunt have been known to have periodic fallings out where she'll stomp off from a visit and arrive home early without warning."

The chance of this was remote but not totally beyond the realm of possibility.

"You mean she could just pop in tonight and catch us…"

"In flagrante delicto."

A frown. "'In…'?"

That cultural gap again.

"In the act," I said.

"Yeah." He grinned. "That could be embarrassing. My place then, for sure."

"For sure."

His arm tightened around me as he nuzzled my neck, sending chills down that side of my body. "Too bad this place is off limits. We could do an appetizer *and* dessert."

That sounded wonderful—tingle-in-the-pelvis wonderful. So wonderful I was tempted to forget my father's ghost and say let's do it. I even had Janie's ribbed accessories ready. But no. With Dad nearby I knew I couldn't lose myself in Trav the way I wanted to.

I gathered myself and tried to sound totally in control. "Well, first off, I'm in the middle of cooking our dinner. And second, didn't your mother ever tell you that you must eat your dinner before you're allowed dessert?"

"I've also heard 'Life is short so eat dessert first.'"

"Good advice, but not tonight."

"Well, then, why don't I channel my desires into the piano and serenade the chef with some familiar tunes?"

"Sounds like a plan."

He cut himself another wedge of Brie and wandered toward the front of the house. A moment later I heard the piano keys start tinkling out the strains of "Für Elise." Marge had all her students learn it, and her "homework" between lessons had been to play it ten times a day, every day.

I stuck my head through the kitchen arch. The piano was around the corner in the living room so not visible from here.

"Tempo! Tempo!" I called, "C'mon, Trav, you can play faster than that!"

I heard him laugh. He'd been playing it at the proper speed but suddenly he broke into a frenzied tempo, bordering on the speed of someone totally cranked on meth. I cracked up at the memories it triggered.

Those ten times a week Marge demanded became a bore, especially when played at the eighty beats a minute she set on the metronome. But I'd ignore that and up the tempo to run through them quickly. Sometimes Trav and I would practice together before a recital and those sessions would devolve into a contest to see who could play "Für Elise" fastest without a mistake. He even brought a stopwatch once so we could time each other. Just for the record: I always won.

By the time the lard had melted and was just showing hints of smoke, he'd started in on "Au Clair de la Lune," another Marge standard, at normal speed. I fried the meatballs until their outer layers were crisp and brown, then set them on some paper towels to drain. Just as I turned off the flame, my phone rang.

I didn't recognize the number, but possibly Rocha's, so I took it.

"Noreen?" said an accented voice I immediately recognized.

"Rocha! How are you?"

"Thanks to you, I'm still alive. I will be forever grateful. I had three stents put in this morning, but I am feeling better than I expected to."

"Excellent. No more stinky cheeses for you. I'd don't want all that CPR I did to go to waste."

I started stirring the gravy. The pasta would hit the water momentarily.

"It won't, I promise you. No more cheeses of any kind. But listen, I have an important matter to discuss with you. I'm sneaking this call and I don't know how much time I have with the phone." He paused, then, "How do I say this?"

"One word at a time usually works."

Okay, a bit snarky, but I had Travis Lawton here and he was playing piano in the next room. I didn't need the distraction of some long, drawn-out tale from a psychic medium.

"Very well. You told me your father was a good man—"

"I believe I said 'the best.'" Because that's what I always say.

"Correct—'the best.' A good man who died a hero and everybody loved him."

"That about sums him up."

In the background Trav's piano playing went off key into some atonal mess and then stopped.

"Well, then, Noreen, I fear I must tell you that whatever has taken up residence in your old house is not your father."

My hand froze in mid-stir.

"That ridiculous. Of course he's my father. He knows things only my father and I know."

"I can't explain that. But I do know that you have a malignant entity there. The longer I stayed, the stronger I felt its evil. So evil it shook me to the core and then—"

"And then?"

"I woke up in the hospital."

I was getting a little steamed now. "You're saying my father gave you a heart attack?"

"What I'm telling you is it's not your father. You must understand *that. You're a doctor, so let me ask you: If you have a bad heart, stress can give you a heart attack, yes?"*

"Yes, but—"

"The doctor who put in the stents saw my arteries and said I was a heart attack just waiting to happen. Well, I'm telling you, Noreen, being that close to such evil was too much stress for my ticker and it almost killed me."

This was too much. "You're saying my father's evil?"

"No, I'm saying it's not your—"

"I have to go, Rocha."

"Noreen, wait! Tell it to go, to be gone! Listen—!"

I ended the call and stared at the phone. What was he talking about? *Not* my father? The ghost knew the meats that went into these meatballs and about Calabro's. He knew I'd called him *Babbo*. That was my father. And as for evil, I knew my father and he was anything but evil.

Some people had cognitive changes after heart procedures and anesthesia. That was the only explanation. I'd call the hospital tomorrow to check on him. He should be better by then and we'd have a laugh about this. But as for tonight, I wasn't about to let a self-styled psychic medium's post-procedural delirium rain on my parade.

Wondering why Trav had fallen silent, I wandered through the dining room to the living room to see what was up, but he wasn't there.

Then his voice: "Norrie, come here."

I turned and saw him through the doorway to my room. He stood a few feet inside with the lights out.

"What are you doing in there?"

"Come here. I need to speak to you."

I headed toward my room. His voice sounded strange. I hoped he wasn't thinking it was sexual appetizer time because that wasn't going to happen.

"Why are you in here with the lights out?"

I reached for the switch but he roughly grabbed my arm. "No lights."

I felt a flare of anger. I don't like being manhandled. I reached for the switch again and he grabbed me and yanked me deeper into the room, then he shoved me against a wall.

"I said, *No lights!*"

"Trav, what's gotten into you? I told you not now—later."

Although with the way he was acting, I was beginning to doubt there'd be a later. I didn't like this new Travis.

"This isn't Travis Lawton talking to you now, little girl!"

That was scary. Travis's voice but then again, not. Different inflection, a slight Italian accent. I could see his face in the light wash from the dining room and his expression was one I'd never seen on him—mean, twisted. That was when I noticed the faint, ghostly glow around his head. The same glow I'd been seeing every night since last week.

"Dad?"

"It's not your father either, you stupid *mucca!*"

Mucca... Italian for cow. Rocha's words from just a few moments ago came back to me:

...whatever has taken up residence in your old house is not your father... you have a malignant entity there...

Fear... deep, cold fear crawled up my spine and wriggled through my gut. I made for the door but he grabbed me roughly again and slammed me back against the wall. Harder. It hurt this time.

"Stay there! You're not going anywhere!"

I had no weapon and he was bigger and a lot stronger.

"I'll scream," I said. "I'll scream like you've never heard before."

A smirk. "Go ahead. Scream all you want. All the windows here are closed against the rain. All the neighbors will have done the same. And your father built a wall of trees around this place. We're as good as soundproof here. Scream. Go ahead."

I could have, but he was right. No one would hear me. My heart hammered, my mouth went dry. I was trapped.

"You're not my father... you can't be my father."

"No, mucca. I'm *his* father."

"*What?* How can that—?"

"Because back in the day I was slipping the *salsiccia* to Al Lawton's wife-to-be, and that slut loved it. Hot little Barbara was younger than us—not as young as I like but young enough—and she couldn't get enough of me. I must've knocked her up.

She never told me—and I'm dead sure she never told Al—but as soon as this boy walked into the house, I knew he was mine."

"Corrado?"

A smile and a little bow. "Uncle Corry, at your service."

After what I'd learned about him, I could never think of him as "Uncle" anything again.

"But I thought you were—"

"Your father? You're supposed to be such a smart one, but you were so easy to fool. Those 'test' questions you asked? Anyone close to Rocky could answer them. And no one was closer than me. Rocky... *mi fratello*... always talking about his kids and his cooking and his fucking gardens. That's what made you so easy. Kinda pathetic, really."

"Don't be too proud of yourself. It's easy to make someone believe what they want to believe. But what have you done to Trav?"

"Borrowed him for a while. He's blood after all."

"But you said I was the only one you could contact ..."

"Because you and me was blood?" He laughed. "Completely made up. I coulda contacted anyone in this house at any time, but I never bothered. What for? I wasn't interested in them. But you bought it, didn't you. Bought it hook, line, and sinker. What a dumbass you are."

Dumbass... yeah, I'd been a chump. It made me sick to think I'd been so completely fooled. But why would I ever suspect Corrado of hanging around our house?

"When you moved back in it was like a dream come true. It wasn't easy, but I managed to contact you and start playing you. I tried real hard but I couldn't influence you. My son here, though, he's an entirely different story. I'm so glad you brought him around last Sunday night. I learned I could control him when I made him play my song. He didn't know I was pulling his strings, but that's when I knew that, after all these years, my time had come at last."

"Time for what?"

"For the 'unfinished business' you asked me about when I first contacted you."

"What business?"

"Fucking your brains out, of course. That why I came here in the first place."

I could barely speak. "You came for *me?*"

"Yeah. You. To fuck you—fuck you up and down, just like I did this kid's mother. At least that's what I wanted to do, but I couldn't do nothin' to nobody. Even now I won't be doing the actual fucking. Travis will. But I'll be getting mine along with him." He curled his hands into fists and shook them before my face. "So good to have a body again, to be able to speak, to touch. I'd given up on ever getting even, but here we are."

"What do you have to get even for?"

"For my murder, mucca! By finishing up what I came here to do all those years ago. Rocky killed me, you know. Your wonderful father murdered me! Stabbed me in the heart—right in this room."

This was insane!

"What? He'd never—!"

"He did! Not a word did he say, not one word. Just drove that knife into my chest. Murdered me, his *fratellino,* murdered me in cold blood. I saw his face as I died—like ice, like stone."

"And you've been waiting twenty years?"

"No, mucca. Maybe five. I couldn't come back here while Rocky was still alive. But once he was dead... as dead as he made me..."

"You don't think you deserved it?"

"Maybe. Maybe I deserved it for being careless. You were a juicy little piece back when you were twelve."

"Twelve? Oh, God!"

"Yeah. Twelve. Such a sweet age."

I could have vomited on him. That was how old Angelina had been when he raped her.

"I'm thinking maybe your father spotted me slipping a little roofie into your milk during dessert. I don't think that was it. I been thinking on it and I think maybe he saw me sneak into your bedroom and unlock the window."

Oh, God, that was what he'd done to Angelina—drugged her. And like her that first time, I wouldn't have remembered a thing.

"I had it planned perfectly. After I left here that night I parked far enough away so no one would spot my car and walked back to your window. All the house lights were out and I thought I had it made, but your father knew. Somehow he knew. He was waiting for me right in that corner by the window when I crawled through. Didn't say a word. Just rammed some sort of big knife straight into my heart. I couldn't believe it. Hurt like hell, but only for an instant, and that's all I remember."

God, I hated this man. "So much for your perfect plan. But I know you're lying."

He laughed. "You can't imagine how many lies I've told in my life, little mucca, but this isn't one of them."

He was so confident in what he was saying, so smugly assured, he had to be telling the truth. My father... a killer... and a cold-blooded one at that. Sure, he was protecting his daughter, but I never would have dreamed he had it in him. Then again, for my father, his family meant everything.

I needed to keep Corrado talking. And besides, I had questions.

"But why have you been sending me on this wild goose chase to find out what happened to you when you knew all along?"

"It wasn't supposed to be a wild goose chase, mucca. You *made* it into one. I wanted to know *where* I was and you kept returning with news of *who* I was."

"I don't under—"

Trav's face twisted with the fury of the one controlling him. "I want to know my final resting place, mucca! Where am I buried, if I'm buried at all?"

"You don't know?"

"How could I know? I was dead and gone by the time I realized a part of me had stayed around. That was what I sent you to find out: What happened to Corrado Piperno? I thought if I was lucky you'd somehow find out along the way that your father killed me. Wouldn't that be a nice surprise for the little mucca? Dear sweet daddy was a killer! And once you got over the shock you might learn what he did with my body. But no, you weren't clever enough to figure out the truth. All you did was keep digging up shit about me."

"That's because there's so much to dig up!" I shouted.

He raised a fist. "Watch that fresh mouth of yours. You always were lippy. What did he do with my body? If he buried me, I want to know where. Or if he dumped me in the Chesapeake, I want to know. Or if he cut my body up into pieces and fed me to the pigs on some farm somewhere, *I want to know!*"

"You'll never know," I said coldly. "It was twenty years ago. Nobody cared what happened to you then, and believe me, nobody cares now."

"*I do!*"

"Why? Some ego trip you're on? Your family doesn't miss you. They thought your disappearance was the best thing that ever happened to them. I was down the Block today, checking up on your old hangs to see if I could get a clue as to what happened to you. Only a few old timers remembered the name—just barely—and only because they have bad memories of you. You know what someone down there said to me just a few hours ago? 'He was nobody. Good riddance.' That's your legacy, Corrado: a nobody. A *bum.*"

He grabbed me and started pulling at my blouse. "A bum, eh? I'll show you what kind of bum! I'm gonna finish what I came here to do in the first place!"

"Travis!" I cried as I slapped and clawed at his face. "I know you're in there! Don't let him do this!"

He leaned close with a nasty grin. "Go ahead and fight me, slut! I like that!! Because I know just how to make you agreeable."

He raised a fist and I closed my eyes and cringed as I raised my hands to ward off the blow—but it never came. I opened my eyes to see the fist still raised above me, but shaking with a severe tremor. And Trav's face—the glowing cloud still framed his head but his features were contorted like someone in severe pain.

"No!" The word came out strangled, distorted. "*No!* Not... gonna... happen! No... fucking... way!" Trav's other hand released me as he spoke through clenched teeth. "Run... Norrie... go! *Go!*"

Oh, my God, he was fighting him. Travis wasn't going to allow him to hit me. I was so proud of him I thought my heart would burst. But I couldn't leave him like this. And then I remembered Rocha's final words before I hung up on him.

Tell it to go, to be gone!

"Get out, Corrado!" I screamed. "Get out of Trav, get out of this house. Go! Be gone! Out-out-out! *Get out!*"

The glow began to fade.

"Say it, Trav," I said. "Tell him to get out of you!"

"Leave me!" Trav shouted, his voice stronger and more like his own. "Leave me *alone!*"

The glow began to trail off in all directions. In the past, when it disappeared, it would fade evenly, uniformly. Now it seemed to be tearing apart, exploding in slow motion.

And then it was gone.

Trav sagged against the wall and slid to the floor as if his legs had turned to water. I dropped to my knees beside him.

"Trav! Trav, you okay?"

He nodded weakly. "Think so." His voice was hoarse, rough. "Or maybe not. I may never be okay again."

11

"My, God!" Trav said. "What *was* that? What happened in there? Was that really my father?"

We were sitting at the dining room table. I'd helped him here from the bedroom on his still weak legs and poured us each a couple of fingers of my mother's Bushmills. He'd downed his in a gulp, wincing at the burn.

"I have to believe it was," I said, "although for the past week or so he's had me convinced he was *my* father."

"Turns out he's *mine*? I can't believe that. No, I won't believe that."

What an awful fact to be forced to face.

Now that I looked back I could see things that should have sounded alarms, but I'd been so taken by the idea of having my father back, even as a ghost...

Corrado's words from last night—which I had believed came from my father—echoed back to me: ... *there's only one outsider I can think of who I want in the house and that's that Travis fellow...*

I hadn't paid it much mind when he'd taken an interest in Travis, repeatedly asking about him. And Travis playing "That's Amore"... all the seemingly disparate pieces floating about during the last week or so had coalesced tonight. They all made sense now.

"Probably better not to buy into it. He was an awful excuse for a human being. Barely human, if you ask me. What happened? How did he get control?"

Trav shook his head. "I don't know. I was playing the piano—I don't even remember what song it was now—when all of a sudden the strangest feeling came over me. Suddenly my hands were pulling away from the keys. I tried to force them back but they kept pulling away. And then my legs were making me stand when I didn't want to. I tried to yell to you but my mouth wouldn't work. Before I knew it I was walking into your bedroom."

"You had no control?"

"None at all. I was like a passenger in my own body... completely helpless. Until he went to hurt you, that is. I just couldn't let him do that. But how come he could control me like that and not you? He had to use me to get to you."

Corrado had said it: *He's blood.* But I didn't want to repeat it. Trav didn't want to believe it—in his place, I'd feel the same—and I didn't feel right forcing the issue. But Trav apparently couldn't stay in denial.

"It's because he fathered me, isn't it." He wasn't asking a question.

"Why don't you think of it as 'sired' you. That's more like it. Because he was never your father. He was never anybody's father."

"Yeah... *sired.* Just like he said: We're blood. That's why he could control me." He shook his head. "That explains so much. Too much."

"What do you mean?"

I had a pretty good idea where he was going, but I wanted him to talk this through and talk it out. He needed that.

"Well, first off, it explains why I failed the match tests for my father's kidney transplant." He looked at me with tears in his eyes. "And my father's name is *Albert Lawton.* Make no mistake about that. No matter what the blood tests and DNA tests say, he's my dad, now and forever."

My heart went out to him. "Of course he is, Trav. That's what he believes and that's what you believed until just now. He loves you and raised you as his own and that's the way it should stay."

"It will. Forever. But do you think that could be why my mother deserted us—because of what she did with this guy? Could it have been guilt?"

"Could have been, sure. That and living a lie." I was guessing here, trying to put myself in the shoes of a woman

I'd never met. "Every time she looked at you she was reminded of what she'd done and how she'd not only betrayed the man she'd married, but how the boy he was raising as his son was fathered by another man. Maybe she just couldn't face another day of lies. Maybe Corrado kept coming on to her and she just had to get away."

Maybe true, probably not, but it sounded good. I found it difficult to bend over backward to give this unknown woman the benefit of the doubt. Because maybe she was just the slut that Corrado had labeled her. Maybe she was a female version of Corrado. Not easy to put a positive spin on a mother abandoning her child like she had Trav, but I was trying for his sake.

"Whatever," he said with a resigned tone. "She's long gone and it's all over and done with."

"The relationship might also explain why you got that strange feeling whenever you crossed the threshold here."

"I was sensing him?"

"That has to be it. I never felt it."

"But I used to come here in high school, remember? Why didn't I feel it then?"

"Because Corrado wasn't here then. He said he was blocked from the house while my father was alive and was able to get in only after he died. You're the only one who sensed him. Well, you and the psychic I had here last night."

His head shot up. "Wait. You were with a psychic last night? I thought you said it was a 'family matter.'"

"Yeah, well, in a very real sense it was. I didn't want to admit consulting a psychic medium, but I brought him here for my father's sake. At least I thought it was for my father. Which reminds me: I need to ask him something."

"The psychic? Now?"

"It has to do with what we just went through."

I retrieved my phone from the kitchen and noticed the pasta water had boiled almost dry. And the gravy was caked in the pot and totally ruined. I turned off the heat under them and returned to the dining room where I sent a text to the number of my last caller.

> If you can call me, please do.
> Immediately
> Must talk to you about entity.

I didn't know if Rocha still had that phone.

"His name is Rocha and he called me while you were playing piano. He told me that whatever was in my house wasn't my father, that it was evil. I got insulted and hung up."

Travis gave me a look best described as *askance*. "You believe in psychics?"

"Two weeks ago I didn't believe in anything I couldn't run a blood test on. But after tonight..."

"Yeah... tonight." He leaned back and squeezed his eyes shut.

"Right," I said. "After tonight I can't *not* believe in ghosts *and* psychics. Rocha was right on the money—'a malignant entity.' Corrado was as malignant as they come. But Rocha had a near-fatal heart attack right next to where you're sitting."

"Jesus! Lucky he had a doctor with him."

"Even so, he almost didn't make it. He had three stents this morning."

My phone rang: Rocha's number.

"Rocha?"

"*I don't know how long I can talk,*" he said in a whisper. I clicked the speaker button on so Trav could hear. "*Noreen, you're okay?*"

"Barely. But you were right. It wasn't my father."

"*I was about to tell you that on Friday night but then I had my heart attack.*"

"I still wouldn't have believed you. He had me totally fooled."

"*But you believe me now?*"

"Absolutely. This entity exerted influence over a relative of his and things got nasty tonight."

Travis opened his mouth to speak but I held a finger to my lips as a signal to just listen. Rocha might be less forthcoming if he knew a stranger was listening in.

"But you're okay?"

"A little shaken up but—"

"Did you learn the entity's real identity?"

"Yes, someone close to the family."

"Do you know why it was there?"

"Unfinished business."

Yeah... business with me.

"What—?"

"It's a long, complicated story I'd rather not get into."

"I understand. But he's gone now? You sent him away?"

"Yes. I heard what you said before I hung up on you—for which I apologize."

"That's all right. I realize it was upsetting news. But I told you when we met—prolonged hauntings are rare."

"You told me to 'Tell it to go, to be gone!'"

"Right. If you tell a spirit to go, it must leave. That was all you had to do."

"I didn't think it would work. I mean, it seemed too easy. How do I know it's gone?"

"I'm sure it is. But when I'm able, I'll stop by and confirm it for you."

I didn't want him dropping in on Mum with a story about a ghost in the house.

"Arrange it with me first. This is my mother's house."

"Will do. I'd better go."

I ended the call and Trav and I sat staring at each other.

Finally, I said, "This was *not* the evening I had planned."

He stared off into space. "I feel like my world's been turned upside down."

I reached over and grabbed his hand. "I'm sure it seems that way, Trav. Al Lawton may not be your biological father, but he's still your dad. There's no reason for that to change."

He nodded. "I can see that. But my biological father was a monster. He came here to rape a twelve-year-old. It's so sick. I can't help worrying that I might have inherited some of that."

I squeezed his hand. He shouldn't have to be asking himself these questions—no one should. But then, after tonight, how could he not?

"Look, you're thirty-two years old. In all your adult life—in all those years have you ever once lusted after a twelve-year-old?" He made a face. "Hell no! Not even close."

"Well, that should be proof enough. If you were going to have any of those tendencies, they'd have reared their ugly heads long before now."

"I hope so."

"I know so. Trust me. Look how you resisted that monster's control in there. As long as I live, I'll never forget that moment. He was going to beat me into submission but you wouldn't allow it."

He looked away, his expression grim. "Yeah, well, no way that was gonna happen."

"I believe you said, 'No *fucking* way.'"

Finally, a grin. "Did I? Well, I wasn't about to allow him to use *me* to hurt *you*."

The matter of fact way he said it gave me a warm rush all over.

"Like I said, I'll never forget it. But me, I've got to somehow wrap my head around the fact that my father murdered his best friend."

"Yeah," Trav said, "but you've got to look at the circumstances, and when you do that you can see how Corrado Piperno needed dying real bad. That guy was inside me and he was..." He fumbled for a word. "He was *foul*, Norrie. Toxic. Pure toxin all the way through. What your dad did made the world a brighter, cleaner place."

"I can't argue with that, but still...it's pretty clear Corrado's death wasn't an accident. My father *planned* to kill him. He didn't set a trap for him, didn't simply injure him and hold him for the cops. He stood there in the shadows by the window, holding a knife, and waiting. And when Corrado arrived, he killed him. Didn't wound him, didn't disable him. He stabbed him in the heart."

"Maybe your dad had learned some hinky things about his friend and this was the last straw. Maybe he realized the courts would give Piperno a slap on the wrist at best for sneaking through an unlocked window, 'cause when you think about it, that was all he was really guilty of that night. We'll never know." That obvious truth came as a shock. "God, you're right. He never got near me, so what could they charge him with?"

Dad must have known he'd get off, and then he'd have to worry about the pig making another try at me. He'd protected me by going for a permanent solution, by making sure Corrado would never be a threat to me or any other child again.

"But Piperno's story answers a lot of the questions in the MCMUP report. The abandoned car always puzzled me. Now we know he left it where he did so he could sneak up on your house on foot. But after he killed him, your father was left with a corpse. What did he do with the body?"

"Good question. That's what Corrado wanted to know. Apparently I'd been drugged and so I was unaware of anything that went on."

Where were Corrado's remains? I thought about that. Besides cooking, my dad's other big passion was gardening. He had his vegetable garden but he also loved flowering plants—roses especially. And then I knew.

"If I had to bet," I said, "I'd bet the ranch that Corrado is buried somewhere in our yard."

"How can you be so sure?"

"Because my dad was a careful man, a planner. He wouldn't want Corrado's body to float up from the bottom of the Chesapeake or the Harbor or have a dog dig up his remains in the woods. He'd want Corrado right where he could keep watch over his grave. Right outside in his yard."

I got up and walked out the door to the front yard and looked around. My folks' little ranch sat on half an acre of grass and flower gardens. The vegetable garden was long a thing of the past—not gonna happen without my father. But the rose gardens remained.

"He's somewhere out here," I said.

Trav was nodding. "And that's where he'll stay. Unless,

of course, your mother decides to dig up the yard for some reason."

An icy bolt of alarm spiked through me. Trav had said it so casually, naturally assuming that would never happen. But I knew something he didn't.

"Oh, hell!" I said, grabbing his arm.

"What?"

"My mother will never renovate, but you heard her Sunday night: She's talking about selling the place. If the new owners decide to put on an extension..."

I could see it happening. In fact, I couldn't see it *not* happening. This old-style three-bedroom ranch was too cramped by today's standards. And with all this extra land around it, who could resist?

If they dug in the wrong place, they'd unearth Corrado's remains. And then my father's secret would be out and he'd be branded a murderer. And my mother would live out the rest of her days known as the wife of a murderer.

No way could I let that happen.

"We've got to dig him up!"

Travis's eyes came close to doing one of those eye pops you see in Saturday morning cartoons. "What? How?"

"With shovels."

"No, I mean how are we going to dig him up when we have no idea where he's buried? And even if we did manage to find him, what would we do with an old dead body?"

I liked that he was saying "we."

"He's a skeleton by now."

"You're sure? I've read where they've found bodies of cavemen that still have skin and clothes."

"Body farm studies have shown that a human buried in dirt with no coffin will skeletonize in ten-twelve years. It's been twenty for Corrado. He's just bones now. He'll fit in a garbage bag—just the place for him."

"But what do we do with those bones?"

"We'll figure that out after we've dug them up."

"But how do we find him? This is one big yard, in case you haven't noticed."

"I grew up here," I said. "Believe me, I know how big it is. Let's take a walk."

I took his hand and led him on a tour. We shared a new closeness now. We'd survived a harrowing, horrifying experience, something we couldn't share with anyone else because who'd believe us?

The lot is roughly square, running about 150 feet on a side. A thick, twelve-foot wall of arbor vitae lined three of those sides. The house is situated toward the front, facing west, which allows for morning sun in the kitchen. The sun was still well up as I guided Trav around the north side and stopped by my bedroom window.

"Here's where he climbed in twenty years ago," I said, pointing.

Trav looked around. "Okay. But where did his remains exit? And where did they end up?"

There had to be a way to figure this out. I knew the man who had done the burying. He'd never, ever, *ever* bury Corrado in the vegetable garden. Let his remains seep into the produce dad brought to the table? Corrado cucumbers? Piperno peppers? Uh-uh. No way. And dig up the lawn? My father loved his lawn. Besides, the body would take up too much room under the turf, and that would leave a very noticeable mound—something my father would never stand for. He'd have had to find a way to get rid of the dirt. Or... find a place in the yard where mounded dirt would not be noticed. And the only place that fit that bill...

"A garden!" I said. "Corrado's buried in one of the gardens."

"Oh, well, that really narrows it down. We're all set then." His tone dripped sarcasm.

I understood. Three gardens on this side, and more in the back and even more on the south side.

"We can disregard the ones in the front," I said. "I don't see him planting a body where anybody driving by could see him do it. My money's on the back. With all those arbor vitae, no one would see him do anything."

I led him toward the backyard.

"But you and your mother and brother could see," Trav said.

"Yeah, if we were home. But he might have convinced my

mum to take me and Sean for new shoes or new clothes or something—anything to get us out of the house."

Travis groaned when we reached the backyard. "Six gardens? Was he nuts?"

"About roses? Yeah."

I surveyed the landscaping. A brick patio, a round wrought iron table with a wind-up umbrella, chairs, and in the right rear corner, against the arbor vitae, his tool shed. A scenario formed in my head.

"How does this play for you, Mister Deputy? My father tossed Corrado's body back out the window and let it bleed out there in the dark, then he carried it around and hid it in the shed. First thing the next morning he started digging a new flower bed, then found an excuse to get his family out of the house for a few hours. Once the hole is big enough, he quick-drags Corrado from the shed, drops him in the hole, and mounds the dirt over him. Then he goes out and buys rose bushes to plant atop him." I winked at Trav. "Dead bodies make great fertilizer."

He shook his head. "You always were a bit of a sicko. Even as a kid."

"No, seriously. When my father planted his vegetable garden, he'd always drop a fish head or fish tail into each hole where he placed a tomato seedling. They grew like crazy."

He looked around at the gardens. "So does that mean we look for the biggest rose bushes?"

"He fertilized everything back then, so they all grew like crazy."

"Okay, which one then? We can't dig them all up. That's a big, big job. And didn't you say your mother is due back tomorrow?"

"Yeah. Damn. There's got to be a way to narrow it down."

I racked my brain for a shortcut. Trav was right: We couldn't dig up every garden. The sun was setting around eight these days—less than two hours from now. And we couldn't set up lights and dig in the dark. Even with the arbor vitae wall, that would attract too much attention.

"Wait-wait-wait," I said. "Corrado disappeared a few weeks after my confirmation. My folks threw a party for me right out here on the patio." I headed for the back door. "I think I may know where to find the answer."

He followed me inside but stopped when he crossed the threshold into the utility room.

"Oh, no," I said. "The chill—you still feel it?"

He shook his head. "No. But let me test it at the front door. That's where it always hit me."

He ducked out and ran around the house while I walked straight through into the living room. I watched him step cautiously through the front door and stop. His frown turned into a slow smile.

"Nothing... absolutely nothing."

"Then he's really gone?"

"I think we're safe."

I had to trust Trav as my canary in the coal mine. Corrado was gone for good.

"Great. Next stop: the basement. We're going to take a trip down memory lane."

12

"Wow," Travis said as he flipped through one of the albums. "Your father was a real shutterbug."

He'd helped me drag out all the old family photos from the basement. Boxes and boxes of them. The vast majority were arranged by date in albums, and only fifty or so remained free in rubber-banded stacks. We'd dumped everything on the dining room table to search through.

"These were all taken by my mother. And 'shutterbug' implies she knew her way around a camera—you know, F-stops and all that. But she was strictly a Kodak Instamatic gal. She was definitely a bug about recording family events, though. And trips. Didn't matter if it was a major trip to someplace like Disney World or a day at Rehoboth Beach, she photographed us in all our glory."

"And so organized," he said. "All these albums arranged by year. That had to be a lot of work."

I held back telling him my mother had had nothing to do with the albums.

"It was. Each one used to be marked with the dates on the spine but it looks like all the labels fell off in the basement.

"The moisture, probably. Did you help her?"

Okay. I had to come clean.

"No, I did it all."

He grinned. "Really? What did she promise you? Or did she hold a gun to your head?"

"I did it on my own. Because I wanted to."

I didn't tell him that I *had* to, which would have been more accurate. My mother would take all these photos, get them developed, look at them once, then throw them in a box with no sort of organization. Drove. Me. Crazy.

Okay, maybe I was already a little bit crazy. But by the time I hit senior year, I was coasting through high school. Not the least bit challenged academically. Sean was off at college, so I was the only child in the house, with few friends and lots of time on my hands. The lonely fat girl, with her o-c tendencies kicking in big time.

So I told my mother if she'd buy the albums, I'd sort the photos and arrange them all chronologically. She liked the idea. Took me weeks and weeks but I finally got it done. We had a few fun nights poring through them, resurrecting old memories. I remember gazing wistfully at my younger, trimmer self. I'd been a fairly skinny kid through grammar school and junior high. But now, by the end of high school, I'd become so used to my excess weight that I'd subconsciously resigned myself to a life at that size. The photos had shown me that I hadn't been born fat, I'd *become* fat. And if I'd become fat, I saw no reason why I couldn't reverse the process and become slim again.

That was when I came to the decision to remake myself. So I owe these albums.

Travis gave me his askance look again. "You *wanted* to?"

"I like things neat and orderly."

An understatement but still true. I *need* things neat and orderly.

"Yeah, you always did. I remember you straightening things up the few times you ever came over to my house."

Good God! Two men living together with no woman around. You can imagine. I never liked going over there. Made me itch.

I said, "Why do you think we'd do all our studying and piano practicing over here? Your place made me crazy. But let's get moving through these pics. Look for my confirmation. You'll see twelve-year-old me in something like a red graduation gown, only without the cap."

All kinds of photos, all sorts of quality, from group shots to portrait shots, posed, candid, landscapes, buildings, underexposed, overexposed, you name it. I tried not to dwell

on them. Sean, me, Mum, and Dad—all so young. I remembered
how the number of photos per year dwindled with time. Fewer
once Sean went to college, and after I left they virtually stopped.
Those were the ones with no album now. But during the time
we were both kids—hundreds per year.

"Here we go," Trav said. "Is this it?"

He turned an album toward me and there I was—slim, pretty,
longhaired Norrie in her red gown, a freshly minted soldier in
the Army of Christ. Religion seemed so simple back then.

I scanned the photos, rushing past the ones taken during the
ceremony and outside the church, and flipping to the afterparty
in the backyard. Mum had taken about a dozen there—one
of them was of my father and Corrado, *fratello* and *fratellino*,
both smiling and holding beer bottles. Was Corrado even then
planning his late-night visit to my bedroom? I resisted an urge
to tear off his half of the photo and burn it. Because once I
started down that road, I'd be consumed with the need to purge
him entirely from the family archives.

Instead I concentrated on the portion of the backyard
pictured behind Dad and the monster. A couple of others
showed a lot of background as well. I pulled them out.

"Let's go out back," I said, rising.

Travis followed me to the rear steps where we looked out
onto the patio, grass, and gardens. The sun had sunk below the
front of the house by now, so the backyard was in shadow. But
the sky remained bright, with plenty of light to see the layout
of the gardens.

I held up two of the photos to compare the past to the present
and the difference was immediately obvious.

"That garden over by the shed," I said, pointing. "It's not in
the photos."

Travis leaned in for a look. "And these were taken when?"

"A couple of weeks before Corrado's late-night visit."

"Seems like a good bet," he said nodding. "But your dad
could have added it years later. Got any pics taken later that
same year?"

I thought about that. "Maybe Sean's sixteenth birthday. That
would have been in the fall."

We trooped back inside and, yes, there it was: Sean and our dad standing exactly where he and Corrado had stood, Sean grinning, Dad looking serious, each holding a beer. I remember age sixteen being a big deal in our house because it meant Sean was free to have beer or wine at home as long as he didn't go anywhere after.

I homed in on Dad's somber expression. I'd always written off his dark moments during my teenage years as anger at Corrado for running off and deserting his family. Now I knew the real reason why he'd never allow mention of Corrado's name in our house. He'd caught his *fratellino* in an unforgiveable act. And Dad had killed him for it. He'd played cop, judge, jury, and executioner, and it had changed him. I can see now how that act must have followed him around. And I have no doubt it contributed to the heart disease that finally did him in.

Last night I'd asked him—at least I'd thought it was him at the time—how he could have had no inkling about Corrado. And Corrado had answered in the guise of my father, but now I realized he'd been speaking for himself.

…maybe he needed one person who thought he was a good man, an honorable man. And so he kept his bad, dishonorable self hidden…

Corrado's last words before fading away last night had indicated that maybe my dad did have an inkling, but only a faint one. Maybe he'd heard an ugly rumor. And then when he'd seen Corrado put something in my milk or unlock my bedroom window, he'd decided it was true, and that it had fallen to him to administer some Old Country, Camorra-style justice.

But that had been then. Right now, in the photo, back by the shed… a new rose garden bloomed.

"That's it!" I said, totally convinced now. "That's where he's buried. Let's start digging."

"Whoa-whoa-whoa!" Travis said. "We're losing the light. We need to figure out how we're going to go about this. We'll need to dig up the rose bushes, and we'll have to do that carefully, because we don't want to kill them. We'll need to preserve the root balls so we can replant then when we're done—unless you want to come up with an explanation for your mother as to why we destroyed one of her late husband's gardens."

"Good point," I said, nodding. "But—"

"And then, assuming we find Piperno's bones, we need to make sure we remove *all* his bones—every last one. And that's going to take light—lots of it."

"You mean, wait till daylight?" I shook my head. "I don't know…"

"Sunrise is currently running somewhere between five thirty and six these days and—"

"How do you know that?"

"When you're out patrolling on the night shift, you want that sun up ASAP. Makes everything a whole lot easier. So you keep track of sunrise. Anyway, sunrise is five thirty-ish, but the sky brightens well before that."

I saw where he was going. "So if we start digging a little after five, we'll have plenty of light and plenty of privacy if we keep quiet. Because who in their right mind is up at that hour on a Sunday morning?"

"Exactly. Again, I'm assuming you're right about that being Piperno's grave. But once we find his bones, what do we do with them?"

"Told you: garbage bag."

"Okay, but what do we do once they're in the bag? Can't just leave them out at the curb for pickup on trash day. And you can't very well drive around with them in the trunk of your car. I don't have access to a crematorium, do you?"

"Nope."

"So where do we dispose of them?"

I leaned back and thought about that, then decided: "Why don't we table that until we actually have the bones in hand—or in bag, rather?"

"Fine with me." He patted his stomach and looked around. "Feels good to have a plan. And that episode in your bedroom is seeming less and less real."

"What are you saying?"

He grinned. "Got anything to eat?"

13

Nothing held Trav's appetite down for long.

I had a dozen semi-warm meatballs, cold garlic bread, and the chopped salad I'd made earlier. I pulled the salad from the fridge, put the garlic bread and meatballs in the oven to heat, and brought out the very-well-aerated Ripasso. By the time we finished the salad and the remains of the Brie wheel, the meatballs and bread were warm. That was how I served it: naked meatballs with garlic bread.

"Sorry about this," I said. "Not what I'd planned. The gravy's ruined so there's no point in making pasta."

"Do not apologize. If it tastes half as good as it smells, it'll be great."

"Well, then, dig in."

He speared a meatball, quartered it, and forked a piece into his mouth… chew-chew, and then his eyes lit.

"My God, Norrie! You made these?"

"With my own little hands."

"This has got to be the best meatball I've ever tasted!"

"Oh, go on." I brushed off the compliment, but inside I was glowing. "They're passable but—"

"Are you kidding me? I've never tasted anything like this. You should drop medicine and open a meatball shop. Marconi's Meatballs. You'd clean up. Truly."

I wondered if he was just buttering me up, but from the way he attacked the rest of the meatballs, I had to believe he was sincere. I tried one myself and damn if it wasn't delicious. Just the right amount of crisp on the outside and smooth and juicy inside. The double-grind on the meat helped a lot, and it tasted like I'd gotten the right balance of spices and parmesan. But how much of each had I added? Well, damn, I'd already forgotten.

By the time the wine was gone, Trav had eaten eight meatballs and three-quarters of the garlic bread, I'd eaten two and finished the bread. This man loved to eat and I loved to watch him chow down. I also loved how he'd fought for me against Corrado. He'd protected me, wouldn't allow Corrado to harm me. How many times in a woman's life can she call a man her hero? I'd always had a soft spot in my heart for Trav, but now I wanted him—I wanted his arms around me, I wanted my legs around him, in wanted him *in* me. And I wanted him *now*.

"You're not going to leave those two meatballs, are you?" I said.

He patted his stomach. "Couldn't fit another bite. But man, was that delicious."

"No room for dessert?"

His eyes lit. "If it's the dessert we talked about earlier, most definitely."

I rose and held out my hand. "Come on."

"Where?"

I pointed to my bedroom. "There."

My main objection to staying here had been that I'd be making love with my father hanging over me. But that was no longer an issue. And besides, my ovaries were doing the Macarena.

Trav said, "After what we went through in there?"

"Corrado's gone, banished. And this will permanently exorcize him."

He stepped close. "But you said your mother might—"

"If she's not here by now, she's not coming. We have the place to ourselves."

All true.

I pulled him toward my room and shut the door behind us.

We'll leave it there. What goes on behind my bedroom door stays there.

14

By 11:30 I was back in the kitchen, dressed only in Trav's golf shirt, and still glowing from our lovemaking. The first time had been rushed, frantic—as expected. The second time more leisurely, and more intense. Note to self: Next time you see Janie: *Viva las ribs!*

Travis was asleep but I was wide awake and up and about. I couldn't leave dirty pots in the kitchen and used plates on the dining room table all night. Simply not possible. Earlier, while putting the meatballs and bread in the oven, I'd poured the cooled but still-liquid lard back into its container and dropped that into the garbage, then put the pot into the sink to soak with some Dawn dish soap. The gravy pot had joined it.

Now I cleaned all the pots and put them, along with the plates, into the dishwasher for a final cleansing. Once I had that running on the pot-scrubber cycle, and set my phone alarm for four thirty, I was done.

Now I could go back to bed and consider sleep.

No, it ain't easy being me.

SUNDAY

1

We didn't get quite the early start we planned. When my phone alarm went off at 4:30, I got up to make coffee but Travis grabbed me and pulled me back under the covers and, well, let's just say we were delayed. And again, Viva las ribs.

But eventually we made it to the kitchen. My mother had left my father's toolshed pretty much untouched after he died. So after coffee we raided it for work gloves and shovels. The gloves were necessary since we were dealing with roses.

The morning broke chilly and cloudy with more rain predicted for later. A good morning for the neighbors to stay inside with their windows shut. All the better for us.

Mostly we worked in silence, not wanting to attract the least bit of attention. I noticed that Trav seemed to know his way around a garden. He preserved nice root balls around the bases of the rose bushes he dug up. He removed the three center bushes first, since the center seemed to be the place where we'd have the highest chance of hitting pay dirt—or bones, rather.

And sure enough, about three feet down, my shovel clunked against something. We dug around it and there it lay: the left iliac crest of a human skeleton. We'd found what was left of Corrado Piperno.

2

Two hours later we were satisfied we had bagged his remains. They required two bags. I didn't count to see if we had all 206 bones. We might have missed a toe or finger phalanx, but that couldn't be helped. We came across the murder weapon in our digging—at least we assumed the knife we found was it. I didn't know if my father had left it in Corrado's chest when he buried him, but it lay loose in the dirt. We stuck that in one of the bags as well.

With all that done, we replaced the dirt and the rose bushes and Trav set up a sprinkler to give them a good soaking.

We sat at the patio table, sipping more coffee and surveying the reconstituted garden. Not a perfect job, not one that would pass close-up inspection, but plenty good enough to pass muster when viewed from the house. The two bone bags rested on the bricks by the grass.

"Now that we've got him," Trav whispered, "what do we do with him?"

I doubted anyone was within earshot, but I kept my voice low too. "I'm thinking the harbor."

"What? We can't just dump a whole skeleton in—"

"We don't. I'm thinking you and I can rent one of those paddle boats and we'll give ourselves a nice romantic floating tour of the Inner Harbor as we drop one bone at a time. Bones don't float, especially ones as damp as these things after the wet spring we've had. We'll spread Corrado all over the harbor."

He shook his head. "That doesn't mean one of them won't ever be found."

"Okay, should someone find a bone and it's identified, at least it won't be in my father's old rose garden."

Now a nod. "True that."

"And what are the real-world chances of it being identified? Do you think Corrado's DNA is on file?"

"Doubt it. They wouldn't have taken a sample for simple D and D. Especially not twenty years ago."

"But even if they do find it and identify it, being dumped in the harbor is consistent with the theory that he ran afoul of some bad people on the Block. My only worry is his skull."

"Why?"

I pointed to the rounded lump bulging in one of the bags.

"I'm afraid it'll trap some air and won't sink."

Trav rose and walked over to the bag, where he touched the lump with the toe of his shoe.

"This?"

"Yes. I might have to drill a hole—"

He stomped on the lump, flattening it with a loud *crunch!*

"—and… never mind."

He returned to the table, sat, and took a sip of coffee. He caught my stare.

"What?"

"Feeling a little hostile, are we?"

"He wanted to hurt you. Tried to get me to do it for him. Nobody does that. Nobody. So, yeah, you could say I'm feeling a bit of hostility toward him."

Did I tell you I love this guy?

I grabbed his hand and tugged him toward the back door.

"Let's go."

"Where?"

"Breakfast."

"I feel ridiculous," Trav said as he worked the pedals of the paddle boat.

Well, not just a plain old boring standard paddle boat. The ones down on the Inner Harbor are formed of green molded plastic and shaped like sea monsters with a dragonlike head and neck rising from the bow. Bright red spines run down the back of the neck to complete the picture.

"You don't find this romantic?" I said.

"Not in the least."

"My-my. You've turned grumpy."

"I think my blood sugar's low. I need food."

Yes, well, our "breakfast" burned calories rather than added them.

"I'll treat you to Sunday brunch at Miss Shirley's when we're done here."

He immediately brightened. "You're on."

"Look at it this way," I said. "Who'd suspect a lovely young couple like us to use a silly Loch Ness monster paddle boat to aid and abet a murder."

"We're not aiding and abetting," he said. "That means to assist in the commission of a crime."

"Okay, I'm not up on law enforcement lingo. What are we doing?"

"We're acting as accessories after the fact: We're hiding evidence."

The threatened bad weather was good news for us. Only one other paddle boat out on the harbor and nowhere near us. We paddled close to the *USS Chesapeake*, an old lightship permanently moored in the harbor and now a museum. You couldn't miss it with its name printed in huge white letters along its bright red hull. We'd decided beforehand to start dumping our hidden stashes of bones here.

We couldn't very well step onto a paddle boat carrying bone-filled garbage bags, so after—ahem—breakfast I went down to the basement to search for suitable camouflage. My mother's not big on throwing things out. She's not a hoarder by any means, but she's frugal. If something's in decent shape, she's not about to toss it, even if she has no further use for it. She'll gladly give it to someone who wants or needs it, but if that person isn't handy, she'll stick it in the basement.

In no time I found an old backpack of mine from high school and stuffed one of the bone bags in there. My mother favors huge shoulder bags and I found an old one of those that could fit the second bag.

We glided alongside the red hull with the paddle boat positioned so that I was on the inside. I wore latex gloves to keep my hands clean, and started dipping into my backpack. The knife was the first thing to go to into the harbor. Bones followed, slipping one by one into their watery grave. As anticipated, they quickly sank from sight.

After we ran out of *Chesapeake* hull, I curtailed my disposal activities as we passed the water taxi dock, then resumed as we glided along the hull of the *USS Torsk*, a submarine from World War Two. Dropped more by the bulkheading outside the aquarium, deserted now because of the weather, and sank the last of them along the bulkhead outside the marine mammal pavilion, also deserted.

"Done," I said, peeling off the gloves. "Corrado Piperno rests in pieces."

Trav barked a laugh. "That's a terrible pun."

"But it's true. He's still officially a missing person and will remain that way."

"Amen, sister. Amen."

We paddled our sea-monster boat back to its dock and made the short walk to Miss Shirley's Café.

4

So here I sit in Miss Shirley's watching Trav consume a humongous brunch. I'm nibbling on an order of fried green tomatoes and sipping a mimosa while he's gorging on both the Cuban Huevos Sandwich and the Chicken 'N Cheddar Green Onion Waffles.

I guess you could call this our third date. And I have him spend it disposing of what's left of a murdered body. Really, do I know how to show a guy a good time, or what?

I love to watch Trav eat. My fellow accessory after the fact, my partner in crime. What we just did is indeed a crime. But so what? Corrado's *life* was a crime. He's gone and forgotten and that's the way he'll stay.

I find my thoughts drifting back over the past week. And what a week it was. Last Sunday at this time I was sure Stan Harris had murdered Marge, but otherwise the world seemed to be on an even and predictable keel.

Monday was when the dominoes started falling. That was when Sam showed up jaundiced. As a result, Ken decided to stock Tezinex goodies into the office which helped send Anna Divisova's and Martin Gale's lives off the rails. That was also the day I was assigned the task of looking into Corrado Piperno's past, which almost sent my own life off the rails.

And if not for the brave, strong, noble man stuffing his face across the table from me, who knows if I'd even be alive now?

We're bonded, Travis and I. We've always had a tenuous bond of shared adolescent experiences, definitely more on my part because of my crush on him back then. But all that pales to what we have now.

Together we survived an encounter with a supernatural entity who just happened to be Trav's biological father. I can't jeopardize my professional reputation by talking about something like that; and neither will Trav because he wouldn't want anyone to know that Al Lawton is not his real dad. The only one we can discuss that with is each other.

We're also accessories after the fact of a murder. Certainly a justified murder, and one that no one knows occurred. As a deputy sheriff, he can't mention that to anyone. Anyone but me, that is.

And so we're bonded. And you know what? I like that. Like it a lot.

As I'm sitting here I'm feeling an all-pervading glow of happiness. That's a new experience for me. I've had brief episodes of contentment in my life, but real happiness? Never. At least not like this.

I don't think my life has ever been in a better place. Don't worry, I'm not kidding myself it will last forever. But I'm determined to enjoy the hell out of it as long as it does last.

The only piece missing is my father. I wish he were still alive so I could share this time with him. But you can't have everything—I'm well aware of that cliché. But right now I feel like I have damn near everything, so I'll go with that while it lasts. And make sure to glory in every minute of it.

About the Author

F. PAUL WILSON is an award-winning, bestselling author of seventy books and nearly one hundred short stories spanning science fiction, horror, adventure, medical thrillers, and virtually everything between.

His novels *The Keep, The Tomb, Harbingers, By the Sword, The Dark at the End,* and *Nightworld* were *New York Times* Bestsellers. *The Tomb* received the 1984 Porgie Award from *The West Coast Review of Books. Wheels Within Wheels* won the first Prometheus Award, and *Sims* another; *Healer* and *An Enemy of the State* were elected to the Prometheus Hall of Fame. *Dydeetown World* was on the young adult recommended reading lists of the American Library Association and the New York Public Library, among others. His novella *Aftershock* won the Stoker Award. He was voted Grand Master by the World Horror Convention; he received the Lifetime Achievement Award from the Horror Writers of America, and the Thriller Lifetime Achievement Award from the editors of Romantic Times. He also received the prestigious San Diego Comic-Con Inkpot Award and is listed in the 50th anniversary edition of Who's Who in America.

His short fiction has been collected in *Soft & Others, The Barrens & Others,* and *Aftershock & Others.* He has edited two anthologies: *Freak Show* and *Diagnosis: Terminal* plus (with Pierce Watters) the only complete collection of Henry Kuttner's Hogben stories, *The Hogben Chronicles.*

In 1983 Paramount rendered his novel *The Keep* into a visually striking but otherwise incomprehensible movie with screenplay and direction by Michael Mann.

The Tomb has spent twenty-five years in development hell at Beacon Films.

Dario Argento adapted his story "Pelts" for *Masters of Horror*. Over nine million copies of his books are in print in the US and his work has been translated into twenty-four languages. He also has written for the stage, screen, comics, and interactive media. Paul resides at the Jersey Shore and can be found on the Web at www.repairmanjack.com.

Repairman Jack*

The Tomb
Legacies
Conspiracies
All the Rage
Hosts
The Haunted Air
Gateways
Crisscross
Infernal
Harbingers
Bloodline
By the Sword
Ground Zero
The Last Christmas
Fatal Error
The Dark at the End
Nightworld
Quick Fixes—Tales of Repairman Jack

The Teen Trilogy*

Jack: Secret Histories
Jack: Secret Circles
Jack: Secret Vengeance

The Early Years Trilogy*

Cold City
Dark City
Fear City

Collaborations

Mirage (with Matthew J. Costello)
Nightkill (with Steven Spruill)
Masque (with Matthew J. Costello)
Draculas (with Crouch, Killborn, Strand)
The Proteus Cure (with Tracy L. Carbone)
A Necessary End (with Sarah Pinborough)
"Fix"* (with J. Konrath & Ann Voss Peterson)
Three Films and a Play (with Matthew J. Costello)
Faster Than Light – Vols. 1 & 2 (with Matthew J. Costello)

The ICE Trilogy*

Panacea
The God Gene
The Void Protocol

The Nocturnia Chronicles
(with Thomas F. Monteleone)

Definitely Not Kansas
Family Secrets
The Silent Ones

Short Fiction

Soft & Others
The Barrens and Others
Aftershock and Others
The Christmas Thingy
Quick Fixes—Tales of Repairman Jack*
Sex Slaves of the Dragon Tong
Secret Stories

The Rx Mystery Series

Rx Murder
Rx Mayhem

Editor

Freak Show
Diagnosis: Terminal
The Hogben Chronicles (with Pierce Watters)

Curious about other Crossroad Press books?
Stop by our site:
http://www.crossroadpress.com
We offer quality writing
in digital, audio, and print formats.

Made in the USA
Las Vegas, NV
19 July 2022